W9-BVB-661

AUG - - 2010

ROY & LILLIE

· A LOVE STORY ·

Books by Loren D. Estleman

*A Forge Book

ROY & LILLIE

· A LOVE STORY ·

LOREN D. ESTLEMAN

A Tom Doherty Associates Book
New York

ST. THOMAS PUBLIC LIBRARY

This is a work of fiction. All of the characters, organizations, and events portrayed in this novel are either products of the author's imagination or are used fictitiously.

ROY & LILLIE: A LOVE STORY

Copyright © 2010 by Loren D. Estleman

Edited by James Frenkel

All rights reserved.

A Forge Book
Published by Tom Doherty Associates, LLC
175 Fifth Avenue
New York, NY 10010

www.tor-forge.com

Forge® is a registered trademark of Tom Doherty Associates, LLC.

ISBN 978-0-7653-2228-9

First Edition: August 2010

Printed in the United States of America

0 9 8 7 6 5 4 3 2 1

ROY & LILLIE

· A LOVE STORY ·

FOR STARTERS

He was a scoundrel on the large scale of West Texas, a killer, thief, and corrupt public servant who imported the custom of public lynching to the Lone Star State. In the saloon he used for a courthouse he sold grizzly-bear jism as an aphrodisiac and charged a penny extra for "ice-cold" beer poured ostentatiously over a lump of glass he used repeatedly until he dropped it and it broke. The citizens of Langtry, Texas, called him the "Law West of the Pecos," and it seems he was for a time, or as much of it as one could expect to find out there among the fangs and spines. When at long last he died, the town went dark in a display of public mourning.

She was an actress of almost unearthly beauty, with a voice like a silver flute and a waist as slender as her neck. She collected jewels and lovers, including the Prince of Wales, and paraded them through the gas-lit theaters and oil-smudged music halls of London, San Francisco, and the gold camps of the frontier for a quarter century. Whether she could act is of no consequence.

Portrait painters and the press called her the "Jersey Lily," although many considered the horticultural variety drab in comparison. In her day she was world famous, but history remembers her chiefly as the platonic love interest of Roy Bean, whose notoriety in life stopped at the Arkansas border.

She smoked cigarettes in carved ivory holders and bathed with rose petals. He spat tobacco into a fire bucket and put on a clean shirt over a dirty one to receive important visitors.

They corresponded. No letters survive.

Theirs was the perfect romance—unalloyed with squabbles or disappointments or unpleasant revelations or the boredom of familiarity.

They never met.

This is their story—after the native fashion of tall tales, illegible journals, newspaper fantasies, self-serving memoirs, axes to grind, and bald-faced lies that historians ferret out and present as fact.

Most of what follows happened. The reader will sort the remainder into separate piles of implausible truth and acceptable legend.

Roy said it best: "There are more ways than one of doing business."

TO ABSENT FRIENDS

*C. L. "Doc" Sonnichsen, who rescued Roy from the ash heap;
and Fred Bean, who bore the family burden with humor.*

The fable taught man that there is sometimes a deep truth behind an obvious falsehood.

—Isaac Bashevis Singer,
introducing *Aesop's Fables*

I

THE COCK AND THE JEWEL

A cock scratched up a precious stone and said, "If you had been discovered by your owner, you would have been taken up and displayed with pride; but I have found you for no reason. One barleycorn is worth more to me than all the world's jewels."

—Aesop

ONE

His reputation, like the lust for Stetsons and high-heeled boots, started at the state line, and he made the most of it by plastering the front of the Jersey Lilly with signs (ICE-COLD BEER & LAW WEST OF THE PECOS) and placing himself on display in a rocking chair on the porch at train time. Earlier he'd bribed conductors and porters to prime passengers for the big attraction, but the railroad men were willing enough to spread the stories free of charge, so eventually he returned his poke to his pocket. Roy was scrupulous when it came to his own money.

Pilgrims who witnessed this exhibition of living waxworks noted that physically, the man matched his legend, and assumed he was born fully fleshed out in his seventh decade, with his belly spilling through the banker's waistcoat buttoned only at the top, tumbleweed whiskers, and eyes that glistened like damp plums under a sombrero with a buggy-wheel brim. But in his youth he was a frontier Apollo, tall and rawboned, with a bristling black beard; a land-locked Pirate Prince who shot a man in

San Diego, California, over an affair of the heart and spent his period of incarceration accumulating poundage from a steady supply of cold chicken and enchiladas smuggled into his cell by pretty señoritas of the old pueblo. In Roy Bean's universe, a pirate was never anything less than a prince and señoritas were invariably pretty.

Was this man, loose-gutted and musty-smelling, the lean young panther who'd crouched behind bars, fastidiously licking grease from his fingers and grinning at the giggling spectators outside?

"I have an old injury from a fall from my horse while serving with the U.S. Cavalry during the battle for Mexico City," he wrote Lillie Langtry many years later, by way of one of his literate children. "The pettifoggers in Washington have held up my pension, but there is one less Spanish despot walking the earth for my effort, and that's sufficient reward."

He was anticipating a face-to-face meeting with the actress and the need to explain the stiff neck that had plagued him for nearly fifty years. The complaint was actually the result of a lynching that failed to take. He'd cultivated the facial hair, it was said, to mask the hemp scars. The circumstances were cloudy but had something to do with the honor of a young woman. (A pattern was forming.) It happened—if it happened—in Los Angeles, California, more than six years after the ratification of the peace treaty between the United States and Mexico.

He never defended the Union, and his subsequent attempt to bring it down at Glorieta was neglibile. In the last year of the Mexican adventure, most accounts place Roy in Independence, Missouri, with his brother Sam (who *had* served with the American expeditionary force below the border), arranging to join a wagon train with the intention of establishing a trading post west of the Rockies. Roy was always an entrepreneur first, a colorful character second, and a man of justice only because he refused to relinquish possession of the only book on Texas statutes for two hundred dusty miles.

If, however, he could be said to have come by anything honestly, it was his interest in the disposition of the law. Another brother, Joshua, presided over primitive San Diego as alcalde, a post that settled disputes among natives and passed sentence for capital crimes such as the theft of a neighbor's sourdough starter. Josh, too, claimed service in Mexico, but no record ever surfaced. He stepped into the more Anglo-sounding office of mayor when American interests prevailed, and in 1850 secured an appointment as general with the California state militia, shooting claim-jumpers from the goldfields and the occasional Chinese. Subordinates with a good sense of an international play on words addressed him as "General Frijol." As the brother of so prominent a man, Roy basked in reflected esteem, romancing girls in his fine new clothes obtained on Josh's credit, until he suggested a shooting contest with a rival named Collins—from horseback, with each man presenting himself as the other's target.

Collins accepted. The combatants made a few galloping passes in jousting fashion, wheeling their panting mounts and firing Paterson revolving pistols across the pommels, while spectators cheered and ducked stray rounds; the challenged party missed his challenger by a Texas mile and fell from the saddle when a ball tore through his leg. Roy drew jail time and the generosity of the Mexican girls with their cornmeal concoctions and baskets of cooked fowl. When he tired of that, his Indian drinking companions freed him with picks and shovels, to the annoyance of the judge, who was proud of the new construction of fieldstone and poured concrete. In a fit of pique he released the recovered Collins from custody.

The melodrama in Los Angeles followed. Roy wrote Lillie: "It was my privilege to slay Joaquin, the legendary highwayman, after he murdered my dear brother Joshua from ambush over a difference of principles."

He neglected to mention that a friend of the great bandit's had fallen out with General Frijol over the affections of a young Indian woman and had lain in wait for him with a musket.

All his long life, Roy clung to the quixotic notion that his favorite brother was one of the last victims of the great Joaquin Murietta, or at least of the road agent's machinations behind the event. It would not do that a barefoot cobbler named Cipriano Sandoval was anything more than the instrument in the passage of a Bean, or that the affair was triggered by nothing more poetic than simple lust. Eventually he may even have come to believe that he was the slayer of Murietta, and not a company of Rangers under the command of Harry Love, a character nearly as colorful as Roy, but one who came without punchlines. Like the prehistoric hunter who wore the skin of the lion he vanquished, Roy adopted the gaudy costume of the New World Spaniard, favoring black sombreros chased with silver, embroidered waistcoats, and tight pantaloons vented at the cuffs and trimmed with bells, until age, girth, and the dignity of public office counseled a more conservative form of dress.

Roy's only recorded brush with Joaquin was the time he failed to put in top bid for the bandit's severed head preserved in a pickle jar—presumably as a trophy to support his claim—a failure lamented by collectors of grisly border memorabilia, who lost a prize when the saloon where the jar was displayed fell to the 1906 earthquake in San Francisco. All the souvenirs Roy assembled in the back room of his own liquor emporium, they pointed out, survived well into the twentieth century, and when lumped all together fell short of that one item in value.

Lillie, reading Roy's letters on the chintz-covered chaise in her West End flat, admired the Spencerian penmanship and ruthless prairie-school attention to vocabulary and syntax, suspecting they were transcribed but unaware of how much they had been altered from dictation. She assumed he was Canadian, and not from its wilderness; her middle-class British upbringing would countenance no origins less civilized than Toronto or Montreal. She pictured him adjudicating from a high mahogany bench in a room that resembled the inside of a gentleman's stud box, like Oliver Wendell Holmes in a rotogravure in *The Strand.*

She could not know that he presided from behind the bar in a frame shack surrounded by dry riverbeds, wrote his name only laboriously with his tongue clamped between his teeth, and was once observed consulting the big mustard-colored volume issued in Austin upside-down. When his court wasn't in session, the book reposed either under his broad bottom or beneath the weight of a big yellow-handled Colt to accommodate the broken spine. Its pages were stained with whiskey and Levi Garrett's, Roy's choice of chaw, and welded together in spots, very unlike the pristine condition in which he maintained the revolver. Bruno, the tame black bear the Law West of the Pecos kept chained outside the saloon, made deep, contented rumbling noises when Roy used the muzzle to scratch him behind the ears.

But then the book was just an emblem, like the notary seal its owner employed to crack pecans when he had the misery in his fingers. The pistol, the noose, and in one instance Bruno himself made the better point in practice. The incessant hot wind did not blow from the direction of published precedent, but from the predators' dens in the Indian Nations and the caves south in Chihuahua where bandits hid.

Roy must have cut a *figura muy hermosa* in the vain splendor of his youth. Any pictures that might have been struck at that time have not come down to us, but when in his December days he set aside his bung-starter gavel and straddled old Bayo, his beloved gray, for his only known form of exercise, he changed his rumpled suit of town clothes and put on a broad Mexican hat and strapped big silver rowels on his heels, gulling uninformed visitors into mistaking him for an ancient grandee. This uniform, and certain things about his conduct, suggest that in convincing himself he'd deprived the world of its most scarlet brigand, he had chosen to offer his own life in place of his victim's, representing Joaquin as he might have looked and behaved had he survived to a crepuscular old age.

Then again, a skillful liar overlooks nothing in his effort to appear sincere.

At the time of the fabled encounter, of course, Roy was biding his time at the end of a green rope, supporting himself on his toes and waiting for one of his inexhaustible supply of sympathetic señoritas to come along and cut him down. In his eagerness to impress an actress, he superimposed Murietta on the Mexican officer he'd killed for the affections of a woman, who was by some accounts his rescuer later. (By others it was a combination of hemp rot and a stiff breeze.) A weakness for the patient sex ran through Roy Bean's family like typhus; and a good thing, too, or our story would have no theme.

But we have a thousand miles to cover before Langtry and old Bayo, thirty years before Vinegarroon, and have still to get to the Channel Islands.

TWO

Fame stalked and swallowed her whole, only to spew her back out forty years later when her beauty would no longer respond to brush or camera. While it lasted, there was nary a brick wall nor a barn nor a cigarette card between Vienna and the Barbary Coast that didn't bear her image. When she died, the only place it remained on display was in the Jersey Lilly Saloon. (Not all the pictures were of her, but of impostors; but then, fewer still of Roy's stories could be taken at face value.) She was a passive accomplice in her rise, a thing that couldn't be said of her most constant admirer, but a seed planted by hand has as much chance to flourish as one sown by the wind.

Begin with an unspectacular first London season, followed by a marriage of convenience. This is the formula for cautionary tales of wicked young ladies of good family.

Jersey, the gem of the islands in the Channel, loses its emerald brilliance when the wheat ripens for harvest, assuming the yellowish hue of a topaz, flecked with the reddish brown of the breed of cattle that bears its name. From a cartographer's point of view, it's more properly French than English; but in Emilie LeBreton's childhood it was known as a place for West Enders to escape the poisonous fog in summer and as a source of lumber, produce, and farm girls, whose peach-colored complexions were expected to help lift the gloom from Old Blighty when the muslin came off the ballroom chandeliers in spring.

Lillie, as her family called her, was no farm girl, but the daughter of a rector. However, her skin was particularly striking for its luminous quality, burnished by the reflection from her chestnut hair, which glowed like copper under the sun, and which most days she wore in a simple chatelaine twist behind her neck, a tomboyish, time-saving decision that inspired a generation of imitators away from the elaborate tonsorial architecture of Europe and America at mid-century.

She was no goggle-eyed *naïf*, but a woman of the world in miniature, or so she thought; an active participant in the rough-and-tumble play of six brothers, each a prime example of the dreaded parson's spawn, and an experienced eavesdropper on gossipers at church social functions. (That wasn't a mouse fidgeting beneath the pews in back when the voices fell to a murmur.) She also presented a faithful audience to the genuine farm girls who attended St. Saviour's Parish, and who had witnessed stock breeding at first hand. A steeple is no shelter.

By the time she was fourteen, Lillie knew more of the ways of man and nature than most of her urban counterparts in that third decade of Queen Victoria's reign, or as much as one could know and still remain a virgin. Late at night she crept into one or another of her brothers' rooms and acted out for them in pantomime the wisdom she'd attained, to avoid rousing a parent. Years before she stepped out upon her first stage, she knew all her marks and cues, what delighted her public and what attracted its scorn.

These revelations did nothing to prepare her to face savage civilization, as she would discover two years later.

"Your accounts of red Indian depredations and the grim wages of war," she wrote Roy through her secretary, "put me in mind of Lord Suffield's ballroom during the '69 season, where I learned that lace fans and whispers can be weapons as deadly as arrows and cannon."

Stricken by her physical charms at a picnic on the beach in St. Helier, Suffield propelled Lillie into the social world of London at age sixteen. But a parquet floor bears no resemblance to a sand beach, and a string orchestra cannot be mistaken for a brass band playing on a platform. Her unfashionable clothes and lack of conversation (plainly, small-town scandal and barnyard observations were inappropriate fodder, leaving her bereft) exposed her to the cutting remarks of rivals and the sheep-faced, stony silence of dance partners: "Lillie Le Cretin" made the rounds of all the drawing rooms in succeeding days. She fled back across the Channel.

There she ripened like the native wheat for four years. The bitter memory she boxed away, to be opened and studied whenever she became self-exalted, and put back once humbled. In this way she acquired a perfection of beauty all unaware, a faculty that would survive the early years of her glory, contributing to the effect she made. When at glory's peak it abandoned her, her descent was imminent. (It was at this precise time in life when Roy discovered that he could exploit himself as a commodity, and started his climb.) An inestimable gift, this ability to deny the evidence of compliments and of the mirror in her boudoir— deny it and mean it—which would at a critical juncture win her a reputation for modesty among her male admirers and blunt the thorns of female jealousy. Salome did not possess it. La Montez thought she did, and in the thinking surrendered all title to it.

When in time jealousy returned, in tandem with Lillie's acknowledgment that she was, indeed, beautiful, and judgment was in season, some would say that when she came of age she fell in love with a boat and married its owner, only to cast him adrift when the boat was no more. While the first part is true, the second is unfair, even if there is truth in it. Relationships begin simply, but seldom end in anything but confusion.

In point of fact, the boat was long gone when Lillie decided that Edward was the least part of the bargain.

Siblings are too often dismissed as mere stage business in dramas about great personalities. Roy Bean's obstreperous nature might never have blossomed except in the heat shed by his brothers, Josh and Sam; the quiet reserve that made a success of Lillie LeBreton's reintroduction to society built a shell that protected her from the relentless teasing of *her* brothers, who sensed her failure even though it was never reported to them. She learned to defend herself physically, and grew lithe and athletic; alertness to possible ambush taught her to stand erect and to meet the male gaze halfway, her violet eyes keen and watchful, gently defiant; her lips, curled in sardonic response to spoken jibes, resembled Diana's bow rather than Cupid's—the weapon of a huntress—above a chin round and firm and lifted in perpetual challenge. Lesser poets who encountered her in the full blaze of her incandescence wrote in private that she had the heart of a woman and the brain of a man; Oscar Wilde, a great poet gifted enough to squander his wisdom on fellow guests at dinner parties, said she kept both in jars.

We outdistance ourselves, however. It's still Jersey 1874, with London 1876 yet to come.

At the age of twenty, when Lillie was gilded with the surname that would capture three continents and christen a town, fate sailed into her life quite literally. Edward Langtry hadn't the imagination to see the artistic imagery in the January gale that swept his beloved *Red Gauntlet* toward the beach where she stood, merely which steps must be taken to avoid physical calamity: canvas struck, course adjusted into the wind. To Lillie, who had imagination enough to carry them both, the scene belonged to the opening of *The Tempest.* The flutelike quality that so many attributed to her tones was shaped reading the works of William Shakespeare aloud to her father evenings in the rectory.

A white craft flying the Union Jack, the trim vessel sprang full-size into the mouth of St. Aubin's Bay, as if perspective were a painter's quaint invention. It had a bellyful of wind and rain in its sails. Just as Lillie put her eye to the glass she'd snatched from the rector, the sun burst like a mortar through the overcast, turning the water brilliant blue and catching the flapping end of Edward's white scarf like a banner. God is a skillful stage manager, as well as a cynical manipulator of audiences. Sun and paint and bright brass obscured the fact that the boat had as many liens upon it as lines, and the resolute expression worn by its master at the bow his lack of the basic seamanship required to pilot it across the gulf that separated his resources from his debts outstanding. He was that creature peculiar to the theaters and reception halls of the nineteenth century: the gentleman pauper.

He was Irish, but not one of those knuckly Celts who brawled at weddings and wakes and never ventured out without a flagon of the blue ruin. He seldom ventured at all, and when he did it was always in yachtsman's woolens. Born in Ulster to a well-set-up shipping agent of revered stock, he preferred deck to pavement and suffered from an almost tangible horror of mobs. In his panic to avoid them he'd spent his inheritance on improvements to the *Red Gauntlet* and its sisters, the *Gertrude*, the *Bluebird*, and the *Ildegonda*, and gone into the hole maintaining them. This reclusiveness was an attraction to Lillie, for whom that long-ago experience in London remained a throbbing ache. The prospect of life in some sleepy port, with the occasional escape to the sea, supported one's faith in divine mercy.

They were introduced. She thought him handsome and admired his quiet good manners. He was dismasted by her beauty. They courted. He proposed. She accepted. Her parents gave reluctant consent. They would miss her spark about the staid old place, but also had heard the rumors of insolvency. She dismissed their cautions as exaggerations intended to keep her at home, the sentimental old dears. All her life she beheld events as scenes in a script she'd already committed to memory. She knew a good entrance when she saw it, and Edward's had been stellar.

Lillie could not know that her husband's finances, whatever they were, would never be a serious issue—although she would miss the boats when they changed owners, marooning her in the parlor with her unresponsive mate. She did not suspect that her antisocial condition was temporary, and that once survived could not be repeated, like the pox; or that Edward's complaint was chronic. She would recover from her estrangement. He would not. That a sailor with a family crest should be pathologically shy, that a daughter of a provincial man of the cloth should turn out to be an extrovert, are matters of irony; that they should be matched for life borders on pernicious design.

A story persists that on the night before she wed, Lillie

scratched her maiden name on a pane of glass in a window of her old room, using the diamond Edward had given her as a pledge of his troth. It's the kind of contrived, cloying detail that belongs to a fairy tale bowdlerized from a Black Forest original, but it happens to be true, or supported by evidence at the least. The jagged letters may still be read by visitors to the cramped drafty space, most of them pilgrims to the haunts of Roy Bean who have exhausted everything in California, New Mexico, and Texas. They trace the scratches with the same fingers that stroked the shrunken wood of the Jersey Lilly Saloon in Langtry and the characters cut into Roy's stone in the cemetery in Del Rio. A century of such contact has required the stone to be replaced three times, but it has not yet worn smooth the scrapings in the glass at St. Saviour's.

Why this inscription? Fear of the loss of identity (the bride-to-be's lament)? Or preamble to the larger billing on outdoor marquees and stone lithograph posters? Could she have been pondering re-exposing herself to public scrutiny so soon? Said Roy, in a different context: "Only a damn fool that climbs back on a hot stove would mount the same horse that throwed him once."

Edward and Lillie exchanged vows in a chilly, pre-dawn ceremony, the rector officiating, and sailed aboard the *Red Gauntlet* to their home at Cliffe Lodge in Southampton, attended by servants who had not yet given notice. The marriage consummated, they divided the spring and summer between there and excursions on the *Gauntlet* and, when it was sold to satisfy the couple's more impatient creditors, the larger *Gertrude*, an eighty-ton racing yawl they entered in a series of regattas. When they weren't competing, Mrs. Edward Langtry enjoyed the quietude in a deck chair, wearing lounging attire from her trousseau, drawing a heavy blanket to her chin during flintier days in the Channel. She thrilled to the races, but found these casual cruises idyllic, and would remember them years later when she asked that charmingly pompous Mr. Shaw if he would consider her for his Cleopatra. (He responded bluntly that she was twice the age of his adolescent Queen of the Nile; thereupon his charm failed to exist for her.)

But the somnolent days grew long; she became restless. Life as the mistress of Cliffe Lodge proved undiverting. The *Ildegonda* went on the block, followed by the *Bluebird*, as quickly as if it had sprouted wings; when the *Gertrude* vanished, Edward consoled himself reading maritime publications and rearranging his trophies. For Lillie there was only the house and tedious card games and sewing parties with the wives of Southampton. She had been brought up with boys and had seen enough of women and their secret arsenals in London. Their company would always be endured, never sought.

London, however, seemed very far away just then, and that old humiliation farther still. The music, lights, and bright chatter of Lord Suffield's ballroom grew larger in her reveries, the shame of her social experiment smaller. Ships put into and out of the harbor, their passengers bound for Paris and Lisbon and disembarking for the boat train to the English capital. She watched them from her window, a seabird in a cage overlooking the water. This imprisonment, these everlasting days and nights confined to a stranger's house, measured by the arrivals and departures of happy peripatetics, were working a cure more painful than the disease.

Ironically, she became ill.

Literally so, with fatigue, fever, and nausea. Edward thought she was with child, but the doctor suggested typhoid and prescribed rest. When her recuperation proved glacial, he reassured Edward that his wife was strong and would recover, but recommended a change of scenery to improve her spirits and allow her to assemble her defenses.

"London is gay this time of year," he said. "It will distract you both. I'll give you the name of a specialist there."

The misanthropic bridegroom paled. Lillie pouted, protested, but squirmed in secret delight. Her husband attributed this to an inflammation of the bowels.

Her later detractors would accuse her of conspiring with the doctor in a plot to destroy her marriage. She never stirred herself to deny the charge, but in all honesty she could not agree with the conclusion. There were no valedictories in a life still being lived, only intervals; *intermissions*, the Yankees called them, in their direct way. The first act had ended, that was all. The curtain was rising on the second.

THREE

Roy arrived in Old Mesilla in little but his long-handles and left in a Confederate uniform. He stole the uniform.

Friends of the Mexican officer he'd shot in Los Angeles for the favors of a woman had stripped him of his Spanish finery and strung him up with an imperfectly cured rope, so that his weight stretched it and enabled him to stand tip-toe on the ground until that same woman found him and cut him loose.

Either that, or the rope was old and worn and broke with the strain, allowing him to free himself; there are two stories to go with every incident in his life, and one is as likely as the other to be a lie.

Whatever the details of his escape, we have the testimony of his surviving brother that he showed up in Sam Bean's place of business "practically naked"; not knowing at the time how close Roy had come to that condition.

"What brings you here, apart from that short-legged dog?" Sam inclined his battered bucket head toward the one-eyed gray burro drooping splay-footed at the hitching rail outside the door. The elder brother was the least photogenic of the clan, which explained his un-Beanlike lack of interest in señoritas and the trouble attendant. He had never killed a man nor deflowered a virgin, not counting his wife.

"I came for my health."

"Law?"

"Mexicans."

"Ah."

Roy had asked an old mestizo woodcutter if he could borrow the animal. When the ancient offered to trade it for his long-handles, Roy, modest to a fault, had conked him with a cotton-wood limb. Nothing the victim wore would fit, including his wooden *zapatas*, so the desperate man had left him fully clothed to come to himself or feed a mountain lion, whichever came first, and ridden the rest of the way into New Mexico Territory with his toes dragging in the rocky soil. Corns and bunions would plague him the remainder of his long life.

"But he was my brother," allowed Sam with a sigh, and let him clothe himself from the dry goods he had in stock, fed him a plate of beans and chili peppers ("chili peppers and beans" was the only other item on the bill of fare), stood him to a soak and a shave, and gave him a fistful of cash from the El Humo box behind the counter to amuse himself with while Sam attended to his business empire.

The term is preposterously grandiose only for those who would compare the seat of Doña Ana County with St. Louis or San Francisco, or even bloody Tombstone, where the locals had the proverbial "man for breakfast" every day and washed him down with French champagne. Mesilla was trade center to a rapidly developing Southwest, crawling with bullwhackers, prospectors, tinhorns, lawyers, and women of negotiable virtue, but never covered more than a few acres in a county the size of Portugal. Sam sold rooms, meal, liquor, overalls, tobacco, patent medicines, and games of chance, all under one roof made of sticks and mud, and served as sheriff. His constituency was light on registered voters, heavy on rattlesnakes, gila monsters, scorpions, and renegade Apaches, but by the time of his reunion with Roy he'd long since given up on trying to run outlaws to ground within two weeks of their infraction; his jurisdiction was too big for any army to patrol. He'd even forgotten where he'd put the pistol that came with the office.

Which was just as well for the safety of anyone who stood in front of it or behind it, or for that matter off to the side. Sam knew nothing about the care of firearms, and might have tried to discharge it with a mud-dauber's nest plugging the barrel. He was regarded as the gentle brother, if not the quietest, who would rather bellow a man deaf than gun him down.

Roy, who was neither gentle nor quiet, throttled back. The circumstances of his arrival seemed to have embarrassed him— a character stretch, perhaps, but less so than regret of his past behavior or fear of landing back in trouble—and to work off his debt and demonstrate he'd reformed, he took a shift behind the bar. (He'd spent part of the money Sam had given him on a silver-mounted saddle to impress women and had the rest stolen from him by one before he could buy a horse to stick under it; a sort of "Gift of the Magi" tale, frontier style.) There he stayed for two years.

Tying that apron string was one of those illuminating moments, like physical relations with your first willing partner or when you descended through the mist of the Rockies and California sprawled glistening at your feet like the green felt on a faro table. Roy discovered he liked pouring drinks and jawing with customers, and as with everything else, including making love and shooting jealous suitors, he found a talent for doing something he liked. Beer and whiskey were easy, no challenge there, but if a fellow just down from Denver ordered something he hadn't heard of, he dissolved rat poison in a glass of tequila and served it with a sprig of juniper. The pinch of poison wasn't enough to cause death, just bring on a thumping headache and loosen the bowels, and judging by the condition of the outhouses in town, loose bowels were nothing novel there. If the victim had a sense of humor, here was a friendship in the making, but if he squawked, there was the bung-starter close to hand. Many years before he took the oath to defend the constitution of the State of Texas, Roy learned the authority of a smart smack with a mallet.

Most of the time he mopped the bar, refilled Hermitage bottles with hog piss distilled locally, and topped tall stories with largely unembellished anecdotes from his frisky youth. Word got around that Sam Bean's was a place of entertainment as sure as Madame Cucaracha's Hotel for Unmarried Women down by the river, and that the barkeep's conversation split more ribs than a single-bladed plow hitched to a three-legged mule, with a floor show featuring pilgrims moaning and holding their guts thanks to Roy's arsenite-of-lead special. Sam, no micromanager to begin with, came in from the emporium side to see what all the hooraw was about, saw his brother scooping greenbacks and silver into the cigar box, and reckoned one or the other of them would be governor someday.

Then Civil War broke out; or maybe Indians attacked. The order of events is muzzy after all this time, and in the heat of the fighting was probably not much clearer.

Displaying the family entrepreneurial spirit, Sam exported Roy's gift of gab to Pinos Altos, a mining camp in a barely accessible area of the Black Range, where a strike was rumored imminent. Along narrow switchback trails the brothers freighted goods and fixtures, including a billiard table they cursed and unloaded often in order to heave the wagon free when it sank to its hubs in muck, and spread their wares at last under a tent on America's newest and muddiest Main Street. Next door on either side was the second establishment in the Madame Cucaracha franchise and an assay office specializing in butcher's thumbs.

Miners, prospectors, and the odd tame Indian browsed among shovels, picks, pans, Dutch ovens, sacks of flour and coffee, and Mr. Levi Strauss's new line of heavy-duty work trousers fashioned from sturdy cotton fabric milled in Nîmes, France ("cloth *de Nîmes,*" the advertising said), saturated with deep blue dye that came off on sweaty hands and reinforced with copper rivets. Before they left, they drank their fill of putative Hermitage (all except the Indian, whom Roy politely crab-walked out the door and deposited in the alley) and spent the rest of their ore samples exploring the mystery of billiards. The rumors of bonanza were confirmed, and the brothers were considering investing their profits in a board-and-batten place with a proper roof and possibly a piano, when the South fired on Fort Sumter.

U.S. troops decamped to engage the enemy, ceding New Mexico to the Apaches, who had plans of their own for the Black Mountains. For generations, they had withdrawn to the shelter of caves and impregnable promontories when Mexican *federales* pursued them across the border following Indian raids on pueblos, and being Chiricahua and grumpy after so much hard riding and some loss of personnel, were vexed to discover the white man's civilization taken root in their ancestral retreat. Small of stature, smooth-skinned over surreptitious muscle like pearl-divers in the tropics—a species as foreign to them as top-hatted financiers strolling Fifth Avenue with their sticks—they had faces made up of bunched ovals, like boulders stacked by gla-ciers, with neither a whisker nor an eyelash in the band; ugly little buggers, by the standards of anyone but an Apache, and nearly indistinguishable from their scrawny mounts. They had fought with Cochise and that rabid whelp Geronimo and deco-rated themselves with hair plaited from scalps lifted throughout southern Arizona Territory. They announced their intentions by capturing two miners and boiling their brains suspended upside-down over a mesquite fire, then proceeded to the tent camp, barking and yelping like a prairie dog town on the march and abusing their horses with the ends of their hackamores.

"I lost three close friends in the Battle of Pinos Altos," Roy confided to Lillie, meaning customers in good standing, "and know not how many braves I dispatched personally. Between Sam, myself, and other citizens of the camp, fifteen savages did not survive to plunder another settlement."

The remaining twenty-five did; but there is no use quibbling over details. Roy may have gleaned the casualty count from *The Mesilla Times*, in part because no one keeps tabs in the heat of fighting, and bloated Indian corpses are better flung into steep ravines than collated, but also because by the time the story was published, he and Sam were back in town, having abandoned their inventory and billiard table to competitors more deter-mined to carry on after the raid. Old-time Mesillans swore that on the day of battle, Sheriff Sam at least was behind the bar at home, still scratching his bucket head over what had become of his pistol, which he was obliged to pay for when he left office if it failed to materialize. At least one witness claimed to have seen Roy doctoring bottled spirits with water from the cistern out back that same day.

But in that first year of national fratricide, skirmishes with the aborigines were telegraph-column stuff at best, with no room for them on the front page (or page three, if like *The Times* the newspaper was wrapped in advertising). Roy, no friend of authority he wasn't related to, went for States' Rights and supported the Confederacy. An alternate account, which seems more in character, suggests the decision was made when he formed a covetous attachment to the splendid butternut uniform worn by a lieutenant serving under General John R. Baylor, followed him to the bathhouse, and snatched it from a chair while the officer was marinating in a tub of scalding water, under the cover of steam.

The story may be a canard. Ostentatious articles of apparel were common casualties in towns where gambling was present—boots made to order were a popular medium of exchange—and Roy may have come by the uniform either by honest barter or across a table surrounded by sporting gentlemen. However it entered his possession, when at length the disgruntled lieutenant donned mufti to rejoin his regiment headed for Glorieta, Roy fastened the double row of brass buttons, buckled on the belt with its ceremonial sword chased with gold, and wore them proudly until Lee's surrender. After that, the uniform accompanied him in mothballs through all his travels until he reached Vinegarroon, Texas, where he had it let out to accommodate his more generous proportions and hung in a wardrobe to smooth out the wrinkles, the better to strike a *figura muy hermosa* when one day he presented himself to the Jersey Lily in the flesh.

He may have exposed it to damage in the Battle of Glorieta,

which secured New Mexico for the Confederacy for a delirious few days, until dwindling provisions and lack of reinforcements compelled the rebels to retire from the field and return the Southwest to the Union. Personal accounts credit him with organizing a company of irregulars christened the Free Rovers. More jaundiced observers referred to its recruitment from among loyal patrons of Sam Bean's saloon as the Forty Thieves, who roamed freely through chattel belonging to neighbors suspected of Northern sympathies. They said the closest the band got to the arena of honor was to seize the supplies intended for it.

For himself, Roy laid claim to having performed duties of espionage, possibly with justification: It's been said that the Union victory might have taken place years sooner but for the secrets that flowed so promiscuously in establishments where liquor was served.

Roy was philosophical in defeat. He wrote Lillie that a man who would spend thousands on traps to prevent a fox from robbing him of hundreds in chickens, and went bankrupt on the purchase, was no less noble for the struggle. She thought this a fine sentiment, and felt that a man of principles would obtain a fair hearing in Judge Bean's court. Roy wrote the letter, or rather dictated it in his own less sculpted style, many years after he robbed brother Sam of his cash and a good horse and saddle and joined a wagon train bound for San Antonio.

FOUR

In 1876, as its foster child celebrated the centenary of its emancipation, Great Britain straddled the globe. It had broken Napoleon, crushed mutinies, acquired territory, and set democracy back a generation; thanks to its treasury, there were no noxious republics yammering on its frontiers. The empire was still three years away from its spectacular first defeat in Africa, and had yet to experience the series of disasters that would eventually reinstate England as a nation of humble shopkeepers. The Widow of Whitehall ruled half the world's population from Glasgow to the Gulf of Siam, and a fellow couldn't find a place in her whole bloody capital to rest his aching feet.

Edward Langtry was the first to suspect that his wife's illness had been a combination of simple ennui and an intrigue with her physician to transport the couple to London. Perhaps the man could not be blamed for having fallen under her spell. Edward had, after all, and was still under it, although each man who joined him pushed him a little closer to the outer edge. He was a bit of a hypochondriac, who maintained a well-stocked private medical library, and had read up on typhoid. Fatigue was its most persistent symptom. Yet within days of their arrival at Waterloo Station, Lillie had dragged him almost non-stop through abbeys, museums, galleries, and every blasted shop on Regent Street and Savile Row and in Piccadilly Circus, that recluse's nightmare where all the souls that could not find shelter at the same time barked and bustled and jabbed a fellow's ribs with brollies and parasols and walking sticks.

He could not keep up with her. Breaking trot to maintain sight of her plumage lest he lose her in the mob—the sinister, snarling, gluttonous mob—made his legs wobble and the soles of his feet erupt in ulcers. If Lillie was ailing, he must be at death's door.

That door had opened, in fact, although not for him. God forgive him, it had allowed him to draw breath, but now here they were back in the maelstrom. If anything she seemed more determined than before to place her dainty heels all over the city of four million. It was as if she were fleeing grief at top speed.

He lunged and grasped her arm. "Madam, I beseech you."

Turning with an expression of impatience mixed with pain—for Edward's grip was desperate—she saw his own physical distress writ plain on his face and relented. "Very well, Edward," she said. "Eaton Place it is."

Eaton, their furnished quarters in a building erected on land newly reclaimed from swamp and rendered respectable, was for Lillie a repository of reflection and sadness, to be avoided until she was too exhausted to do anything but sleep. Their London adventure had scarcely begun when a telegram came announcing that Reggie, the brother closest to her in age and confidences, had been killed in a riding accident.

Reggie had tormented her the least, had accompanied her on neighborhood forays stealing door knockers and tipping privies, and the brief return to Jersey to attend his services had reminded her of these things, and of her past. Despite charting a course toward a new horizon, she was still tied up at the dock. It was the second time fate had taunted her with her humble origins, and once again the setting was London.

By the time she confessed these conclusions to Roy, the seagoing metaphor had become elaborate. "From that sad day to this, I have ever remained under full sail, lashed to the mast, no matter what lay ahead. Whatever it was, it was not half so frightening as what I had left behind." (Roy, refolding the letter and his spectacles on his dusty front porch, felt seasick and sent son Little Roy to fetch him brandy. The busthead he sold from barrels was recreational; fortified wines strictly prescriptive for gastric complaints.)

Lillie shared with this distant correspondent impressions she kept from her own daughter; not to be secretive, but because Jeanne would only pretend to understand challenges she herself had not yet been called upon to confront. Roy, too, had lost a beloved brother, and lived the vagabond life of furnished rooms and strangers with hidden motives. More important, she found in him a credible substitute for her sibling accomplice. Early in the association, the Jersey Lily had sensed something of the anarchist in the Law West of the Pecos. His attempts to gentrify himself in her eyes had not been entirely successful; she was an experienced actress, after all, well-versed in euphemism and subterfuge. She was part barbarian herself. She was also a woman reared in the faith, and trusted him not to break their unspoken seal.

He did not. From the day he received her first letter, carrying a stamp with Queen Victoria's portly profile upon it, he'd committed himself to struggle his way from salutation through signature without assistance. In time he even learned to discriminate between Lillie's schoolgirl hand and the more businesslike cursive of her secretary, and to know from them whether she was responding politely or opening her heart. Male acquaintances celebrated the cleverness of his escapades or condemned their crudity; females he had known, in and out of the biblical sense, swore that he was a gentleman from start to finish. His wife, who knew him best, gave thanks to the blessed Virgin for the distance that came to separate them, although she acknowledged his kindness toward children, his own among others. He possessed charm: The Carmens and Rosalitas of San Diego and Old Mesilla had not brought him comforts in jail out of impersonal Christian charity. He enjoyed the company of women for its own sake. They sensed this and appreciated it as something rare in their world.

His inner circle insisted that in his last years, in great part because of the happy ordeal of reading Lillie's letters, Roy's literacy had progressed to the point where he was often seen in conference with a threadworn copy of Scripture. ("Looking for a loophole," muttered one sour fellow who had come out on the short end of a land transaction with the founder of Langtry.)

But this is not Roy's time onstage. Parallel lives that follow so many similar curves are at times mistaken the one for the other, and apt to intersect.

Edward was no less sensitive to the feelings of the woman who shared his bed; neither was he beyond exploiting them to his own end. What may be dismissed as caddishness in another must in his case be assigned to the weakness of his arches and lingering unease with the stream of humanity that seemed to flow constantly past the door of even so quiet a place as Eaton. If she would employ poor health to transplant them to that mortal cesspool, he would use her sorrow to return them home.

"This house has sad associations," he said in their parlor, fixed and decorated by unknown hands, foreign tastes. Even the copy of *The Times* he'd just set aside belonged to a subscription arranged by the previous tenant. "This was where we got the news. You know, the racing season starts next week."

"Which racing season is that?" Though she knew very well which. She was sitting perpendicular to her husband, staring at her hands twisted in her lap.

"Southampton, of course. Just because we haven't a boat is no reason not to take part in the festivities."

"You forget I'm in mourning."

"You can't be forever. Reggie wouldn't want it."

"He never liked you, you know. He didn't even attend our wedding."

He looked away, drew on his pipe. At times like this he seemed a scolded puppy, an object of equal parts pity and contempt. Was this the young Viking she had first laid eyes on at the prow of his gallant craft, scarf flying, his face a determined mask? Disillusionment and grief were closely related.

"I'm sorry," she said. "Truly I am. I can't go back to Southampton. All our friends would be sympathetic. I should drown."

He did not return to the subject; personal confrontations upset him and drove him deeper into retreat. That night they had tickets to *The Merchant of Venice* at the Prince of Wales's Theater, purchased before the bereavement. A tragedy offered no solace. She considered letting the seats stand empty, but could not endure another evening in that room, listening to the grinding of the clock's gears and Edward turning pages, the stem of his pipe gurgling unpleasantly. They dressed and hailed a hansom.

The evening was only partially diverting, and for the wrong reasons. Some remnant from an earlier period of acting mugged and postured as Shylock, looking like a Chinese villain from melodrama in his skullcap and sackcloth; she wondered, were there Jews in the Orient? Ellen Terry's Portia, on the other hand, had already made her a required feature in every successful drawing room from Balmoral to Buckingham, where Her Majesty was Not Amused but His Highness the Prince preened in her presence. Both performances were lost on Lillie, for whom play-actors' travails on a painted set had no resonance. The time would come when she would compare her carriage and gestures, the pitch of her voice, with Terry's out of professional necessity, but now was not that time. She willed toward faster motion the hands on the watch pinned to her bodice and waited for the gaslights to come up.

Racing season came and went. Winter crept in aboard a scow of brown fog, one part mist, nine parts exhaust from a hundred thousand coal fires that warmed little but themselves and settled soot on curtains and carpets through the ductwork. Lillie traded the smutty air and deathly quiet of the hearth for solitary tramps through Hyde Park, where the falling snowflakes at least were unsoiled until they mixed with the slush at her feet; she was learning to appreciate the comforts of the moment.

Her twilight wanderings did not pass unmarked.

A young Irish writer hurrying toward his paying job at the Lyceum Theatre mistook her, in her cerecloth and bonnet, for a shopgirl, albeit one uncommonly beautiful and ineffably sad. She crossed his path without turning her head or speaking, a bewitching phantom straight out of Mallory, and when the fog enveloped her he was uncertain he had seen her at all. Twenty years later he would change her attire from black to white and create an unforgettable image in his only enduring work, a novel about an aristocratic vampire from the barbaric Balkans and the English woman he chose for his bride. (Ironically, the wordsmith would fail to connect his youthful vision with the glittering woman he would meet in the presence of Henry Irving, his tyrannical partner, at the height of her vogue; the visions of one's impressionable youth are seldom so easily put to rest.)

Spring arrived, and with its celadon shoots and timid tiny blossoms appeared the promise of change. At the new Royal Aquarium at Westminster, among transparent tropical fish and the good-natured grin of the odd bottle-nosed dolphin, a voice from what had seemed the buried past hailed her.

It belonged to Lord Ranelagh, a friend of the LeBretons and a frequent summer visitor to Jersey, who expressed astonishment at finding her so far from home. Lillie introduced Edward to the tall, florid man dressed in immaculate morning attire. The men exchanged cards. That afternoon, their landlady presented a silver tray holding an invitation written in flawless calligraphy on stout linen stock requesting the Langtrys' presence at the peer's house in Fulham that weekend.

Edward was a pragmatist. The two men discovered they had mutual friends in shipping, and Ranelagh had shown interest in Edward's passion for sailing, but Edward knew full well the man had been impressed more by his wife's appearance and quiet speech than by any distinguishing characteristics of her consort's. He doubted His Lordship would recognize him on the street without Lillie on his arm, but he was accustomed to his near-invisibility in her presence. He agreed to the weekend because it promised a holiday away from the throngs and an opportunity to draw his wife out of her melancholy. At the aquarium, they had paused before a creature in an elaborate carapace partially interred in gravel at the base of the tank. Edward had been struck by Lillie's reflection in the glass, superimposed over the image of the half-hidden crustacean. Her shell was thicker even than his own. It was one thing for a colorless specimen like himself to be shut away from the rest of the populace; to deny it any approach to the angelic figure here at his side seemed a sin.

In later years, when he was scorned as a weakling who could not keep the Jersey Lily in his own planter-box or simpered over as an unwitting step-stone in Lillie's ascent, Edward would draw strength from this early awareness that he'd have been wrong to try to keep her for himself alone. Greater love had no man than that he would give his wife for another.

They packed for a stay of two nights, strolled through the estate's gardens and among old-growth oaks that had witnessed the passage of Richard Lionheart, stood awkwardly holding hands like newlyweds where the lawn swept down to the bank of the Thames, and watched the excursionists sail past; she observing the barges filled with bright dresses and brighter chatter, he contemplating the lines of trimmer craft rigged out for racing. On Sunday, more guests sat on scrolled outdoor benches, clicking their cups in their saucers and laughing when someone repeated something someone else had said at some similar party. It all belonged to a world where grief had no meaning.

And then it was over, and they were back in Eaton Place, although with a difference. Lillie found herself humming a tune played by the string quartet Lord Ranelagh had engaged for the gardens, and stopped herself abruptly to suggest to Edward that they go to a concert. Without a word, Edward abandoned his argument in favor of a quiet evening at home and opened *The Times* to the culture section.

When they returned, wrung out and sotted with cantatas and fugues, the landlady was waiting with her tray. Lady Sebright, a patron of the arts who conducted a salon for writers, actors, and painters, had invited them to a Sunday At Home. She had met the Langtrys at Fulham, it seemed, although neither could place her: The grounds had been filled with eccentrics, titled and otherwise. Belatedly, Lillie remembered hearing her name during their first whirlwind tour of town.

Edward, one shoe off a throbbing foot, felt a stab of panic. First a weekend, then an interminable concert, now a dreaded evening in some stuffy parlor jampack with strangers and—depend upon it—an amateur coloratura squalling next to a piano. What had he wrought in his innocent concern for his wife's humor? He grasped at flotsam. "Guests at such affairs get themselves up like peacocks. You're still in weeds."

But she had something she thought not inappropriate, a black evening dress her mother had pressed her to order from Madame Nicolle's during her visit home for Reggie's services. Trying it on before the mirror, she disapproved of its high neck; her months in London had taught her to discriminate between city and country fashion. A few ruthless minutes with shears and a needle and thread and she had a daring frock that left her neck and shoulders exposed. If she was to embarrass herself as she had on her first trip to the capital, it would be for appearing too bold, not timid.

With her hair in its chatelaine braid and Empress Josephine curls on her forehead, she and Edward were announced at Lady Sebright's in Lowndes Square—and promptly abandoned by their hostess, a product of paint and powder who wore diamonds the way a general wore his decorations of valor, to attend to a crisis in the kitchen. Marooned among strangers, the pair fled to a seating arrangement in a far corner. Lillie was convinced that it was to be Lord Suffield's all over again. She owned no jewels, wore no paint, and felt dowdy in her funereal apparel.

But by the time the lady returned with apologies, she found Mrs. Langtry quietly holding court. Seated on her skirted chair, she offered a slender hand to a reception line of men in tails, her husband standing beside her seat, stiff as a dress dummy.

Lillie suspected mockery, and kept her responses guarded. One man in particular offered the prospect of torment, however different from her brothers' brutish ways. He was a bantam sort with a corseted waist in a ruffled shirt, with black-dyed hair and a monocle, Lillie's first; it was an affectation of social climbers who never seemed to notice that no one of breeding appeared to own one. He snatched up her hand with a sharp yelp of a laugh, like a terrier's bark. He was a popinjay straight out of newspaper caricature, belonging in a frame on the wall of some gentleman's club devoted to whimsy, and reeked of gardenias. She assumed he was a pederast, a common affliction in the artistic set.

"I observed you entertaining Johnny Millais and Freddy Leighton just now," he said in that same high, affected note. "I've no doubt they asked to do your likeness. Pray do not allow them to tarnish your beauty with Royal Academy paint. Let Whistler paint you, madam, and posterity will cherish your memory."

She smiled, her face warm. She guessed he was American, for all his ludicrous attempt at a West End accent. If this was mockery, he was a target far broader than she. "When you put it that way, Mr. Whistler," she said, "no lady can possibly refuse."

FIVE

For every tooth in every gear there is a corresponding notch, waiting to be filled in order to set a great machine in motion. For Roy Bean, that notch was Texas.

He found it a place of infinite variety. The panhandle country was as flat and without feature as its name implied except where it opened suddenly into columned canyons deep and dark and crawling with Comanches; the green hills of Austin reminded him of his native Kentucky; and in San Antonio, a man could walk the length of an adobe-lined street and follow every step of the chili-cooking process with just his nose. The town looked and smelled like San Diego of happy memory, Josh's murder notwithstanding. The young women in such places invariably had good teeth, trim ankles, and high complexions—flowers soon to fade and transform themselves into stout harridans grinding corn in the plaza, but more precious still for that—as well as an eye for a handsome young stranger who dressed like a *picador* turned out for a night of *celebración*. There he stepped down and led brother Sam's horse down to the river to drink, and while wait-ing decided that he would die in Texas.

He was thirty-eight years old, after all, and a man was not ex-pected to live much past fifty, if he was lucky enough to make it that far. He calculated he'd used up most of the luck he'd been dealt at birth at the end of that rope in Los Angeles.

There was just enough left of the money he'd taken the bor-row of from Sam to refresh his Spanish wardrobe and, when he found a buyer for the horse and saddle, secure a wagon and team. He'd learned most of what needed to be known about the freighting business hauling that blasted billiard table up the ver-tical road to Pinos Altos. The layout of south central Texas was at least sideways, and the mesquite grew too close to the ground to conceal even so contrary an obstacle as a band of renegade Indi-ans, giving a man a fair chance at a warning shot into the heart of the first brave who rode within rifle range. With the railroads confined to the extreme right and left of North America until the war ran its course, any fellow willing to pack goods and pas-sengers from the San Antonio River to wherever was assured a living so long as arrow and rattlesnake permitted.

Then, of course, there was the blockade; but breath was scarcely worth the trouble it took to draw it if someone else wasn't determined to deliver you from the burden.

It was 1863, the dead middle of the War Against Northern Ag-gression, as Roy would refer to it in his letters; certainly there was nothing civil about it from the point of view of one who had heard the thunder of Yankee naval cannon punching holes in French trading vessels attempting to run supplies from the sym-pathetic Louis Napoleon to the Confederacy. Not that Roy had been among those who'd heard it. With so much commotion in the Gulf of Mexico, fording the Rio Grande to collect and ship

salt pork, cornmeal, burlap, and liquor—that thief that robbed
men of their good sense and so fueled the conflict on both sides
of the issue—and resell them for a confiscatory profit in the
states, required no more consideration than wading through a
puddle. The trade ran both ways, with a bale of Louisiana cotton fetching gold from dressmakers in Paris to shore up the
Virginia scrip that in other circumstances was only good for
starting fires. At the height of the fighting, depending upon the
size of his audience, Roy enjoyed setting flame to Union currency and using it to ignite a quarter cigar. He had by this time
acquired a fleet of wagons and oxen and mules sufficient to re-
open the Oregon Trail. Just how he acquired them would prove
to be an important point in his passage.

In letters he forebore mention of profit and wrote instead of
sacrifice. As he put it, the struggle for States' Rights taught him
the satisfaction and hardship of breaking the law of the land for
a cause greater than himself. He did not add that it taught him
also the pleasure of manipulating the law in his favor. Both lessons would pay him dividends in the fullness of his years.

Breaking first. Manipulation later.

Supporting the South was hard work, particularly in the beginning. He never owned a slave. It's questionable if he ever saw
one close up. But he found in oxen the embodiment of Uncle
Tom: loyal, resolute laborers that only ceased to lean into the
traces when the bullwhackers' lines grew so taut that forward
motion seemed futile. Mules, on the other hand, were beasts
bred by sodomy from the Devil out of Cain, responding to neither carrots nor caresses nor soft words, but only to the sting of
the lash. But they were plentiful and cheap, cutting less deeply
into profits, so Roy made up the difference with a stout whip in
a good right hand. Then there were chuckholes and broken

wheels, the jack and the shoulder, and before them the inevitable off-loading of heavy cargo to make the replacement possible. Roy quickly shed the blubber of the sedentary life behind the bar, packed on muscle, and with it the reputation of a wagon boss not to be challenged over some slight; in time he had two full sets of knuckles broken and healed over that would bring him fiery pain during the winters of his extremity. Busthead was the nearest thing to a cure.

That first year in Texas he spent more time fighting men on his side of the conflict than he did the enemy. Freighters were hot-tempered and thin-skinned, but a smart blow to the bridge of the nose with the knotted end of a pack rope usually finished the argument and spared a fist. A more personal technique was required with San Antonians who took a dim view of Mexicans and of white men who fraternized with them. When someone called him a greaser-lover, Roy was almost always just in from a long haul, tired, irritable, and empty-handed. He didn't always come out on top in these brawls, but those who did suffered gouged eyes, ear lobes bitten off, and sundry other inconveniences. Roy was intolerant of the intolerant. "A man that takes it against a fellow just because he ain't the same as him is no better than a Chinaman," Roy told the sweet young amateur nurses who bathed and stuck his hands with plaster.

Such considerations aside—in his experience, violence was a necessary evil in any successful enterprise—he found blockade running largely to his liking. His personal antagonists feared him, and for similar reasons he had the respect of the men he commanded. He established comfortable living quarters in an unassuming adobe off North Alamo Street with a cozy kiva fire-place, a fine horsehair armchair, and the only feather mattress between New Orleans and Santa Fe, which he shared with his señorita of the season. His neighbors looked up to him as *un Anglo simpático* and a prominent local businessman who tipped their children generously when they ran errands for him, and he kept enough cash under a floorboard in his bedroom to offset damage to his bottom line caused by his own consumption of the spirits he provided to customers. It was the best living he'd known, but also monstrous hard work. He counted his rare moments of leisure the way a poor man kept track of his pesos and racked his brain for a way to enjoy monetary wealth without stirring from his armchair.

In time, his own larcenous nature would light that very way. That the law would provide the fuel to set it burning, that these two seeming opposites would ever perform in concert, could not have entered into his thinking at this juncture.

It happened in this order:

First, the war ended, reversing his fortunes when the blockade was lifted.

Second, he was slapped with a lawsuit.

The compensation demanded was 350 Yankee dollars, an impossible sum in Reconstruction Texas. It would buy thirty suits of clothes, waistcoats included; fifteen pump organs, assuming a man had urgent need for such an appliance; a similar number of fine cemetery monuments carved from Florentine marble, an item far more practical in a Texas teeming with stirred-up Indians and former guerrillas. Roy didn't have it, but he was sanguine: "The only times in a man's life when what he owes don't worry him is when he's stinkin' rich and when he ain't got a pot to piss in."

He wasn't as badly off as all that, but he wouldn't be lighting good stogies with greenbacks again anytime soon. The sudden finish to four years of bloodshed and inflation had caught him short. The price of merchandise once held dear fell below wholesale, and he'd had to sell half his assets at bargain rates in order to pay off his men, who weren't easily gulled and who were too many and too motivated to be pacified with the knotted end of a pack rope. What remained of his outfit represented all his working capital.

The legal trouble went back to one of his earliest ventures in the smuggling trade. Pat Milmo, a dyspeptic general store baron in San Antonio, supplied Roy with teams and equipment and engaged him to freight forty bales of cotton from outside Galveston to Eagle Pass on the Rio Grande, a distance of some 350 miles across the entire bottom third of the state. The train battled desert heat and outran Comanches who had taken advantage of the army's distraction to reclaim all their old territory and a large tract that had never belonged to them. Roy rattled up to the storage barn in Eagle Pass sunburned and dusty, only to be told by Milmo's man there that he knew nothing of any shipment. It could rot in the wagons for all he cared.

Roy fumed and sent a letter to San Antonio by the Overland. After nearly two weeks of enforced inactivity, a communication arrived from Milmo instructing his agent to accept delivery and pay compensation. But the delay had cost Roy business and eroded the black side of the ledger with living expenses for himself and his crew and fodder for the animals at bordertown rates. He made up the difference by seizing the wagons and teams that had been entrusted to him for the journey. What would become a substantial accumulation of wagons and animals by the end of the war was founded on someone else's property. This was nothing new in the history of New World capitalism; Vanderbilt had made much the same start. But no one was erecting statues in honor of such sharp practice on the raw frontier, only scaffolds.

Milmo might have considered a lynch party, but it wouldn't restore his chattel. Instead he went to court. Roy's immediate response was to raise a stake on a pair of loaded dice and file a countersuit seeking redress for himself in the amount of two thousand twenty-eight dollars.

He was an unlettered man, but a mathematical savant when it came to figures preceded by dollar signs. The unexpected diversion in Eagle Pass from the twenty-ninth day of December, 1863, until the tenth of January, 1864, had let eight wagons lie fallow and reduced thirteen laborers and one hundred eighty mules to a state of immobility for thirteen days. ("A mule takes exactly as long to start as it spent stopped," Roy pointed out.) Calculated on the wartime market at twelve dollars per wagon per day, Roy's deposition demanded of Pat Milmo the aforementioned sum.

The complainant-turned-defendant threw a proper Irish fit. When it was over he requested a writ of attachment, to be served the moment Roy showed his face with property to attach. The writ was granted by a justice of the peace who had had personal experience with Roy's trained dice.

Whereupon this bartender, freighter, smuggler, duelist, seducer of women, and all-around wastrel demonstrated a talent for legerdemain. Man and tackle disappeared, along with six bulky elmwood wagons and ninety mules. The house off North Alamo stood abandoned, with an empty hole in the floorboards under the bed with the feather mattress. The sheriff's men asked around the saloons, brothels, and barbershops where their quarry had been known to pass time, interviewed a number of attractive young women in the glowering presence of their black-clad *dueñas*, and drew only eloquent shrugs. Subterfuge on their part was dismissed. Even Roy's enemies—cuckolded husbands, broken-nosed teamsters, a number of men who'd been fleeced in games of chance—swore ignorance as to his whereabouts. No one had witnessed the leavetaking.

"Ground's too hard this time of year to dig a deep hole," the sheriff reported to an incredulous Milmo. "We'll get him when he sticks up his head to bark."

The barking didn't take place until March 1866, when a train of eight wagons trundled into town from the south laden with barrels of molasses and vanilla extract bound for El Paso, a town well known for its sweet tooth. During his self-enforced exile, the wagon boss, huskier and hairier than ever, had managed not only to flush out a customer, but also to acquire two additional wagons and teams as well as a fine new chocolate-colored sombrero with gold thread woven around the brim. Many of his drivers were *mestizos* with humorless faces and, it was alleged, bounties on their heads in old Mexico. Machetes swung from their belts and there didn't appear to be a complete set of fingers among them. ("Dumb greasers probably took ahold of the wrong end," commented a man who'd come off the worse in a dispute with Roy in the street over his associations.)

Word reached the sheriff, who waited until the boss and crew put in to a saloon to settle the dust, then installed a party of newly deputized men in the drivers' seats. Wagons, teams, and cargo were removed to an impound yard. The barrels filled with perishables were placed in the cellar of the jail.

The court was scheduled to rule on the disposition of the goods in August. Ferocious rumors spread that Roy had raised the seed money for the molasses and vanilla extract and two extra wagons by robbing a bank in Nacogdoches or by hijacking a shipment of Springfield rifles on its way to Fort Worth and selling it to Comancheros for trade with renegade Indians, or that he'd simply rolled for it with his talented ivories. As summer dragged on and the only activity Roy showed was to fan himself slowly with a palm leaf in a rocking chair in the shade of a porch roof, speculation supported the last suggestion as the laziest and most likely. The hell-for-leather blockade runner of fighting days had subsided into the contemplative life of the weary veteran.

When court opened, all of the principals were present except Roy. Assuming from his recent demeanor that the defendant had surrendered his case, the justice of the peace found for the plaintiff and ordered that the mules and wagons be turned over to Pat Milmo and that the cargo be auctioned off and the proceeds awarded to him as well for his trouble and suffering. The gavel had just come down when a deputy entered and whispered in the sheriff's ear. It developed that while court was in session, Roy Bean had stirred himself from his rocking chair long enough to assemble his *mestizos*, hitch up the wagons in the impound yard, and drive them out of San Antonio.

When this had in fact been established to everyone's satisfaction, the man behind the bench informed Milmo that his opponent was now justly in his debt in the amount of 350 dollars, but as the property under examination was no longer inside court jurisdiction, the plaintiff was unlikely to collect upon it.

The summer recess followed, a two-week period during which no legal action was important enough to compel both sides and a magistrate to swelter in a close room. Meanwhile, the vanilla and molasses earmarked for auction vanished from the jail cellar. Some blamed pilferage on the part of the new deputies, but public opinion ran strongly toward a bribe provided by the man who'd brought the barrels to San Antonio in the first place, with the deputies lending their own backs to the reloading. The portion of the process that kept it in conversation long after later atrocities should have taken its place was just how Roy had engineered the thing, spiriting a hundred braying mules and eight clattering overloaded Conestogas out of a city of thousands, where a boll weevil could be overheard farting in a bale of cotton, without raising a whisker of suspicion.

The answer was simpler than the question. The jail and impound yard were square in the center of the Mexican quarter, where Roy's friends were thicker than the stuff in the barrels. The men sat on porches smoking and passing bottles of mescal back and forth and the women watched from behind lace curtains as the train disembarked for El Paso.

Roy carried an extra bit of ballast in the form of a book the size and weight of a cinderblock in the compartment under the footboard of the lead wagon: the 1866 edition of the *Revised Statutes of Texas*, which contained the precedent that had enabled him to delay his opponent's case with a countersuit long enough for him to recoup his fortunes south of the border. His attorney, a carpetbagger from Massachusetts who'd come West to help settle claims between cattlemen, didn't miss the volume until after his client left, neglecting to pay him. It traveled everywhere with Roy from then on, along with the loaded dice and his yellow-handled Colt. He knew an ally when he saw one, as well as one that would not crawfish in the face of adversity.

SIX

"The Jersey Lily."

Lillie started, breaking her pose. The sudden presence of a human voice at the end of twenty minutes filled with nothing but bristles stroking canvas and lips popping on the stem of a pipe, and the words spoken, caught her unprepared. "I beg your pardon?"

John Everett Millais used the edge of his stained smock to wipe excess paint off his brush and repeated what he'd said, the pipe clenched between his teeth. "I've heard of the plant, although I've yet to see so much as a blossom. Is it native to the island, like yourself?"

"I am, but it is not. Mama told me it was introduced to the north shore when a ship from Africa fetched up on the rocks."

"Much as you fetched up on London. Do you, please, write your mother and send for some."

"I hope you won't be disappointed."

"I rather hope I shall. You are the most exasperating subject

I've ever painted. You look simply beautiful for about fifty-five out of sixty minutes in the hour."

She considered this carefully. City banter was a tiger trap, best approached with a cautious step. "Praise be to mercy you choose those five minutes to rest."

"Quite the opposite. During them, you surpass beauty. A man cannot perform under such conditions. They require a machine like Jimmy Whistler."

She smiled and inclined her head. Mention of Whistler reminded her the little peacock was all chirp and no flight, always taking her to task for her decision to model for a "popular" painter like Millais and repeating his intention to immortalize her; but when she said, "Very well, when?" he seemed distracted and never returned to the subject until the next time. She wondered if there was truth in Mr. Millais's flattery and that Whistler suspected she was beyond his talents. She'd seen his work in galleries and thought it dull in comparison to his plumed and scented person. The monochrome portrait he'd rendered of his own mother might have been George Washington done by an uninspired hand.

Lillie was beginning to realize that in London imagination was in as short supply as sunshine. In Whistler's case it extended only to his outlandish dress and tea party tittle-tattle, and would likely be forgotten the moment he drew his last supercilious breath, while the spirited, more modern work of Millais and Lord Leighton and George Frederic Watts would be hung and discussed and reproduced for generations to come. Still, they were all splendid company, including that glittering fellow Wilde, who had a habit of dropping in unannounced during a session and observing his friend furiously painting, as closely as if he were planning a picture of his own.

Absurd impression, that; Wilde's reputation was that of a poet, not a painter, although to her knowledge he hadn't yet published a word and seemed to invest all his time in smoking aromatic Egyptian cigarettes, uttering witty remarks about the decay of society, and growing his hair to his shoulders. She had to remind herself not to give voice to her private conclusions. In London, the prevailing wind lifted an indiscreet word and carried it far and wide, spreading it like—well, like the Jersey Lily.

"By thunder, there it is again." The man at the easel quickened his strokes. "I'd trade a queen's commission to know what's going through your mind at this moment."

"You'd be swindling yourself. My thoughts are all quite ordinary."

She clung to this view—sometimes subscribed to it—from a deep sense of self-preservation. Gentlemen she trusted to a point; publicly professed connoisseurs of beauty, they cared less for the interior workings of a woman's mind than for the pleasures of her face and figure, and were disposed to overlook evidence of provincial limitations as unimportant. Women were keen for it and fed upon it. With them she was particularly circumspect, and in the absence of material for public humiliation, they directed their animosity toward easier targets, and for the time being were content to tap into the conventional mode of thought and consider the young lady from the Channel Islands demure and unthreatening, a model of feminine modesty. Such a position was precarious and commanded eternal vigilance: There would be no whispers of "Lillie Le Cretin" as long as repose could be maintained. Life under the acetylene spot of social acceptance was a field of unexploded charges, to be crossed with skirts lifted and the lightest of treads.

On occasion, when she was early for a session or Mr. Millais was delayed by an Academy project, she spent the time in the anteroom outside his studio, paging through periodicals of the day scattered across a library table fashioned in Rome of native marble. They included West End ephemera, of course, but copies also of *Harper's Weekly* and *Frank Leslie's Illustrated Newspaper*, trumpeting blood-and-thunder accounts of savage happenings on the American frontier. Accompanying pen-and-ink illustrations depicted scalpings, female abductions, and guerrilla massacres featuring satanic red Indians and white savages with long hair and quills. Such pamphlets were popular in a country whose masses kept smug faith in the eventual return of its lost colonies to restore British order. A woman educated in the bloodletting and charnel houses of Shakespeare's plays could scarcely be blighted by these scandalous goings-on, but detailed reports of General Custer's gruesome fate at the oxymoronically named Little Big Horn made one appreciate the veiled violence of drawing rooms in Westminster.

Texas seemed especially harrowing, with its slaughters at Goliad and the Alamo, Comanche atrocities, and outlaws on the run; a place as large as western Europe with a population smaller than Ireland's and a history more sanguinary than the Hundred Years' War all in the space of four decades. She read of it the way she read of cities under the sea and settlers on the moon, with as much anticipation of ever seeing any of them.

"Such is the path of empire if Mr. Disraeli has his way."

Startled by the unexpected voice, she slapped shut the periodical in her lap. Standing in the doorway from the studio was a man well past middle age, bald and sidewhiskered, with the down-drawn brows and rat-trap mouth of an Anglican elder.

He resembled one in his black Prince Albert coat and cutthroat collar, and his grip on his stick suggested an imminent caning. She was stuck for a reply.

"No politicking on the premises, that was the understanding when I agreed to the commission." Mr. Millais, appearing behind the stranger's shoulder in working gear of smock and pipe, was visibly peeved. "I apologize, Mrs. Langtry, for this lapse on the part of this morning's subject, most probably brought on by enforced inactivity. In that I claim the honor of accomplishing something the conservatives in our parliament could not. Sir William Gladstone, may I present Mrs. Lillie Langtry."

Lillie stood, as if for royalty. "I know of you, sir. The news even gets to Jersey—after a time."

The former prime minister loosened his lips a millimeter, assuming the semblance of the phantom of a smile. "And when did we take Jersey?"

"That would be 1066," said Millais. "The Norman Conquest? It was in all the journals."

"I seem to have overlooked it." Gladstone appeared impervious to jibes in the salon. "Lady Gladstone and I rarely find time to socialize when parliament is in session. But I've certainly heard a great deal about you, Mrs. Langtry, and seen your photographs."

Lillie demurred—her unfailing fallback position. She'd sat for a host of photographers with their cumbersome equipment, but knew too well the opinion of most painters in regard to their science to take a part for or against it.

The artist ground his teeth on his pipe stem. "Those obscene black boxes are making great strides, all in the wrong direction. They're an insult to art, but we'll be rid of them when their novelty is passed. We survived powdered wigs."

"Let us hope we can survive the current administration." Gladstone retrieved a bowler hat from a peg. "I hope to see you again, Mrs. Langtry."

"Undoubtedly you will," said Millais. "She's been elected prime ministress of London by unanimous vote."

"Couldn't think of a better choice. Thank heavens comeliness is not another of Disraeli's gifts. Good day, madam. You must allow me one day to introduce you to His Highness. He has a great eye for beauty." The statesman bowed over her hand, exposing as he did so a curious pinkish welt snaking up from under his collar and coiling nearly all the way around his neck to the front. Talcum failed to cover it completely.

Back in Eaton Place, Edward was less excited by the prospect of meeting the Prince of Wales than by Lillie's brush with Gladstone, who had announced his intention to stand again for prime minister when Benjamin Disraeli's run was through. Edward was keen on politics; it occupied nearly as much of his conversation as sailing. During the interrogation, she gleaned the fact that the Great Men's chief difference was that the incumbent favored expanding the empire through exploration and conquest while his challenger held firm for consolidation of its recent gains. It seemed a small point upon which to lavish so much time and oratory, and didn't explain that funny blemish upon Sir William's neck.

"Oh, blast the slice! His razor slipped. Why must you fix on trifles?"

Wounded by Edward's fit of pique, she did not again bring up the subject, or Gladstone himself. But her curiosity would be laid to rest.

The higher one rose in the caste system, the more one was exposed to its dark secrets. The goddess and the servant of the public would be at their respective crests when whispers reached her that Gladstone punished himself periodically for his brothel visits by flagellation by his own hand. Only his personal physician knew the full extent of his self-imposed injuries, but refusing to remove one's shirt in the emporia of flesh could not conceal them from touch, nor providing a generous gratuity silence gossip. Thereafter, whenever Lillie heard him referred to as the "Scourge of Whitehall," it was as if the wind had changed from the direction of an open sewer, wallowed in by the press and those who wandered the corridors of power—paraded by them, in fact, within full view of an unsuspecting population. At the height of her celebrity she resisted all overtures by suffragists to enlist her as a spokeswoman for their cause. The polling-place was no fit venue for a woman who considered herself a lady. It was suited only to swine and scribblers.

"I envy your New World its fresh air and bright outlook," she wrote Roy. "Sins cannot long remain hidden in its strong sunlight, but must shrivel and die or be rooted out as soon as they break surface. 'Daylight bank robbery'; what a phrase! I would rather sacrifice my life's savings in such an event than accumulate wealth and power in the damp blackness of foul night."

"We have sins enough of our own manufacture," Roy wrote back, "and some that commit them smell pretty foul when left suspended too long." But after reading his daughter's transcription, he scratched out the last part and had her rewrite the page.

As Lillie had feared, Millais was disillusioned by the small, fragile red blossoms she brought him in a vase. He considered using the more assertive ruby lily, but his subject's own charms did not assert themselves; they were insinuative, and their effect lingered the longer for it. Then there was the fact that the rumor mill had gotten hold of the name Jersey Lily (Good God, but what a provincial village was the hub of the universe), and was already applying it when Lillie's carriage first appeared on Rotten Row, that promenade of the glittering and fashionable. A popular painter couldn't ignore the will of the people and remain popular. ("I'm frightfully jealous of John," Whistler trilled to two separate sets of listeners. "When inspiration is required, he needs look no further than the nearest crowded boulevard.") He painted over his canvas and began again.

The new picture was the talk of town before anyone had even seen it, including the woman who had sat for it. The artist routinely emptied his studio of all but its two principals the moment he picked up his brush; now he tightened his security further, throwing a cloth over his work and refusing to remove it for anyone, including the smitten Gladstone. He placed Lillie in a snug black dress tied with bows of the same drab hue, with only a white lace collar for contrast and of course the daily bouquet of Jersey lilies, which burst bold and scarlet against so somber a palette. When the portrait was unveiled at last, she would be known in every corner as the Jersey Lily.

Edward attended the little ceremony as his wife's escort, but was in animated conversation with a somewhat distracted acquaintance when the painting was revealed to a clatter of applause. He'd seen quite enough of her likeness in every shop window in Piccadilly, and held Millais's same dim view of the photographic process, although for a different reason: the ease with which it lent itself to duplication and distribution.

"Copying a painting requires talent at least," he told her as their carriage rolled past yet another display. "Any fool with the price of the chemicals can reproduce a photograph. It's an offense to decency to place oneself on exhibit like a baboon in a cage."

"I'm afraid it can't be helped." She brushed damp soil from

her skirts. It seemed half of London waited for the chance to fling fistfuls of lilies into her carriage whenever it paused. For some time now it had no longer been necessary to ask Mrs. LeBreton to send the flowers. They were available at every florist's.

"Why do they call it Rotten Row, do you suppose?" Edward asked. "Because it's rotten with people?"

"I understand it's a distortion of *Route de Roi*. That's Mr. Wilde's view, at any rate. You can imagine what he makes of it."

"That fellow is too clever for his own good."

"Fortunately, not every man suffers from his affliction."

After a moment he said, "You've developed a mean streak, Lillie. Your new acquaintances are an unhealthy influence."

She watched the people lined up along the pavement, turned out for the two-hour daily procession of the anointed as faithfully as for the Changing of the Guard: the gentlemen lifting their bowlers, the workmen touching their caps, serving women holding parcels to their bosoms, and the typists in their shirtwaists and trim little hats, some of them resting bicycles, faces turning with the traffic, and now and then a man or a woman bold enough to dash up and toss a bouquet through a window. (Lillie had been terrorized the first time it happened, thinking it was a rock or a horse-apple.) Little boys ran alongside the green fenders and yellow wheels, hoping to touch a hand or a fine linen sleeve. She watched them all and thought what a colossal difference a single invitation made; how short the distance between the pavement and the place where she sat, and yet how long. Only months before, she had stood where they stood and watched Sir Randolph Churchill pass accompanied by his much-discussed American wife and pudgy, pasty-faced son. What an odd place was London, stranger in its way than the Texas of Mr. Millais's library table.

The carriage turned off that glistening stem and picked up speed. Edward sat back with a great whoosh from his lungs and stuffed his pipe, a short black bulldog far less eloquent than Millais's briar with its long amber stem. She noticed such things now, found herself making comparisons between her husband of two years—was it two only?—and her new acquaintances, as he called them. He always dressed as if he were going to a funeral, while she herself had put down her weeds in tissue and moth powder; if she'd laid out so much as a printed waistcoat for him, he'd have demanded she return it to whatever shop in Bohemian Soho had sold it. And his habits were as predictable as his wardrobe. Such close attention paid to packing a bowl with Cavendish always preceded a pronouncement.

"Well, Lillie, you've had your London adventure. You're sound as the pound sterling and ready to return home. If we start packing right away we can be in Southampton in time for the second regatta."

"We shan't." She turned to look at him, her eyes as clear as amethysts. "*I* shan't."

SEVEN

In the autumn of 1866, Roy Bean founded a town, after a fashion, and took a wife. The town would not be his last. The wife would.

San Antonio was a hard place to stay away from, even for a man facing forfeiture of all his possessions if he returned. The cool dampness of its winters beckoned to him in hot dry El Paso and in the sun-battered pueblos of old Mexico, and even in summer when breathing the air was like inhaling boiled cotton, solace awaited him in the dim corner of some adobe cave with a bottle of mescal and a little heap of salt. This image pricked him like a cocklebur and drove him finally back inside the jurisdiction of the Bexar County Court.

Poverty was on his side, or so he avowed. On the face of it, his situation seemed nearly identical to the one that had brought him to his brother Sam aboard a stolen burro with only a sixteenth of an inch of faded red flannel between himself and his modesty. The deflated market and competition from railroads, which had resumed construction after the war, battered the freighting business; Roy presented scribbled receipts to support his claim that he'd settled accounts with his teamsters by turning the wagons and mules over to them, and when the sheriff came for what he owed, he spread his hands. The windbroken bay he'd ridden into town wouldn't bring a cartwheel dollar at auction, and once again there was a cloud over just how he'd obtained transportation that brought the horse's ownership into question.

Roy moved into a shack on the bank of San Pedro Creek, a pretty spot where he could sit in a rocker on the dilapidated back porch and throw a line into the water as supper time approached. He didn't have title, and when the owner of the property ordered him to leave, he drew his yellow-handled Colt and shot a hole in the ground near the man's feet, insisting afterward that he'd been aiming at a water moccasin. The sheriff, responding to the assault complaint, found the occupant of the shack on the porch skinning a freshly killed snake, accepted a pull from the jug of whiskey Roy sank in the creek on the end of a piece of twine to keep it cold, and left without pursuing the case. He reckoned that at this point he'd spent nearly as much time in Roy Bean's company as his own family's.

Undeterred, the property owner took the matter to the same justice of the peace who had found against Roy in the Milmo affair. The defendant was ordered to evict immediately and pay damages in the amount of sixty-three dollars plus court costs. Roy lip-read his way through some pertinent paragraphs in the *Revised Statutes of Texas* and filed for an injunction. It was granted. ("I'll never part with this here book," he told a friend. "It's full of stories, with two sides to every last one.") So things stood until the owner, sensing that a deal he'd made to sell the parcel was slipping away, paid a second call on Roy and asked what it would take to persuade him to leave.

Roy rocked and fished and drummed his fingers on the book in his lap. At length he said, "I got my eye on a place on South Flores where the skeeters ain't so thick. If you'll stand the expense of moving my gear and throw in a jug of busthead, I'll quit all claim."

"What gear? You told the sheriff you're down to the shirt on your back."

"That was a few weeks ago. A man's friends won't let him sit on the floor in an empty house. I got a trunk and some sticks, but as to busthead I'm down to my last drop."

"What brand?"

The deal was struck. In the spirit of accord, Roy offered his former unofficial landlord a bargain price on six wagons and forty mules he'd been boarding across the county line.

The man was dubious. "Why would a man with such possessions squat in a shack he didn't own?"

"They say Vanderbilt counts his change. That's why he's Vanderbilt."

After inspection, the transaction was completed. Pat Milmo's reaction when he found out what had become of his fleet is unrecorded, possibly because polite custom prohibited committing the details of a show of Irish temper to paper.

With three thousand dollars cash in hand, Roy was now a wealthy man by most of the country's standards, a stunning reversal of his apparent situation upon his return from exile. ("In America," he wrote Lillie, "a pauper's as good as a pope if he wipes his feet and knows what a spittoon is for.") He prepared to step up to his new station as a man of property, freshening his wardrobe with a pair of hand-tooled stovepipe boots made to his measure and acquiring legal deed to a large lot on South Flores Street, a place where cows routinely wandered outside their pasture into the avenue, shacks leaned at angles that mocked the laws of nature, and chickens strolled into and out of Conner's General Store in the middle of the block. The yellow, slat-sided mongrels that had given the neighborhood its name—Dogtown—were too debilitated by malnutrition and the heat to do more than lie in the mud and follow them with mournful eyes as they clucked past. There was a racetrack at the end of the street and cock-fights daily. Roy was an enthusiastic sportsman and bet heavily. His nest egg shriveled away at a wondrous rate.

It's unclear whether the place came to be known as Beanville in recognition of its most prominent resident or because of its dense Mexican population. In either case the christening appears to have been an act of derision, motivated by race or bitter past experience of Roy himself. In typical fashion, however, he turned it on its head by accepting and using the name as an affirmation of his high standing in the community. The attitude was contagious. His Spanish-speaking neighbors touched their hats when they encountered him on the street, and even though he was never seen paying for his own whiskey or anyone else's, they considered him a man of substance and judgment and sometimes came to him for counsel when they entered into a dispute with their other neighbors. The large impressive volume resting on the lid of the pickle barrel at his elbow singled him out as a learned man, even if he sometimes used its heft to exterminate cockroaches; *el jefe cucaracha*, some called him with affection.

Roy subsisted for a time on the storekeeper's patience founded on his guest's popularity and pocketed the occasional peso he accepted in return for keeping the peace among the citizens of

Beanville, but although he had fallen into the very mode of existence he had sought for so long, he was aware of a mounting feeling of dissatisfaction with the sameness of his days. It occurred to
him that as a respectable man with a permanent address, he was
bound by propriety to marry and raise a family.

His preference in women, like his taste in food and dress, remained Spanish. The girls were ravishing, and even when (before they were out of their twenties) they grew stout and
leathery, they were hard workers who considered themselves
humiliated if their man so much as touched a broom or stirred
from his chair to retrieve a bottle of *cerveza*. His eye fell first
upon Señora Leandro Chavez, a trim exception to the rule
who'd kept her figure, though her age was not much less than
his own. Such a match befit his dignity. She drifted into his orbit
in the company of her eighteen-year-old daughter, Maria Virginia, and a hand from the family ranch a mile outside San Antonio, to purchase supplies and provisions from Conner's store.
Roy assumed from the way she ordered the hand around that
she was widowed and in charge of the spread, but when he
learned that Leandro was very much alive and stood proudly at
the end of a line that extended all the way back to ancient Por-
tugese aristocracy and included the earliest settlers of Texas, Roy
laid dignity aside and fixed his attentions on the daughter.

Disappointment stung him when he found out the Chavezes
had prestige but no fortune; but he still had some money from
the sale of his wagons and mules, and anyway a ranch in the
family could only add to his reputation as *un hombre muy im-
portante*. He pressed his troth in the appropriate Old World
manner, putting on his best suit of clothes and hiring a horse
and buggy to ride out to the modest spread and speak with
Maria Virginia's parents. Leandro, his contemporary in age,

scowled and shook his head, but his wife whispered in his ear and his demeanor brightened. Roy guessed what intelligence had been exchanged. In the East, they said, the marriagable daughters of wealthy industrialists were being farmed out to Europe to shore up the finances of impoverished nobles, and in the process they acquired titles that helped to legitimize their fathers' fortunes. Whether or not Señora Chavez was aware of this fashion, she had probably heard that Roy was a gentleman of leisure and considerable resources in search of a fine old family connection. The size of his wagers was legendary, and when he lost he always paid off promptly in cash. He made no effort to unburden her of the conclusion.

Maria Virginia was not consulted in the transaction, but there is no evidence that she was opposed to it. Pretty Mexican girls fell prey to Roy's charms as a matter of course, and despite an expanding waistline and a beard in need of trimming, *el jefe cucaracha* was a picture of distinction in Spanish tailoring, like the grandees south of the border who sold many heads of longhorns to the Chavezes' larger neighbors for relocation and resale in Chicago. He told fabulous stories of past adventures, like Don Quixote, which if only half were true promised a protective presence in a dangerous world. She would give him the care required to present his best side to the public, as befit the mayor and first lady of Beanville.

They were married in a Catholic ceremony and moved into the first of several houses they would occupy throughout the sixteen years of their residence in San Antonio, including the Chavez home on the ranch; by which time the last of Roy's windfall had gone—on the beak, legend has it, of a fighting rooster named Emperor Maximilian, who in the ring had proven less illustrious than his name. It was under the paternal roof that the first of their children, Little Roy, first saw the light, a beautiful child with traces of his father's obstinance, manifested in the determination to remain awake and loud every hour of the day and night, and his mother's aristocratic cheekbones and black Spanish eyes. But his cries for attention had to compete with his parents' frequent shouting matches; for the union was contentious from the beginning and would remain so sporadically, with intervals of uneasy truce, throughout its run. (Roy wrote Lillie: "I was set in my ways, and Maria Virginia's blood was hot as peppers.") Little Roy, and the three siblings who would follow, would grow up believing that marriage was not unlike the War Against Northern Aggression their father was always talking about: long, stultifying stretches broken up by furious bombardment.

They had been married only a few weeks before the bridegroom learned that his mate wasn't the labor-worshiping handmaiden he'd expected. Maria Virginia had been conditioned from birth to regard herself as the heiress to a fine and noble name; her needs were attended to by the loyal descendants of original family servants who were disposed to work for bed and board alone in return for the privilege, and she never opened a door for herself if someone else was present. Roy would take his leave of her in the morning to station himself in Conner's store, imagining that she would busy herself sweeping their dirt floor and baking tortillas for his noon dinner, and when these events failed to materialize, he called her *Condesa Condenación* ("Countess Go-to-Hell") and growled that the situation must change immediately. She responded by swinging a cast-iron baking pan at his head.

"That's progress," he told the Mexican barber who sewed up the gash in his scalp. "Now that she knows where it is I'll soon have her cooking in it."

This was overoptimistic. When some time after the baking-pan incident he came home to find his wife in bed in the middle of the day, he tore away the covers and stuck her in the thigh with a burning stick from the fireplace.

When she fled to the ranch with the wound and her story, Papa Leandro went for his saddle and a bullwhip, but his wife left off dressing their daughter's leg and counseled legal action instead. Was not their son-in-law a man of wealth, capable of paying damages that would settle their mortgage? At this point the couple had dismissed Roy's pleas of poverty as subterfuge to prevent them from infringing upon his generosity. He was *un mentiroso monstruoso*, a great liar, ask anyone; but his wife's shameful affliction would speak for itself.

The case dragged on for more than a year, with requests for delays and motions for dismissal, but while the requests were granted the motions were not. Roy's stock with the local justice of the peace, who had found against him innumerable times only to be thwarted by the defendant's slippery nature, was low. He'd put aside his book in favor of the services of an experienced lawyer (not the one he'd stolen it from); that party exploited judicial prejudice to move for a change of venue, while hoping for Maria Virginia's thigh to heal and destroy the chief exhibit for the prosecution. Surprisingly, the venue was ordered, and the complaint was heard thirty miles away in the city of Bourne. There Roy Bean was unknown: If he had a coat of arms, its motto would read "Big rooster, small barnyard."

When the victim's testimony came to her injury, the tone of the defense changed from deference to sarcasm. "How inconvenient—or should I say convenient—that all traces of this supposed goring must have vanished by now."

"No, señor. Sadly I shall wear the scar all my days."

The lawyer withdrew to his client's table for a whispered consultation. "How deep must you stab a woman for refusing to get your dinner?"

"It warn't that deep," said Roy. "The stick was hot is all."

"Christ. Why didn't you just hit her?"

"I never raised a hand to no woman."

The lawyer chewed his cheek and returned to the witness stand. "I now ask the plaintiff in this case to show the scar she alleges to have received."

Maria Virginia colored, looked to her parents for rescue. Adroitly, the attorney for the defense placed his person directly in her line of view. Faced with a masculine presence with his thumbs hooked inside the armholes of his vest, she colored deeper and shook her head vehemently.

"I request that the witness's refusal to present evidence of the defendant's guilt be entered in the record."

The judge wheedled, prodding the young woman with an avuncular tone. Maria Virginia stared at the floor and said nothing. With a great exhaustion of breath, the man behind the bench snapped his gavel and dismissed the case without remanding it to the jury.

Roy's grip came within a tenth of an inch of crushing his attorney's congratulatory hand. "You damn jackass, what did you take a chance like that for? One look at that scar and they'd turn the key on me and break it off."

"Chance never entered into it. You know as well as I do that no respectable Mexican woman would lift her skirt above her ankles in public."

"Well, it was risky all the same." And he demonstrated his disapproval by adding the attorney to his long line of embittered creditors.

The Beans made peace once again and settled down to the business of having children. Maria Virginia even learned to cook, setting out a handsome spread when a company of Texas Rangers camped next to their property while in pursuit of John Wesley Hardin, the gunman and road agent who had taken the Comanches' place as a nuisance to be eradicated. The children became accustomed to men with pistols lounging around, spitting and telling stories. They grew up wild as thistledown. Their mother had no experience of boundaries and discipline to pass on to her offspring, and their father was as indulgent of them as he was of himself. Conner learned to dread their invasion when school let out, which he compared to a swarm of Mormon crickets. The breakage and pilferage cut into his profits and for a time Roy and his progeny were banned from the store, but when Conner discovered that the local Mexicans were now buying their corn from the granary three blocks east where *el jefe cucaracha* had taken up his new post, he relented, on the condition that not more than one of Roy's children would be allowed on the premises at one time. Roy, whose hay fever was aggravated by grain dust, agreed, but in truth his authority over his brood was no greater than his wife's. The plundering resumed.

Little Roy, his sisters Zulema and Laura, and kid brother Sam adored their father, whose moods at least were always on display, and who distributed among them pieces of hard candy borrowed from Conner's jar. But they found their mother cool and distant, all the more so as the four grew and began to display evidence of Roy Senior's personality. After he moved on, and when the girls were old enough to leave school (the boys' attendance was less hit than miss), she did not object when he sent for them and they pressed her for permission. She was back home by then, living with her parents.

"I'm a widower with four children and a boy I adopted." For all the contact Roy'd had with Maria Virginia by the time he wrote this to Lillie, it might have been true.

Roy had mouths to feed. On occasion he hauled freight for the firm of Wicks and Hickman using their mules and equipment, and when the owners asked him to keep an eye out for firewood poachers on company property, he made ends meet by poaching the wood himself and selling it to ironmongers George Holmgreen & Sons to fuel their furnaces. Eventually he got tired of all the chopping and stooping and left it to others in return for a fee to gather firewood for themselves. When the wood ran out, he went into the dairy business, but feed was dear and milking was hard on his rheumatic knuckles. He helped along the supply with water from San Pedro Creek, but business fell off when customers complained about minnows in their milk. Roy muttered something about watering the cows at the creek, but for the first time one of his lies lacked conviction. He was restless and distracted.

Conner, sensing an end to his Bean predicament, offered him nine hundred dollars for his dairy and property if he would agree to leave town. Roy, fingering a tooth loosened in a recent domestic row, was tempted. He asked where he might go.

"West of the Pecos, where they say there's no law. It's perfect for you and that nest of skeeters of yours."

Roy drank and slept on the suggestion. Where no law existed, anything that passed for it was bound to be in demand. He'd had a taste of sole responsibility under Wicks and Hickman, and of the benefits of a comfortable seat where the business came to him instead of his going out to find it. His education now was complete, and his wandering days at an end.

II

THE ASS AND THE ICON

An ass carrying a holy icon through a city noticed people lowering their heads as he passed. Believing himself the subject of their respect, he pricked up his ears and refused to take another step. The driver whipped him furiously, crying, "Go to work, you dunce! It has not yet come to this, that men pay worship to an ass."

—AESOP

EIGHT

The press, which was running out of hyperbole to describe Lillie Langtry, referred to her as "society's Disraeli."

When she first heard the phrase, she didn't know enough about politics to decide whether it was a compliment or a canard, either to herself or to the prime minister, and after quizzing Edward on the matter, she was still undecided. It seemed to have something to do with conquest, but as all England appeared to be divided on whether that was a good thing, she remained in the dark.

The mourning dress she had modified all those months ago, and which had brought her to notice, had been copied by designers and displayed in shop windows from Chiswick to Chislehurst as "the Langtry Gown." When nothing the milliners had to offer struck her as appropriate for a day at the races, she made a smart toque out of black velvet, sewed a feather onto it, and almost before she and Edward got home from Sundown Park, "the Langtry Hat" was everywhere. Even when she wore nothing, as it were, she couldn't avoid influencing the British economy: Customers saw photographs of her in the chatelaine braid she employed because she hadn't patience to arrange her hair in an elaborate style and pressed their hairdressers for "the Langtry Knot." Jersey lilies were in such high demand that a prominent Channel Islands botanist declared that the species would soon go the way of the passenger pigeon. Lillie began to think that if she caught a cold, women throughout the empire would rouge their noses to imitate her.

If this was conquest, Edward was a pacifist. "Photographs are for family and close friends," he said. "I can't even relax at the club without seeing your face plastered on every periodical in the reading room."

It was an old litany; she barely heard it anymore. But her husband of what now seemed a lifetime had power still to astonish her. Black for her was the color of luck, but upon learning that Lord Dudley, her forthcoming host at a ball to welcome King Leopold of Belgium, loathed the funereal hue, she commissioned a simple white gown along the lines of Grecian dress, and when she modeled it for Edward, fully expected the customary lecture about unseemly ostentation and unnecessary expense.

"It's stunning," said he. "White is so much more flattering to you than black. I never understood why you would choose to go about looking like Lady Macbeth."

"This was quite expensive."

"My dear, we're not quite reduced to a coldwater flat in Whitechapel. Your position in society requires the best."

"But I can wear black every evening. White is for garden parties, and it isn't the season."

"Buy another. Winter doesn't last forever, even in Old Blighty. Clothes are to London what a trim hull and a shallow draught are to sailing. You're famous now, like it or not, and must keep up appearances."

She suspected she knew the reason for this about-face in regard to her public acclaim. For some weeks she'd been aware of a new langorousness in her husband, and twice she had detected a faint smell of spirits when he returned from his constitutional in the middle of the day. She'd never seen him drunk, never known him to take more than a few sips of sherry to avoid offending his host. Her own schedule, crowded as it was with sittings, invitations, and charity events, had kept her too busy to give much thought to the matter, but if the occasional brandy brought him comfort and spared her another lecture upon what Was and Was Not Done, she would gladly buy him a case.

The exact state of their finances was a mystery to her. Leafing through to the society pages in the papers, she couldn't avoid lighting briefly upon headlines about British investments in South Africa and the like; perhaps Edward had made some cautious moves in the market—she could not imagine him proceeding in any other way—and they had turned out well. When she tested him, asking if they might consider moving to larger quarters in a more fashionable neighborhood, he raised no immediate objections. He was secretive about his own affairs, and it was a compliment to his modest nature that he would not boast of any success. She would not question his motives.

Jimmy Whistler dipped his brushes in paint at last in her presence—to brighten the living room of the Langtrys' spacious new residence on Norfolk Street, gilding paper fans to hang on the walls and painting the ceiling with blue sky, white clouds, and yellow canaries. She thought the ceiling middle-class and slightly garish, but praised it nonetheless; Jimmy was pouty when he thought himself underappreciated, and anyway, who really looked at ceilings? If someone did and his expression turned scornful, she would pre-empt any remarks with the announcement that the work was Whistler's. Such was his reputation among the bourgeoisie that even his most pedestrian efforts hovered beyond criticism's reach. She was convinced now that this dabbler in birds and mothers would fade from the scene with the nasal echo of his final words, no matter how much labor he would put into selecting them, as no doubt he would. His canvases would gather dust in secondhand shops and when they were discarded to make room for the next young barbarian, he would truly be dead.

She shared with no one this dreary eulogy for James McNeill Whistler, whom she adored but had never liked; for if the treacherous gravel path of human discourse had taught her anything, it was that a careless whisper in the wrong ear invariably found its way to its subject. Everything about her new life demanded cautious diplomacy. There was an invisible line between admiration and covetousness, and constant vigilance was required to avoid stepping across it. Extravagant offers of jewelry, furs, and hotel suites were scented fly-paper, leading to entanglement and destruction. Elegant mistresses were as common as ribbons in Mayfair; she was determined not to become an off-color joke. When she learned that Edward had accepted the gift of a fine thoroughbred from Moreton Frewen, a particularly supercilious specimen of inherited wealth, behind her back, she insisted he return it at once.

"I shall do nothing of the sort. We've a stable now, and something in it at last. How often have you said to me how much you longed for a prancer of your own? You're the most ungrateful creature that ever existed."

"What did you promise him in return?"

"Why, not a thing. He merely thought it an injustice that London's fairest flower should lack for a reason to appear in Hyde Park in riding habit."

"And you believed him."

"You're not married to a fool. Between you and me, I think the fellow's in a bind. The income from his trust fund is failing to keep pace with the rising cost of oats, and this is the only way to get out from under without losing face. You might say I did him a good turn."

"What do you suppose *he'll* say?"

"Honestly, Lillie, every lamplighter and publican in the city can throw flowers at so bright a target. The munificence of Frewen's gift, and the identity of its recipient, will do far more for his reputation than the bloody Victoria Cross."

She saw that there was nothing for it but to acquiesce. This new Edward was not the same pallid misanthrope she could bend to her will with a note from her doctor. He'd even begun to dress the part of the boulevardier, with a nosegay on his lapel— decidedly, never a Jersey lily—and a collection of sticks with knobs of ivory and silver and gold; it seemed he'd warmed to the role of escort to the belle of the season. His flushed face put the lie to the licorice on his breath intended to disguise the evidence of drink. "Be it so," said she. "I hope you're prepared to step in to my defense should Frewen's reputation improve at the expense of my own."

"Let's not be dramatic. I'm beginning to think you're seriously considering these preposterous requests to take to the stage."

Distraction was a new tactic for Edward, who in past quarrels had simply withdrawn from the field of battle when his first volley fell short. He appeared to have acquired, if not precisely a backbone, at least a servicable set of land-legs at last. Preposterous? Lillie had thought the repeated suggestions that she share her grace and beauty with theatergoers for material gain not preposterous, merely funny. The mounting number of calling-cards left at Norfolk Street by theatrical managers and talent agents struck her as nothing more than a curious new variation upon the theme of public attention. She was complimented nearly as often upon the musical quality of her voice, which hovered pleasantly among the low registers, as upon her looks, and it was true that her father had told her she needn't preface each line she read to him from Shakespeare with the name of the character who was speaking, as she gave each a distinct tone. But to think that she who so recently had fled to a deserted corner when stranded by her hostess in a crowd of strangers should willingly stand on display in the same proscenium as Ellen Terry and Sarah Bernhardt would be to drop the guard she had held up for so long. She sensed a trap.

The Prince of Wales swept into her life like a storm from the Hebrides. She and Edward were dining after the opera with a K.B.E. named Young—a misnomer demonstrably, as a drier example of human petrification was impossible to imagine—when the air in the restaurant stirred as if a door had blown open and the Heir Apparent boated in, wearing his courtiers like the badges of honor on his evening waistcoat, a large man and loud, inclined toward his mother's stoutness of figure unfortunately combined with the late Prince Albert's matronly hips, but with both characteristics discreetly draped in exquisite tailoring. He made his way to the Young party's table along a bumblebee route, pausing here and there to wrap his great right paw around the hand of a male acquaintance and to acknowledge the presence of a lady who dipped a knee before him. At last he shook

Young's hand and apologized in a deep booming voice for the lateness of his arrival. "If our armies in the field started and stopped on the same schedule as these infernal official functions, we should all be speaking French this day."

"No explanations are necessary. Your Highness, may I present Mrs. Lillie Langtry and her husband, Edward."

The big face—it seemed as large as a medicine ball—turned her way and smiled at her curtsey. His dark beard was tipped with gray, as if its owner had abandoned expectation finally of a timely ascent to the throne and agreed to age. Nothing in the smile or the deepset eyes indicated that he was aware of either her fame or her beauty. "Always a pleasure to meet another Edward." He turned to envelop her husband's hand in his.

Instantaneously, the guest of honor became the host, and as course after course of fish, sweetmeats, venison, and pastries arrived at their table, Prince Albert Edward ("Bertie, please," he reminded Young. "Whenever I hear 'Your Highness,' I look round to see if a sultan has entered the room") showed both a keen interest in and remarkable knowledge of horses, racing, sailing, and the current bill at Covent Gardens. If not yet monarch of the British Empire, he was inarguably the King of London. Lillie wondered briefly if Millais's remark that she was the unanimous choice for prime ministress of London had reached the Prince through Gladstone. For all the attention he'd paid her so far, she decided it had not, or that if it had, he had been unamused by the witticism and had determined to put her in her place. Then he turned her way.

"It's warm in here, Mrs. Langtry. With so many people in town during the season putting out so much heat, one wonders why so much is spent on coal."

"It is close, your—sir." She could not bring herself to address him as Bertie. She touched the back of a hand to her cheek. It felt feverish. She thought she must be as red as a boiled lobster.

"One cannot escape your likeness these days, not that he would want to. I must say the photographs are unworthy of the subject."

She murmured something she hoped was demure and not banal.

"I intend to ask the queen to cite the governor of Jersey for his generosity in letting you go. There should be an order in it for him at the least."

Lillie floated for many days upon the cushion of air provided by these pretty compliments from so high a person. It brought a radiance that drove the next photographer for whom she sat to the edge of artistic despair.

"Blast this monochromatic prison," said he, in his exasperation neglecting to apologize for the oath. He was by nature the gentlemanly sort, his necktie knotted neatly whatever the condition of his smock, streaked as it was with magnesium ash and eaten through with corrosive chemicals from the darkroom. "I almost begin to think that Millais and Whistler are right, and that my medium is inferior to theirs. I cannot hope to capture that angelic glow without resorting to tinting by hand; in which case I may as well satisfy myself with infants and doughy-faced brides and leave the authentic beauties to the daubers." He fussed with his box and tripod and reflectors shaped like parasols.

When she returned to see the results of the session, she was drawn to a print he had made upon a square of glass, which when she held it up to the light produced an ethereal pallor that chilled her to the spine. It was as if she had come upon her own phantom in a dark hallway.

"Ambrotype." The photographer's tone dripped with scorn.

"The poor man's tintype. Glass is less dear, and prints may be purchased by any common groundling who would forego luncheon to possess one."

"It's pretty, though, if a bit unsettling."

"Also fragile. Invariably the oaf who bought it knocks it to the floor with his elbow, and is left with both an empty stomach and only shards to show for his extravagance."

It was something she had seen before, this contempt for the customer who kept him in supplies and the wine he habitually uncorked to celebrate the end of a successful sitting; and not infrequently a disastrous one. The attitude was endemic among the artistic set.

Lillie was distracted, however, and did not dwell upon this dismissal. Her mind was conflicted. Shortly before her visit, an intermediary had approached her at a charitable function and let it be known that "the Prince is much interested in forming a possible friendship with you." A proposition was a proposition, however careful the language in which it was couched; but it had come from Albert Edward, and was therefore in the manner of a command performance. There need be nothing shabby about it.

NINE

"What in hell is an am-bo-type?" Roy squinted at the square of glass, through which charged the white light beating down on Vinegarroon, a parched plot of land split down the center by the tracks of the Southern Pacific. The rails squirmed in a haze of pure heat.

"Ambrotype." The drummer who had offered him the item hooked his thumbs inside the armholes of his checked waist-coat. "It's all the thing back East, Judge. Any poor widow can show off her soldier-boy's face on a wrinkled piece of tin or a *carte de visite* with a flop-ear. That there's as smooth a hunk of glass as you'll find this side of the Crystal Palace."

"I been to the Palace. I seen better saloons in Frisco."

"I mean the attraction in London, England, not the ginhouse in San Antone. An ornament like that's just the ticket to dress this place up proper to a man of your august office."

"It won't last till August, the way the Mexican I pay to sweep out the peanut shucks swings his broom."

"Well, a careful man like yourself knows how to look after his valuables."

The ghost-woman held a bouquet of long-stemmed flowers in her lap, smiling shyly as if she'd just discovered him staring at her. It was enough to make a grown man blush. "Sure is a pretty little thing. Who is she?"

"You mean to say you never heard of the Jersey Lily?"

"Look around you, mister. This place ain't exactly the high line between Chicago and St. Louis." Roy stretched his leg from his rocking chair to squash one of the stingless scorpions that had given the town its name. It was the size of a jackrabbit kit and crunched like a pecan shell.

"Why, she's just the most famous woman in the civilized world. Her name's Lillie Langtry. They say the Prince of Wales is head over heels for her, but she won't even give him the time of day."

"Prince of Whales, is it? A fish that size ought to own a watch. Hell, I got one." He hauled out a heavy silver turnip attached by a stout chain to his waistcoat, won off a railroad conductor at monte, a game that had replaced educated dice in Roy's affections. He kept his pair out of sentiment; they would be found among his effects at the end of his improbably long life.

"I imagine he's got a watch for every day of the week. He's fixed to be King of England if his old lady ever takes it into her head to shove off."

"I don't know about all this England business. My pa was with Andy Jackson the day he shivareed the limey sons of bitches clear out of New Orleans." This romance was spur-of-the-moment. So far as he knew, the old bastard had spent that war selling gold bricks in Kentucky. Truth was he'd taken a fancy to the girl in the glass and had set himself up to jew down the price. "She's a pretty little thing, and that's a fact. She's out of place here. What are you asking to take it off your hands?"

"One thin dollar."

"What's thin about it? This court's self-sustaining. I ain't fined a vagrant nor married a couple with the money for the license since April."

"That's firm. I wouldn't let it go so cheap, but this here's the end of my route and the porters won't change a bank note."

"Tip 'em more than a nickel and you spoil 'em clear down the line. I'll give you two bits."

The drummer found a toothpick in his pocket and plugged his face with it. "I can't let it go for less than four. Any lower and I couldn't slide my end under a snake."

Roy let him broil under his hard hat. The air was cooler inside the tent, but canvas had a way of letting in rain—not a problem in West Texas in June—while preserving chili farts in their original pristine condition—which was. Most days he sat out front in the shade of his sombrero watching skinny little lizards dart past on their hind legs as if they had somewhere to go. "Two bits, and you can water yourself from the well free of charge. That's a generous offer. You see the Pecos on your way through?"

"I seen a gila track in the sand, if that's what you mean." The toothpick traveled right and left. "Throw in a glass of beer and she's yours."

"I have to charge you a penny if you want it ice cold."

"You forgot I sold you that lump of glass you stir in it to soak greenhorns with. I'll take it Texas temperature, like the natives. You're a good customer, Judge, or I'd climb right back on the eastbound with Lillie in my pocket."

"You could try, but I'd shoot you in the leg and fine you for possession of stolen property."

The exchange was made and they went inside, where Roy carefully propped the ambrotype on a barrel against an impressive framed certificate, lettered in copperplate and signed by the governor, proclaiming Roy Bean justice of the peace of Val Verde County; the document leaned in turn against the 1866 *Revised Statutes*, obsolete now that Austin had provided him with a crisp copy of the 1879. He'd been loath to part with its predecessor and hung on to it like the stuffed carcass of a beloved dog; it had followed him to more places, gotten him out of worse jams, and proven more loyal than any bluetick he'd ever owned. A later edition had arrived in January, but had long since gone to start fires in the barrel stove in the corner. If he'd been told there was reading involved, he'd have held out for attorney general. Anyway, he hated writing nearly as much and was disinclined to transcribe all the penciled notations he'd made on the endpapers of the '79; for him, the book was a combination ledger, scratch pad, and family Bible.

He filled two glasses from the keg behind the plane table that served as bar and judicial bench, often simultaneously, and raised it to the lady in the picture. "I clean forgot her name."

"Lillie Langtry, Judge, the fairest flower that ever bloomed."

Roy repeated the name and drank. "She sure does dress up the place. I wouldn't mind if there were more."

"Well, there's Jenny Lind, and Lillian Russell—"

"I mean more of Lillie. This ain't no whorehouse, mister. It's a seat of justice and a one-woman saloon."

"There's lots of Lillie. You'll need walls."

"I'm working on it."

Later, stretching his legs in his Pullman aboard the eastbound train, the drummer wrote Roy's name in the back of his grubby account-book and next to it the initials L.L. That dry country was more fertile than it looked.

Roy was inclined to agree.

How it happened was this (more or less):

Like its namesake, Vinegarroon had broken the dusty surface all of a piece, when the railroad paused there for breath before pushing on to Eagle's Nest to join up with the Sunset line moving in the other direction. The town hadn't existed yet when Roy came through aboard a borrowed wagon hauling freight to the Eagle's Nest railhead, but when he went back for another load, the first tents had sprung up to take the sun off the heads of surveyors and graders, and by the time he returned, entrepreneurs had begun dealing monte on the tailgates of their wagons. By a happy coincidence, the freight Roy was carrying was busthead. He lost no time in turning his canvas sheet into a tent and sold out quickly.

When the owner of the shipment arrived to ask what had become of his whiskey, he was told it had been hijacked outside San Antonio by Geronimo himself, whose braves had slain Roy's Mexican driver, cudgeled Roy, and left him for dead beside the road. Upon coming to himself, he had struck out on foot and put in to Vinegarroon to have his scalp sewn up. He offered the old scar left by Maria Virginia's baking pan as evidence.

The owner was skeptical. "I heard General Crook was chasing Geronimo in Arizona."

"I reckon that's what brung him to Texas."

("Why Geronimo, Judge?" asked a confidant the third or fourth time Roy told the story. "That's simple to check."

"Lie big, I always say. It's easier to keep your facts straight later.")

Roy's Mexican driver related a different account when he showed up alive and unmarked in Eagle's Nest with another freighting firm. He and Roy had had an agreement to spread their pilferage equally among the barrels when they stopped to refresh themselves, in order not to arouse the suspicions of the owner, and he had been fired when he violated the pact because the untapped barrels were too hard to get to. Armed with this intelligence, the owner returned to Vinegarroon with some evil-looking companions, but Roy, who had replenished his stock after running a would-be competitor out of town at the point of his yellow-handled Colt, was forewarned; shortly before the crew entered his tent, the saloonkeeper had bought a round for the packed house in honor of George Washington's birthday. So popular a fellow would not be ill-treated by strangers while his friends stood idle. The hammer-and-shovel men from the Southern Pacific sent the party home bruised, bloody, and in their long-handles.

News of this reception did not reach San Antonio in time to stop the man from whom Roy had borrowed his freight wagon from seeking its return. (A true soldier of fortune didn't always scruple to ask, timing being crucial when it came to enterprise.) Roy described the encounter to Lillie:

"I made him understand I had to burn the wagon stick by stick to keep from freezing to death. As he well knew, that first winter in Vinegarroon had been a hard one. Whenever some pilgrim tells me he's never seen a drier place, I tell him he's standing smack dab in the middle of what used to be a lake, but that December a flock of ducks froze their feet to the surface and took off carrying the whole shebang with them."

Lillie, once she found out what "shebang" meant, thought the story amusing enough to tell Oscar Wilde, who needed cheering up just then, as his suit against the Marquis of Queensbury for libel had taken a sinister turn. He smiled wanly and said he wished her judge were hearing his case.

"Whether you burned it or whether you didn't," the man from San Antonio told Roy, "you owe me the price of a wagon, and if I have to I'll go to court to collect."

Roy, who sat on the *Revised Statutes* when not actually officiating, transferred the book from his chair to the plane table with a thud, indicating that court was in session. "Mister, that winter was a sure-enough Act of God, which no man on Earth can trump. Your suit's dismissed."

The wagonless wagon owner took his complaint to Eagle's Nest, where a company of Texas Rangers had established camp. Captain Oglesby, a grizzled veteran three-and-thirty years old seated on a campaign chair, listened, filled a stoneware mug with whiskey from a bottle Roy had given him, and said there wasn't a thing he could do, as the matter had been settled by a sworn justice of the peace.

"You don't mean to say that old bastard's legitimate!"

"I'm here at the request of the vice presidents of the Southern Pacific and the Sunset Limited, to deal with the bandits and sharpers sowing discontent among the track gangs in places like Vinegarroon. I told the adjutant general in Austin we need a J.P. nearby because it's six hundred miles to Fort Stockton and the nearest court of law, with nary a decent tree between to hang a man from. The general spoke to the governor, and the governor appointed Bean."

"For Christ's sake, why him?"

"He organized a committee of concerned citizens and ran a

gang of hooligans out of town a while back. General King was impressed enough with his initiative to recommend him."

"And what's Bean's end?"

"The court has to be self-sustaining. The State of Texas can't afford to remunerate any of the justices it has already."

"In other words, every penny he squeezes out of the unfortunates who come before him winds up in his pocket."

"You won't hear a word of protest from taxpayers."

"He's a bandit and sharper himself, can't you see that?"

Oglesby drank, wiped his moustaches with a knuckle. "Well, dynamite can blow up a train or make a tunnel to run one through. It's all in who's lighting the fuse."

"You think a fat old pig can keep the peace with a broken-down pistol and a saloon full of drunks?"

"That pistol works. He used it to corner the liquor market in Vinegarroon. It's handy to have, but he won't need the drunks when the Rangers are backing him. I'm assigning Sergeant Carson to that duty, with as many men as he needs. All that's wanting is a warm ass in a chair and a piece of paper from Austin. Bean's got the first and the second's due in August."

"But he's opened court already!"

"Strictly speaking he ain't supposed to, and for the record I oppose it. But if you was to file a complaint today it'd take two months to answer it, and by then he'll be official. *Then* he might have to be removed and we'd have to start over from scratch with somebody else." The captain's eyes were shards of flint. "I wouldn't counsel it. Not over no wagon."

The man from San Antonio took this advice in the spirit in which it was plainly intended, and went back home. When some weeks later his wagon—risen, as it were, from its own ashes—appeared on East Travis Street bold as Gerty's garters, he didn't even bother to stop the driver and ask from whom he'd obtained it. By then the true particulars of Roy Bean's heroic actions against the so-called gang of hooligans had come to his attention, as he was sure it had to Captain Oglesby's before their meeting. He didn't care for the odds of the game he was playing and so folded his hand.

TEN

The invitations came end upon end, like those artillery barrages one saw headlined on sandwich boards worn by newspaper vendors. South Africa was under siege and so was Lillie; but she accepted them all, and to Edward's wonder and chagrin, often stopped at Norfolk Street just long enough to change from her ball gown into riding habit. She adored showing off Redskin on the Row, despite her misgivings as to the circumstances under which Edward had accepted the gift of the horse from Moreton Frewen—who had been pressing her constantly with his affections since that transaction (for that was what she suspected it was)—but in truth it gave her an excuse to meet the Prince. He would invariably be found waiting for her aboard some splendid animal from the royal stables.

There was talk, of course. There was always talk, against which the memory of her first exposure to upper-class savagery made her immune. That long-ago slight was like a broken bone that had been set and had knitted, rendering it stronger at the break than it had been previously. In any case, she was seen with Albert Edward only in public, photographed and lithographed relentlessly for all the popular journals, always in the presence of his court entourage and in full view of the throngs that crowded the pavement pressing their noses, in a manner of speaking, against the glass that separated them from the celebrated. That same entourage spared no pains ensuring that they were never seen alone. Buckingham Palace held architectural features more intricate than a Chinese box; Lillie was escorted down passages and through compartments trod by Lady Castlemaine and the Lord knew how many others before her. The walls dripped with lechery and dark mold.

Unfortunately, those loyal titled minions were of no service when she herself was alone. Visiting Lord Malmesbury at Whitsuntide on his estate in Hampshire, she broke her fast with toast and marmalade while Edward was strolling the grounds, then sat down at the mahogany secretaire in their room to write a letter. The upstairs maid had taken it away safely to post before Edward returned. She was seated at the window awaiting the hour to dress for a picnic when her husband spoke her name in a queer choked tone. She turned her head—and felt the blood slide from her face when she saw Edward standing before the dressing table holding up the desk blotter to the mirror. Every dip and whorl of her schoolmaidenly hand was plainly legible. The absorbent paper she had used to blot the ink had reproduced her letter faithfully.

"A love letter, to the Prince of Wales, of all people!" His face was an alarming shade of magenta. She no longer took notice of the unnatural ruddiness he brought back from his frequent constitutionals, but this was something altogether—*Whistlerian* was the only adjective that suggested itself. It bordered upon apoplexy. "I've known for some time you think me a fool, but this— this—" He blew out a great gust of air, like the stack of a steamboat expelling a clog of cinders.

Her hand went involuntarily to her heart, and touched the small elegant halo of diamonds pinned to her morning dress. Upon the instant her thoughts assumed a plausible pattern. "I was merely writing to thank him for this brooch. You know how generous he is with his friends. It's too beautiful for just a formal thank-you."

Edward was not a thinker on his feet when there was no deck beneath them, and chewed his cheek as he re-read the text of her letter. "You address him as Bertie."

"It's what he prefers to be called. It must be terribly tedious always to be greeted as 'Your Highness.' One looks about for the victor at a dog show."

"Now you're only repeating something you heard in a drawing room filled with your clever friends." He let the blotter drop, upsetting a number of her pots and jars. "It's disgraceful to accept extravagant gifts from a man other than your husband."

"You let me accept Redskin."

"A horse is not a brooch, and very properly he presented it through me."

And what was your commission? thought she. It had been at just about that time that Edward had begun to dress more gaily, and incidentally take more walks. On the girl's day off she had taken his coat off the chair where he had left it to hang in the closet and discovered a silver-and-pigskin flask in an inside pocket. What guilt was he marinating in brandy? Aloud she said, "Edward, the letter is nothing. Perhaps it was indiscreet, but no harm was done."

"That's what people always say when a thing is done and can't be withdrawn. I know very well what you think of me; what everyone thinks of me. I'm that dull fellow people invite to parties in order to secure Lillie Langtry. I confess I haven't been much of a husband, but you've been a failure as a wife. You won't bear my children."

She felt washed over with pity and contempt; pity for Edward, and contempt for herself for wasting the emotion upon a creature of so little consequence. Well, he had self-perception at the least; she could not have summed up his situation so succinctly.

She sent the maid to their host with excuses, and slept with Edward that forenoon for the first time in months. When he rose to bathe and dress for dinner, she lay listening to him whistling some silly little tune he must have heard in Piccadilly and reminded herself to blot her letters with sand henceforth.

Court discretion nothwithstanding, rumors abounded: Lillie and the Prince, Lillie and Leopold, the King of Belgium (a dreary country, she decided, or he would not spend so much of his time in England); Lillie and Sir William Gladstone, as if such a thing were possible in this world or the next. She would more promptly consider Disraeli, with his stringy goat's whiskers and famous wit, which paled beside the least significant quip at the salons she visited; but the mill ground on. She read that she had been trimmed like a Christmas tree with diamonds by Crown Prince Rudolph of Austria and Baron Rothschild, when in fact His Highness had given her only a small and tasteful pendant and the baron a garnet ring for her index finger. It seemed the burden had fallen to her to distract the public of Great Britain from its dismal colonial situation. The editors of *Punch* had rejected a cartoon of Her Majesty's troops stumbling across the Transvaal in favor of Lillie in regal caricature receiving Queen Victoria. In reality the old thing had looked through her with cold dead eyes when Lillie was presented, despite reports that she was curious to see this latest interest of Bertie's.

It was all very hard on Edward, who had given up reading the journals, and she had risked the displeasure of the Prince of Wales by asking him if there might be a title for her husband. She had seen her mistake immediately and made a joke of it, suggesting that he'd earned the order of something-or-other at least by resisting the compulsion to yawn in public after she'd kept him out late at dinner after the opera three times in one week, but it was apparent she'd crossed some invisible line and that their friendship was altered.

She was at the summit. French and Italian journalists crossed the Channel to ask her opinion of England's relations with the Continent, the press in America printed items about her in telegraph columns, sheep ranchers in Australia assembled scrapbooks from cuttings about her taken from periodicals that had required months to reach their shore. The governor of Jersey proclaimed a day in her honor, and when she could not attend because of her social obligations, presented her parents with a magnificent wreath of lilies that hung in the rectory at St. Saviour's until it turned brown and withered. A sour observer at the *Evening Standard* coined a term to describe her: "Professional beauty." She thought it appropriate except for one important point. There was no money in the position.

She shot pheasants and grouse with Bertie in the country, astonishing onlookers with her marksmanship; they had not known her in her girlhood, when the tomboy in her predominated. She sailed with the Prince on board his yacht, the *Hildegarde*, and demonstrated her skill with the lines, acquired on the *Red Gauntlet* during her honeymoon; the witnesses to this were absent when she joined her host for moonlight excursions. In the course of these off-season activities, she was given a diamond bracelet that Edward never saw. The staffs of several country homes were instructed to lodge His Highness on the same floor as hers to avoid catching a chill in drafty hallways after midnight. The British journals, conscious of the broader implications of the Official Secrets Act, were circumspect about such arrangements, but they filtered out of the servants' quarters into the mainstream, contributing to Lillie's mystique. Alexandra, the Prince's consort, was not consulted, and offered no commentary on her own; the term "court morals" had existed long before the current royal family, and would in all likelihood survive it for many years.

Lillie would never be better known, although in time more people would see her in person than had seen George Washington, King Louis XIV, and Genghis Khan combined, and her likeness would be nearly as familiar as Buffalo Bill's when barns and fences would wear the reds and yellows of the Wild West show throughout the civilized world. The fine clear eye of Ellen Terry would flash fire when some well-meaning admirer presented her with an elaborate bouquet of Jersey lilies instead of the usual roses during a curtain call at the end of a performance of *East Lynne*. This incident led to renewed efforts on the part of the London theater to put Lillie onstage.

It was an odd time for her to announce her withdrawal from public life.

On October 4, 1880, the *New York Times* featured the following article from the *London Figaro* on its front page, headed "Retirement of Mrs. Langtry from Society":

Mr. and Mrs. Langtry have given up their London residence and for the present Mrs. Langtry remains in Jersey. Is beauty deposed or has beauty abdicated? The result on London society will be the same. Public pets may be objectionable, but few could so well have survived the ordeal of universal admiration and preserved so much of the natural good-hearted woman as Mrs. Langtry.

ELEVEN

The following notice appeared in the *San Antonio Express* on July 27, 1882:

I would announce to my friends and the public in general that I have opened another saloon, where can be found the best of wines, liquors, and cigars that the house of A.B. Frank & Co. affords. My saloon is at the meeting point of the great Southern Pacific and Western extension of the Sunset railway. No other saloon within a mile and a half of my place, and visitors will always find a quiet, orderly place, where they can get a good drink. In connection with my saloon I have a good restaurant, where one can at all times get a good "square meal." The water is good and the scenery grand. Will be pleased to see any of my friends at all times.

Roy Bean

Within a few weeks of this advertisement, visitors to Vinegar-roon were no more successful at locating Roy's restaurant than in observing grand scenery. For a time, the common-law wife of the Mexican who swept out the peanut shucks and polished the spit-toons prepared beans, chili peppers, and cornbread on a range placed outside the tent to avoid the heat in a closed place, but the accumulation of sand fleas and vinegaroons that had sought sui-cide in the simmering pots and pans had alienated diners. The proprietor, after briefly contemplating charging more for the meat, sent her on her way—in the act losing also the services of her husband—and provided hungry customers with bowls of peanuts soaked liberally in brine to increase their thirst.

Pared to the basics, the Headquarters Depot Saloon (named for the nearby Rangers camp and the train station the rail-roads kept promising) became a qualified success, with overhead expenses underwritten by the fees and fines collected by his court. Construction of a proper depot was delayed when he req-uisitioned the carpenters to build a frame structure more suited to the dignity of justice than the patched-over wagon sheet he had turned into a tent upon his first arrival. That project bleached and shrank half-finished, a pinewood skeleton, when the summer heat forced the workers to discontinue it until autumn. They continued to draw their pay from the Sunset and the Southern Pacific and spent it on whiskey and beer and monte. Roy took naturally to this shellgame-inspired sport. His skill at manipu-lating the elusive ace gave birth to the disgruntled opinion that it came to rest up his sleeve more often than not, and another card substituted in its place. Sharpers from places like El Paso who attempted to upgrade his operation by offering him an interest in the game of faro were ejected forcibly; Roy didn't understand the rules and suspected them of having been engineered for the purposes of cheating him.

It was a bare-bones enterprise for all that, and economizing by deciding not to replace the janitor, and letting the spittoons turn green with verdigris and brown with tobacco splatter and the peanut shucks to pile up on the ground until just walking across the tent sounded like a locomotive chugging up a steep grade, had little effect on the profit margin. He allowed as how he'd have gone belly-up if the place had any competition within easy walking distance.

He'd discouraged the first attempt with a simple fusillade through the half-finished shack across the tracks. After that fellow and his party decamped north at a high rate of speed, Roy appropriated his stock and dismantled the place to feed his stove. (He had only partly exaggerated the severity of that first winter; a San Angelo cowboy told friends he lost his job after using frozen snakes for fenceposts, which crawled off with several hundred yards of barbed wire come spring.) Thereafter, the gift of a bottle to Captain Oglesby, the commander of the Rangers camp, and rounds of beer for his men in celebration of some remembered holiday, ensured their support of his monopoly whilst turning the saloon into a sort of officers' and enlisted mens' club. It was reckoned that more Rangers business was discussed there than in Oglesby's tent, and any prospective rival who dropped in to check out the opposition soon saw the lay of the land and sought his fortunes farther down the line.

Although he'd had no judicial aspirations at the time he staked his tent, Roy couldn't have selected a better spot for his court. A lightning-blasted pecan tree twenty paces from the front flap offered a fine gallows as well as a place to discourage accused offenders from running off in lieu of a jail; the Rangers introduced him to the old trick of shackling together their wrists around the burled trunk. Tom Carson, the sergeant assigned to maintain order at the bench, freed the first of many prisoners from this open-aired cell to stand beside the callow lawyer the man's family had sent from Fort Smith, Arkansas. The young man had distinguished himself by winning a rare acquittal for another client in front of Isaac Parker, the notorious "Hanging Judge" of the U.S. District Court.

Finding himself overruled at every turn, the attorney declared that since his client had been denied a fair trial he was requesting a writ of habeas corpus.

"What's that?" asked Roy.

"Why, it's just the basis for the system of due process. Don't you read the *Statutes*?"

Roy laid his bung-starter gavel across the big book. "I read every word and never came across them two."

"It's Latin. It means 'bring forth the body,' and I intend to use it to secure my client's release."

"Overruled." The bung-starter banged the table.

"You can't overrule habeas corpus!"

"Mister, I'm running short on patience, and I didn't start off with a big load. Keep going on this way and there'll be more bodies than one to bring forth."

"Are you threatening my life in a court of law?"

Roy turned to Tom Carson, standing behind him and to his left. "Sergeant, what are your orders here?"

He shifted his cud to the other cheek. "To stand behind all your decisions, Judge."

"What if I told you to take this squirt out and hang him?"

"I'd take him out and hang him."

"You can't do that! This is a seat of justice."

Roy said, "I know it; I'm sitting on it. I won't even get up from it to take you out in the hot sun and hang you. I'll use the ridge pole right here in the saloon."

"Court, Judge," Carson said.

"Court."

"Your honor, I withdraw my request."

"Thought you might. The defendant's guilty as charged."

This exchange took place during those phantom two months between Roy's appointment and the date when it became official. The presence of Sergeant Carson in his sworn capacity strongly indicates that the gun was jumped with at least the tacit approval of the Texas Rangers, who had been known to engage the U.S. Army in armed conflict over their respective views on such fine legal points as jurisdiction and the rule of law. Carson, a veteran of the Comanche wars some ten years older than his captain, with a formidable set of salt-and-pepper muttonchops and deep lesions on his face and neck burned by the sun, had reported to his new duty fresh from a six-hundred-mile march from Eagle's Nest to Fort Stockton to deliver prisoners for trial—if "fresh" is a term that can be applied to such a journey conducted in just twelve days, a record that still stands in equestrian history. It wasn't in his nature to discourage Judge Bean from putting the cart so far in front of the horse and reducing his travel to a fraction.

This leisurely attitude toward legal technicality would cause Roy no end of annoyance in later years, as an acorn of truth grew into the oak of legend, and the Law West of the Pecos was dismissed popularly as a product of his own whim and the happenstance of the *Revised Statutes* having fallen into his possession. But for those two months (and a somewhat longer period when a later governor replaced him for impropriety and Roy simply refused to give up either the book or the post), he was bona fide; a Latin phrase he took to immediately it was explained to him, as he never did habeas corpus.

Progress continued—in fits and starts, according to the cycle of heat waves in summer, monsoons in autumn, when the Pecos remembered it was a river and stranded lumber shipments on the wrong side, and the level of inebriation in the laborers—on Roy Bean's palace of justice. Meanwhile he adjudicated under canvas and stored pictures and posters of Lillie Langtry in a trunk to await walls to tack them to. The little drummer supplied them faithfully and with an enthusiasm that scooped up likenesses of other professional beauties who bore a passable resemblance to the creature of Roy's not-so-private fantasies. The drummer, who had run away from an immigrant farming family at fourteen, had a Bohemian name no one could pronounce, spoke in a combination Texas drawl with a Middle European bubble and consonant-biting Chicagoese, and grew fat from his stops in Vinegarroon. He sold Roy empty Hermitage bottles to fill with Old Johnston, named for the famed Liver-Eater of story and song; the Judge depended on him for news from the East, and taught the latest popular tunes he carried with him to the local mariachis, who played "Whispering Hope," "O, Susannah," and "I Dream of Jeannie" with a Spanish interpretation that made them all sound like "Cielito Lindo." Unsatisfied, he tried them on a concertina he'd won off a teamster at monte, but he decided the man had given him a bum steer as to how to work the instrument and traded it for a Confederate flag the drummer insisted had been carried at Chickamauga. Roy tacked it up for a time behind the bench, taking it down when a Ranger who had served with the Army of the Potomac complained. The Judge had a dim memory at best of just why the war had been fought, and in any case he had a no-nonsense idea of just where his support lay. His Colt, bung-starter, and even the mighty *Statutes* were just stage properties without the Sons of Texas backing them up.

"We've a saying in West Texas," he wrote Lillie, with the help of daughter Zulema, who had a way with contractions he admired. " 'There is six times more law in the chambers of a Paterson revolver than in Washington.' " He rather regretted the swift justice he'd given the little habeas corpus lawyer, who could probably have translated it into a fine motto to hang on a sign at the entrance to his courtroom. More and more, as white hairs sprouted among the black in his beard and his belly expanded to the girth appropriate to a respected jurist, he regretted the ill-considered actions of his youth. At the same time he contemplated what sentence he would impose upon the teamster who'd given him the squeezebox without providing complete instructions for its use the next time he came through.

As beyond doubt he would. All roads led to Texas. In the fullness of time even the Czar of all the Russias must eventually stop off at Vinegarroon to take a shit. It was one of the four corners of the world, as surely as Paris, Rome, and Beanville.

But when the emporium of law, order, and whiskey-fueled entertainment that would eventually be christened the Jersey Lilly was yet a dream—albeit a noisy one, punctuated with the wheezing of saws, rataplan of hammers, and blasphemies of hungover carpenters—pretty Zulema, her siblings—Little Roy, Sam, and Laura—and Roy's dreams of a venerable old age surrounded by his adoring heirs were stuck in San Antonio with Maria Virginia. Thoughts of them led inevitably to her, and the scar on his scalp throbbed and ached whenever she entered them. A man's accomplishments were as dry chaff without his progeny to witness them and pass them on to their children, and so on, snatched up by the hot wind from Mexico and deposited barren in the desert. It was an easy thing, now that the railroads had linked up (he'd made a mad dash to secure the silver spike that had been driven to commemorate the event, only to lose the race to a carpetbagger), to plead his case to his wife, but memories of that lethal baking-pan always stopped him as he was reaching for the cash to pay the fare. He wired her at irregular intervals at her parents' ranch, beseeching her to permit the children to visit. He gave up waiting for her to respond. Tom Carson, who kept company with him drinking and playing cards after court was adjourned, listened sympathetically to his slurred lamentations and helped him to his cot when his legs were unsteady. No one else saw the Judge brought so low, and the sergeant told no one.

Guilt was part of the reason for intemperance. Roy was ashamed to admit even to himself that he was relieved by his wife's silence. He missed his children, the girls especially, but he wasn't the disciplinarian with them that he was behind the bench, where he had the Rangers to back his play. Evidence of the young Beans' behavior in San Antonio, and certain things he remembered from his own unsupervised childhood, made him wonder if one or all of them might someday stand in his own dock. He suspected the *Statutes* discouraged a justice of the peace from standing in judgment of his own flesh and blood, but the language of the law kept circling back and crossing its own trail like a wounded bobcat, and a man sometimes got lost in it. Little Roy was approaching the age his father had been when he quit Kentucky to chase adventure and Spanish tail in old Mexico; followed a string of colorful episodes, including his own lynching. Roy was loath to own to it, but he thought they were all better off with their mother, rabid she-wolf that she was.

Maria Virginia, meanwhile, was wondering if perhaps she would not be better off without her children.

Not permanently, of course; what kind of mother would she be if she abandoned them, particularly to the care of one such as Roy? Nothing she had heard of the old *puerco*'s activities since he'd left San Antonio aboard a stolen wagon had given her cause to believe that his ways had changed. Scarcely a week passed that some angry creditor did not knock on her father's door, looking for his son-in-law. The sheriff himself came nearly as often as the parish priest, who took tea with them every Sunday. It was a mortal embarrassment.

The addition of J.P. to his name did not sanction rascality. Had not her own ancestors been forced to flee Portugal, leaving behind all their holdings, because of some insult to a king's inquisitor? Nothing was different in America, only the names were more outlandish. Maria Virginia Bean, indeed. She never stirred herself to correct those who addressed her as Señora Chavez, assuming the woman who lived with her children at the ranch was a widowed daughter-in-law, and visited town only when necessary, enduring "Señora Frijole" in simmering silence.

But the children were a challenge. They all shared her physical characteristics, but as to personality they might as well have sprung directly from Roy's loins with no interference from her. Little Roy was long-limbed, lazy, and insolent, with the cruel good looks of a toreador, and knew it; when he did not come home, she lived in terror that the sheriff would visit yet again, this time with her son's body, ventilated by buckshot fired by some ruined girl's father. Sam looked up to his brother and would likely follow his example; meanwhile, he busied himself committing petty thievery, learned at Little Roy's knee. The first time the boys had presented her with a dead chicken, still warm, insisting that it had been run over in the road by a wagon, she had given it to the cook without question. After the second episode, she'd decided to keep an eye on the boys as they played near the fence that separated her family's ranch from the neighbors, and witnessed them fixing a kernel of corn to a hook and dangling it from a length of twine over the other side of the fence. "Chicken fishing" clearly violated the Eighth Amendment. She'd put a stop to the practice, but the taint was there. Wash day almost invariably yielded a bounty of clasp knives, slingshots, and jews' harps from Sam's pockets. Maria Virginia had approved none of these acquisitions, and there was no money for them.

Laura and Zulema provided little more comfort. They were strong-willed and nearing the age dreaded by the parents of daughters. She prayed nightly that by some miracle they would come to resemble their father physically before the young goats caught their scent.

They were all guilty of truancy, the boys more so than the girls. That the deputy assigned this responsibility had stopped coming to the Chavezes' door suggested merely that the school-teacher was just as glad to have them absent and had stopped re-porting them. Maria Virginia was reluctant to make inquiries that would confirm this suspicion.

"Beans don't sprout far from the patch." She overheard this wherever she went.

She thought of all these things with Roy's last telegram before her, crumpled without reading but now smoothed out on the table by the window overlooking the yard, where Little Roy and Sam were hunkered in a corner drawing diagrams in the dirt with sticks; had they graduated from barnyard fowl to banks? With no further hesitation she reversed the yellow flimsy, dipped a pen, and drafted a wire asking Roy to send train fare for four at children's rate.

TWELVE

All London knew the circumstances of Mrs. Langtry's withdrawal from society, or thought it did, and few condemned her. Who, barring the royals and the unassailably rich, had not found himself at one time or another low in resources and high in creditors? Few knew the distressing details. She and Edward had been living astronomically beyond their means for years. The allowance he received from his family would hardly pay the interest on what they owed their landlady, her seamstress, his tailor, stabling for Redskin; even the gas bill was deep in arrears. Letters had come threatening to shut off their service.

Lillie had long suspected her husband of prolonging the inevitable by wheedling gifts of cash and pawnable trinkets from casual male acquaintances seeking an introduction to his celebrated wife. Some were charming, others boorish; they encompassed doddering old age and callow youth, and pressed their affections so fervently that she grew adept at turning them away, either with grace or firm resolution. At times reinforcements were required, and the *illuminati* of artists and poets that fluttered about her flame had learned to look for the arched brow or tilt of a fan intended to summon them to her rescue. Oscar's intimidating height and Jimmie's persistent prattle nudged and prodded the offender to some neutral part of the ballroom or salon for champagne and paté, freeing Lillie for more congenial company. Such support did nothing to relieve her annoyance with Edward, who in her view was nothing more than a common procurer; but his state of near-constant inebriation and the growing gulf between them prevented her from confronting him with the sordid accusation.

They retrenched. The furniture from the Norfolk Street flat was first to go, followed by her jewelry through discreet brokers. They gave up their rooms and with them Whistler's hideous ceiling, dismissed the household staff and stable boys, and paid their most pressing debts, gaining time to attend to the rest. Edward moved into his parents' home in Belfast and Lillie went to live with her family in Jersey to save expenses. London sympathized. What it did not know, what even Edward did not, was that Lillie had gone into the customary period of confinement on the advice of the Prince of Wales's personal physician. She was—oh, *what* was that delicate phrase actors used onstage?— "with child."

She was terrified. Not of the physical challenges of pregnancy, but of Edward's reaction. Counting back three months, she could not assign the moment of conception to Whitsuntide at Lord Malmesbury's estate, when she and Edward had been intimate for the first time in nearly a year, but rather six weeks before. (Caution born of dim suspicion had caused her to turn to Bertie's own doctor.) Edward could count; he was not so far gone as that, and as there had been an epidemic of premature births in their set lately, she could not depend upon the easy excuse to defuse the situation. He never failed to bring up that blasted desk blotter every time they fell out. There would be a suit for divorce, naming Bertie as co-respondent (His Royal Highness' dalliances were an open secret; those who read the agony columns could recite their names in order as easily as they did the kings and queens of England), scandal, the child's custody questioned. As yet the little bastard was nothing more than an hour of discomfort in the morning, but Lillie assumed that at some point the maternal instinct would kick in—and besides, having one's own flesh and blood wandering about unsupervised was a reputation disaster just waiting to happen.

Money would be behind the thing, of course. It would start with a discreet request for a boon from the royal family. When that was refused, Edward would seek damages in court. Brandy was not cheap, certainly not at the rate he consumed it, his club didn't carry members more than two months behind in their dues, he gambled there, lost usually, and his friends, who were his friends only because they had hopes of becoming Lillie's, would encourage him to press any action that would free her from matrimony. Legal contests were all the thing that season, as peacock's feathers had been in the last. Even that strutty bantam Jimmy Whistler had forced himself into bankruptcy when he won a decision against an art critic for an insulting review but failed to collect so much as reimbursement of his lawyers' fees. The public followed the latest sensational trial the way it did races and cricket, and hers would push the war and Disraeli's resignation into the inside pages.

No. She would not be last year's disgrace.

Was it possible? Could it be done? Had ever a wife successfully concealed six months of confinement and birth from her husband? It was not so simple a thing as casting a basket adrift among bullrushes.

Bertie could help; would help. But it ill-behooved a woman who could bring the millinery industry to its knees by mentioning casually that she was weary of wearing hats to petition the heir apparent. Anyway, now was the time to limit contact with the prince, not increase it. Her father, the rector, had given up St. Saviour's for a less demanding parish in London, a fortuitous turn. Through her mother, who wrote him daily from Jersey, she asked for his support in the decision she had made. Mrs. LeBreton was persuasive. He agreed, suitably alarmed by the news of Edward's bibulous and profligate habits and his willingness to accept favors in return for promising his wife's affections. The rectory in Marylebone would be Edward's first stop after he heard from Lillie. He would ask his father-in-law to intercede. The old man would refuse. Her husband, who was so evasive when she asked him for anything directly, was easily manipulated by authority. His father's financial advisors had forced him to sell his yachts to stem his debts, her doctor had persuaded him to move his wife to London despite his horror of the place; he would be no less intimidated by clergy. With all her shuttlecocks thus in position, Lillie wrote him a long letter explaining that their marriage had come to an end.

Divorce was out of the question. She was in no fit place for it, and barring grounds (at all costs he must be kept ignorant) Edward would be opposed to it for reasons of respectability. Separation, whether of bedrooms or residences, was hardly uncommon at a level of society where marriages were arranged for social or financial convenience; affection was for mistresses and the working class. Once he overcame his objections, her husband of six years would be relieved to surrender all his responsibilities and while away his time racing his father's yachts and drinking his brandy. Men were simple creatures, easily mollified by trifles: Bertie and his cigars, dear Oscar and his smart waistcoats and comely male companions. It was no wonder so many thought they could possess her with gifts of horses and jewelry. She kept calm—and collected. Edward had shown her the way.

All things being equal, there was nothing to suggest directly that the child wasn't his. History's pages sagged with unacknowledged royalty, novels were written about it, and the Court of St. James simply boiled with K.B.E.'s, secretaries, and ministers plenipotentiary whose fathers or mothers had been born on the wrong side of the purple blanket. It all seemed sordid, the stuff of melodrama, and altogether too commonplace for the son or daughter of the Jersey Lily. Shakespeare himself had had a go at it. *A Comedy of Errors* occupied a place in the pile of playscripts that had begun to arrive as regularly as milk and butter in her mother's parlor once the news of her financial inconvenience got about. The sensation-starved theater remained high on the long list of her most persistent suitors.

Preposterous, Edward had thought the notion. Perhaps so, and in any case she couldn't entertain thoughts of anything so energetic for another six months at least, however pressing her situation. (The Marylebone parsonage did not pay nearly so well as St. Saviour's; she could not impose upon her parents' hospitality indefinitely.) She was under doctor's orders not to exert herself, and terribly bored without activities or visitors except family. She stretched an arm from the chaise and drew a script from the top of the stack. *She Stoops to Conquer*: Promising title.

My dear Judge Bean,

Please forgive me for the delay in responding to your most recent letter. Rehearsals are a tedious, all-consuming thing, as I'm sure your responsibilities are also.

I enjoyed your account of how you came to be appointed Justice of the Peace. Tell me, are you required to preside at quarter sessions, as are our J.P.s in England?

My entry to my own profession was similar to yours. It came about quite by accident, with no formal preparation, and I should not have accepted were someone whose life I held dearer than mine not dependent upon me. (I envy you your four children; I have but one, and fear that by lavishing all my affections upon her instead of distributing them among a group I have spoiled her beyond reclaiming.)

But, oh, Sir, that child! When first I set eyes upon her, I knew that I had never loved before and never would again. No heart is so stout it could withstand the strain more than once. . . .

I am, Your Honor, yours cordially,
Lillie Langtry

She had attended many christenings at St. Saviour's, so could not convince herself, despite the midwife's blandishments, that little Jeanne was the most beautiful child in the world. She was a tiny, red, pinch-faced thing, like some of the peers Lillie had seen toddling to and from the House of Lords on their sticks, and when she opened her toothless mouth to wail, the lung power she exhibited brought memories of William LeBreton bellowing Job's lamentations all the way to the back pews. Apart from that, she resembled Lillie's family very little and, thank God, anyone else not at all. She might have been Edward's child or Spring-Heeled Jack's for all the familiarity she bore to any other creature on earth.

Lillie loved her with an emotion almost violent. She wept bitterly when her mother and a governess took her away to live with her grandfather in London; she would follow soon after, but the subterfuge that Jeanne was her niece (whether upon Edward's side or hers was left to the imagination of others) required that they live separately, which seemed to her a form of abandonment. But she dried her eyes and selected her most conservative dress to make the rounds of prospective employers. A retired professional beauty had no pension and must provide for her little family somehow.

"You are going on the stage, of course," said Oscar, when she went to him for advice.

"Henry Irving suggested me once for a little part, but I suspect that offer has expired. I'm a has-been, you see."

"Balderdash. 'Age cannot wither her, nor custom stale her infinite sobriety,' or however it goes." Young Mr. Wilde tossed back his lion's mane and presented his arm. "We shall go round and see Nell."

Ellen Terry, five years Lillie's senior, was the first lady of the British stage, and a lovely and statuesque woman who greeted them both graciously in a dressing gown in her parlor. Her French maid bustled about, removing items of clothing from a walnut chifforobe and packing them in a huge steamer trunk. "My costumes," Terry explained. "I'm touring the Continent in *Saint Joan*, and I'm done with having my costumes arrive at the theater the day after I left. I trust them to no one's care but mine."

Lillie considered this her first nugget of sound theatrical advice.

The rest, when the reason for the visit had been explained, was less encouraging. "Beauty is a distinct advantage on the boards, Lillie, but it will only take you so far. Worse, it erodes at almost the same rate as experience expands. Look at Madamoiselle Bernhardt. She's nearing forty and always looked consumptive, but she commands every set because she was born with talent and her skill is frightening. You, however, would be starting at the top, and be judged on her level. They'll expect everything from you, then damn you as an amateur. Forgive me, dear, but your training hasn't prepared you to be flayed alive."

Lillie thanked her for her candor and they left. Outside, Oscar patted her arm. "Mea culpa, darling, for ignoring one of my own maxims. Experience is the name everyone gives to his mistakes."

"You needn't comfort me. I expected something of the sort. I'm in the way of being Barnum's Jumbo, who need merely stand still and be an elephant to be admired. If he were to start spouting Aeschylus, he would bring down the house."

"The critics may object to his diction."

She sighed. "Tragically, I am Jumbo no longer. I am not even Tom Thumb."

"Let's test it," said he. "Johnny Millais has invited me to a soiree at his home day after tomorrow. He's unveiling a picture of the Prime Minister Redux, or perhaps his Scotch terrier; Gladstone is easily mistaken the one for the other. I don't think the maestro knows you're back in town. If with you on my arm I'm turned away at the door, we'll know the Jersey Lily has lost its bloom."

"If that happens I shall kill myself."

"I sincerely hope not. Such an act would be ruled unjustifiable suicide."

She was, of course, welcome, in last year's dress with some hasty personal modifications, and was soon in the center of a jabbering male circle. Oscar, with genteel insults of apology, extricated her and steered her toward a beet-faced stranger in a dinner jacket of a decidedly non-European cut, smoking next to a convenient potted plant. He was Lester Wallack, the American theatrical producer. She was not surprised. Obviously, Oscar had been priming the pump. She asked him what he thought of the British theater.

Wallack, a gentleman of the awkward New World stamp, held his cigar smoldering behind his back. "With respect, ma'am, your players bellow the lines directly at the audience when they should be reading them to each other. The plays are artificial enough without that."

"I always say it's not good for one's morals to see bad acting," Oscar said.

She remained intent on Wallack. "Are American plays less artificial?"

"I wish I could say they were. You'd blush to see *Uncle Tom's Cabin*. It makes natural delivery that much more important. Have you ever considered acting, Mrs. Langtry?"

"I have no background. Would you take that chance?"

He appeared startled. She'd been too eager, and in front of Oscar; she was mortified. "I'm joking, of course. I have all I can do to remember the name of my hairdresser, much less commit a playscript to memory."

"I'll start you off at two hundred fifty dollars a week."

She was relieved—and staggered by the amount—but wary. "But what about natural delivery?"

"An irrelevancy in your case. It's you the public will pay to see." His expression was puzzled. "I don't think you understand,

Mrs. Langtry, how highly you are regarded in America. Just last month a man in Texas shot and killed a fellow for shooting a hole through your likeness on the wall of a saloon. We're a Christian country: Zealotry like that is usually reserved for holy images."

"Surely your theater isn't in Texas."

"No, ma'am, New York. But we aspire to be as big."

THIRTEEN

Roy said, "It don't look right."

"What do you mean? It's level." The Southern Pacific carpenter spoke through a mouthful of nails. He'd just driven one into the board.

"I mean how it's spelt."

The sign beneath the porch roof read "THE JERSEY LILLY," complete with quotation marks.

"I can't answer for that. You wanted a sign painter, you should've hired one."

"I don't want to be no laughingstock from here to England. You better have a look. I left my reading glasses inside." Roy passed a brittle sheet of paper up the stepladder.

The carpenter, who had never seen the Judge read anything, with or without spectacles, studied it. It was a two-year-old hand-bill advertising Lillie Langtry's appearance in *As You Like It* at Abbey's Park Theatre in New York, the inaugural stop on her first American tour. The actress was pictured wearing a daring Elizabethan costume of doublet and tights.

"It don't make sense. When it comes before Langtry, it's ell-eye-ell-ell-eye-ee, but after Jersey it's ell-eye-ell-ell-why. Them Easterners can't spell any better'n Old Blue."

Roy worked on the chaw in his cheek while the spectators on the street awaited his verdict. Any sort of outdoor activity in West Texas in summer was sure to draw a crowd, and when it involved the saloon it was a public event.

Finally the Judge spat. "Well, let's just say we went ahead and split the difference. Nail 'er up and we'll get to the christening."

When the sign was in place, Roy smashed a Hermitage bottle filled with liver-eater against a porch post and invited everyone in for a round on the house; he charged a penny tax on the next, "to cover the cost of moving the court into its new quarters."

The year was 1884, and a big one for Vinegarroon. With order in place and the trains running smoothly, the town was in the staking-out process, with incorporation soon to follow, and Roy had moved his possibles into the new turpentine-smelling build-ing south of the tracks. No sooner had the sawdust settled than he put the Southern Pacific crew to work on a house for himself and his children, whom he expected any time now that Maria Virginia had agreed to let them go. He said the lumber was sur-plus, left over from the completed railroad station, but there was some business about a reported construction-site theft—a com-mon crime in that bald country—and replacements sent; in any case it would be a sin to let it rot in piles or feed stoves in winter, when cottonwood was suited for nothing else. No one com-plained, not even Roy's enemies, who were curious to see just what kind of spawn a man like the Judge had produced.

In August, his appointment expired and he stood for election. His opponent was a land-office attorney, put up by a client, Jesus Torres. An old Spanish land grant entitled Torres to the property upon which Vinegarroon stood—and until recently the site of the Jersey Lilly. He didn't care for the incumbent, whom he accused of cornering him into donating the parcel to the S.P. for the right-of-way. Pressure had been applied by both the railroad and the Texas Rangers, who opposed evicting the Judge for reasons of consistency. The wheels of justice could hardly revolve smoothly if its custodian were forced to pull up stakes like a gypsy.

As the palace of law and also the largest building in town, Roy's emporium was selected as the polling place. The proprietor greeted each voter with a blank ballot and a glass of beer. Torres came in to vote, assessed the situation, and said, "Don't you know the saloons are closed on election day?"

Roy smiled. He liked the big, handsome young Mexican of Castilian ancestry even if the feelings weren't reciprocated. The imposing figure Torres made in silver braid and red-topped boots with big clanking spurs put Roy in mind of his own gaudy youth; although that was where the resemblance ended. For all his show of arrogance, Torres struggled for identity between his autocratic father and overbearing German wife. He was easily intimidated when a man was in a less generous mood than Roy was at the moment.

"It *is* closed," he said. "This here's a private party to celebrate my victory."

"The polls are open for two more hours!"

"I'm optimistic."

"Any fool can see you're trying to buy your way into office."

"That ain't true. There ain't been a word of politics spoke on these premises since I opened the door this morning. Draw you one?" He rested his hand on the tap.

"You know damn well I'm not voting for you."

"I suspected as much, but a man ought to be mellow when he concedes."

Roy won handily, and Torres's complaints fell on deaf ears in Austin. It was a Bean triumph, but it turned a rival into a bitter enemy, one with deep pockets and a long family history of patience and cunning. Old Don Cesario had established a sprawling cattle ranch, the 7D, higher up the Pecos on a tract of land nearly the size of Andalusia, granted by King Philip to a New Spanish ancestor in return for the gift of a bust of the monarch cast in gold; the tract Jesus now owned had been presented to him at the time of his wedding. The bust went down aboard a galleon in the Horse Latitudes, after which it was represented to the court in Madrid as a life-size statue, with eyes of Montana sapphire. Roy, who'd heard this story, told Sergeant Tom Carson that he had to scheme six times as hard to stay ahead of six generations of sharp practice.

As train traffic increased between Vinegarroon and civilization, the barrels and boxes that had supported the backsides of interested parties in the old tent gave way to Windsor chairs ordered from Sears & Roebuck. The moth-eaten buffalo robe Roy had traded off an old hider from Kansas went out back to shed water off a stack of firewood and a bright woven rug was laid on the plank floor in its place. He hung crossed staffs bearing the U.S. and Lone Star flags behind the bar and legal bench, but papered every other inch of wall with posters, handbills, rotogravures, cartes de visite, and cigarette cards decorated by the figure and features of Lillie Langtry. Although it was true that the resemblance in some was slight, customers and supplicants who questioned their legitimacy were obliged to leave or, if court was in session, found in contempt and offered the choice of spending the night shackled to the mangled pecan tree outside or sweeping the floor and polishing spittoons. (One prisoner who chose the latter option took his revenge by scattering grapes on the floor and, when a pilgrim found him corraling them with his broom, remarked upon their fineness. The reply: "Them ain't grapes. They're eyeballs. We had another fight last night." The story traveled down the rails, and for a time visitors to town made the longer trek to the saloon Jesus Torres had established north of the tracks.)

When a drunk scarcely aware of his surroundings scratched a match off a wall, tearing a gash in Mrs. Langtry's peaches-and-cream cheek, a pair of Rangers seized and threw him out into the street, aiming for a pile of horse-apples. Their quickness of action likely spared the county the cost of a funeral, as friends of the Judge were present, and others who didn't know him but were eager to curry favor with the local leading citizen were armed as well as any of Carson's men. Roy was absent, snoring off the effects of the morning's session in back, but when he heard later that he'd either shot the offender personally or sentenced him to hang, he made no effort to correct the misapprehension. It might prevent any further defacings, and if anything such rumors seemed to attract trade rather than repel it; it had begun to dawn upon him dimly that he was the town's biggest draw. Meanwhile, he directed the carpenter who had hung the Jersey Lilly sign to fix the flaw in the picture, which he managed to do by matching the pink with a drop of barn red swirled in a shot glass filled with whitewash.

The carpenter had found ample opportunity to improve his artistic skills. Driven by Roy's whims and added responsibilities, he decorated the front of the building nearly as thoroughly as

his employer plastered the inside, with signs reading JUDGE ROY
BEAN, NOTARY PUBLIC; JUSTICE OF THE PEACE; CORONER; FREE
LUNCHEON SERVED NOON TIL ONE; BILLIARD HALL; and the
painter/carpenter's own favorite, ICE COLD BEER & LAW WEST
OF THE PECOS. New signs were erected and old ones replaced
with such regularity that loafers began to congregate in front of
the building to note the newest developments as often as they
gathered on the train platform to see who'd arrived from San
Antonio and points east. Anticipation began to build whenever
the proprietor lifted his rocking chair off the front porch and set
it down in the middle of the street facing the saloon; there he
would sit for twenty minutes or an hour, chin in hand and elbow on knee, staring at what to him was a blank canvas, while
traffic flowed around him. Within the hour, the painter would
be back aboard his ladder.

All this took place during lulls in business and between court
proceedings. The rest of the time the Judge kept busy settling
property disputes, serving liquor and beer, punishing petty
larceners, telling stories ("stretching the blanket," he called it),
fining disturbers of the peace, and—his favorite—presiding at
weddings. Matrimonial ceremonies offered him the chance to
spout Scripture as he remembered it (fragments from The Song
of Solomon, blushingly unbowdlerized) and slobber over the
bride; for, fat and rheumatic as he was, he maintained his appreciation for the pretty Mexican girls who came before him to surrender their hands to the neighbors' sons. He stocked cases of
putative French champagne for such occasions, and when the
popping of corks was overheard and reported in newspapers as
far away as Nevada and Louisiana as "more gunfire in J.P. Bean's
court," enjoyed having the accounts read to him as he nursed his
aching head with towels soaked in vinegar.

When, as sometimes happened, a couple recovered from the reception to find themselves disagreeable strangers, he listened with sympathy and granted the divorce with a slap of his bung-starter. His authority covered performing marriages, not dissolving them; but he thought this a senseless technicality, as any good Christian was empowered to correct his mistakes.

One day he found himself confronted with two bridegrooms and two brides, each of whom coveted the other's mate. He studied the matter in silence, looking for all the world as he did when he stared at the front of the Jersey Lilly contemplating signs. At length he nullified both unions, "shuffled" the principals, and remarried them according to their preference. The arrangement was successful and produced several children, two of them named Roy, which in later years led to ugly rumors that completely obscured the original violation, and yet another incident to add to his legend.

A challenge to a duel was dry kindling for gossip. When Sergeant Carson discovered Julio Martinez, the father of one of the Roys, drinking uncharacteristically heavily at the end of the Judge's bar, he searched him and found an old ball-and-percussion pistol stuck in his trousers. Martinez confessed that he was on his way to kill a neighbor who had insinuated that his Roy was not his Roy at all, but Roy's. The sergeant charged him with carrying a concealed weapon and manacled him to the pecan tree to await trial.

When court reconvened after siesta, the Judge listened to the particulars and ordered the prisoner's release.

"On what grounds, Judge?" asked Carson.

"On these grounds, where else?"

"I mean how come? There's the evidence right in front of you."

Roy examined the antique firearm and laid it on a shelf among his growing arsenal; he allowed as how he'd saved a number of his constituents from drowning in the Pecos under all that iron. "The charge won't stick. If he was standing still when he was arrested, as you say, he wasn't carrying a weapon because he wasn't going no place. Case dismissed."

The next day, Carson observed Martinez striding down the street with a hitch in his step and relieved him of another pistol nearly as old as the first and in worse condition. In court, Roy made a face at it and dumped it in the slop bucket. "Case dismissed."

"Hold on, Judge. This time I caught him red-handed, in motion and walking down the street."

"In that case he was traveling, and it's legal in this county for travelers to carry weapons. Release the prisoner."

The sergeant, who had grown weary of arresting the same man to no useful purpose, reported this second incident in person to the neighbor whom Martinez had pledged to kill. That fellow gathered up his family and moved to Del Rio.

His personal interpretation of his responsibilities aside, Roy felt respectable. His children arrived shortly after his election; three days later he strolled home during siesta to find his household a picture of domestic bliss. Laura and Zulema were sewing curtains from gingham to replace the pieces of cut-up tent their father had nailed over the windows to keep out dust, and in the footworn path to the outhouse the Judge called the backyard, Little Roy and Sam were using Roy's counterfeit lump of ice as a magnifying lens to incinerate fire ants. There was a new schoolhouse forty paces away, and Maria Virginia had made Roy promise to see that their formal education continued without interruption, but Little Roy had matriculated from the sixth grade, and Sam had told his father that the schoolmistress, a daughter of the Old South, had declared a holiday for the children of Confederate veterans in honor of Jefferson Davis' birthday. Roy wasn't that gullible, but he admired the invention and enjoyed having his family around him. All he'd ever learned in school was how to get around the rules, and he figured he could teach that well enough.

The very presence of the schoolhouse, and of the army of surveyors pacing out future streets in the dust, told him the wild days were drawing to a close. The last inquest he'd conducted over a violent death involved a stranger who had plunged off the Myers Canyon bridge three miles outside town. When the body was stretched out on adjoining tables in the Jersey Lilly, a search of its pockets found no identification, only forty dollars in bank notes and a revolver in good condition. The victim's clothing reeked of Old Johnston, which made it unlikely he'd been helped to his reward. Roy ruled death by misadventure, confiscated the revolver, and fined the dead man forty dollars for carrying a concealed weapon. Sergeant Carson held his tongue as to whether the defendant could be considered standing still or traveling on his way from the bridge to the floor of the canyon.

Well, things had come to a definite pass when crossing a bridge was more dangerous than crossing town. The revolver joined the artillery display, powdered now with dust and looking more like a museum exhibit and less like material evidence.

A man could smell change as surely as the seasons. The guerrillas whose exploits Roy followed in newspapers and nickel novels were getting themselves backshot in their own parlors; that little snot Bonney was dead in New Mexico because he couldn't stay away from Spanish tail, which seemed as good a reason as any to take the risk. The Comanches were learning their letters at Fort Sill, and Wes Hardin had been busting rocks in Huntsville for years. Roy reckoned Geronimo and himself were the last authentic hell-raisers still at large, and it wouldn't be long before General Crook starved the Apache butcher out into the open. Maybe it was time Roy placed himself on display, the way Sitting Bull had done with Cody's frontier circus. He could jack up the price of a glass of beer and possibly bail out that billiard table he'd ordered when the sign went up advertising it; the company in San Antonio was holding out for cash.

Something needed to be done, that was clear. The court couldn't sustain itself on dog-bite complaints, and Jesus Torres—prodded, no doubt, by his interfering, schnitzel-eating wife—had attached an ice cream parlor to his competing saloon to attract ladies. Roy couldn't very well shoot up the place without starting a range war with Don Cesario, which the Rangers would never stand for. They'd take sides against Roy for the same reason they'd supported him in the beginning, to restore and preserve peace. The *Revised Statutes* was silent on the problem. Evidently no law in Texas prohibited the sale of ice cream.

Coincidentally, he was deep in these ruminations when a telegram arrived, addressed to young Torres at his saloon but delivered to the Jersey Lilly by order of the stationmaster as part of a standing agreement; a hard-working entrepreneur needed an edge somewhere, and he had found it in the railroad man's preferred brand of apple-flavored pipe tobacco, ordered on Roy's account from A.B. Frank & Co., tobacconists and distillers to the trade.

The wire was from the office of the Postmaster General in Washington, D.C., informing Torres that his application for a post office had been approved and asking under what name the town should be registered.

Roy grinned. He was impressed by the simple effrontery of it: going over his head to lay claim to the place just because he held the deed to it, when everyone knew who was in charge. The Judge reversed the sheet and licked the end of a pencil stub.

Vinegarroon was out of the question. It was the miserable name of an ugly creature that existed only to be eaten by road-runners and prairie chickens. Anyway, there was no advantage in it. He wrote "Beanville," then rubbed it out, tearing the flimsy with the petrified eraser. Torres had more friends in Austin than he did, and would turn aside any frontal assault with an ease that would reflect badly on the reputation of the Law West of the Pecos.

While he was considering his strategy, his gaze alighted, as so often it did, upon a vision far more suited to civilized society than either himself or a stingless scorpion or even Don Cesario himself.

Langtry, Texas
December 8, 1884

Dear Mrs. Langtry,

You don't know me, and there is no reason you should, but as the duly elected Justice of the Peace of Val Verde County in the great State of Texas, it is my distinct pleasure to be the first to inform you . . .

Yours very truly,
Judge Roy Bean

FOURTEEN

It's you the public will pay to see.

Lester Wallack's words, doubtless intended to flatter, festered in Lillie's dreams. She saw herself as Barnum's elephant, got up in tights and a tutu, gallumphing pathetically to the strains of "The Rogue's March," punctuated by the rude splat of a pig's bladder on a stick. All the world laughed, Bertie and Oscar loudest of all, their faces distorted like malicious imps'. She awoke, clammy and convinced that all the honeyed words all these years had been poured into her ears expressly to trap and humiliate her on a scale so vast it wouldn't be forgotten in a century. Humbling the exalted was a spectacle that never failed.

Wallack's card languished unanswered in her writing desk while she made certain arrangements; or, more properly, surrendered herself to those made on her behalf. For Madame Labouchere was a force of nature, and her appearance was well timed.

Henrietta Hodson, as the madame preferred to be addressed,

was a nervous jerky sparrow of a woman with a somewhat mysterious experience of the London stage. (She claimed to have retired, but Lillie could find no one who remembered having seen her in anything; Oscar pondered aloud whether she was cock's-crow in *Romeo and Juliet*.) She effectively bearded Lillie in her Ely Place den, arriving unannounced and forcing the maid to awaken her mistress from her latest nightmare of public humiliation, and with little preamble offered—no, insisted—upon tutoring her in the theatrical art.

Lillie instinctively resisted bullying, whether by her brothers or presumptuous strangers. "Someone has misled you, madame. I have no interest in going on the stage ever."

"I am organizing a benefit performance for charity." Henrietta, as would be seen, was slightly deaf or affected to be; a useful affliction in one to whom the word "no" held no meaning. "An amateur production, perforce; just the sort of thing to get your feet wet. No press, so you needn't be concerned about embarrassing yourself in front of society."

"I have no talent."

"You have beauty, presence, and poise. Many great careers have been founded on much less. I will provide the instruction."

"Madame Labouchere, really—"

"Henrietta, if you please. I am an actress, not a dog-groomer. This weekend, then. Tell your driver Pope's Villa, Twickenham. Everyone knows where it is. We'll begin as soon as you've rested."

Alexander Pope was a great poet; everyone said so, and Lillie, who in her girlhood had brought her father to tears of laughter reciting the satirical verses in "The Rape of the Lock," wasn't disposed to disagree. She assumed, therefore, that his sardonic humor had been much involved in the design and construction of

Pope's Villa, Twickenham. In truth, Pope had been dead more than a century when the humble stone cottage where he'd wetted his quill was razed by order of an androgynous Swiss architect and replaced by the alpine atrocity where Mrs. Langtry received her first lessons in the craft of acting.

The delirious arrangement of turrets, gables, and gimcrack resembled a great wedding cake dumped beside the Thames, and was so poorly joined that when she walked down the hall to bathe, the draughts twirled round her ankles and up under her dressing gown as freely as if she were naked. Leering satyrs and fat pink nymphs cavorted on tapestries hung in an effort to insulate the walls, but their only effect was to give the impression that she was being spied upon in her deshabille. Monsieur Lebouchere, it developed, was an energetic collector of pornographic books and glassware; one blushed to tip back the hinged lid of an inkwell shaped like a respectable eighteenth-century lady and find oneself staring at a pair of naked porcelain buttocks inside the recess. Lillie would have made her excuses and left after the first night, were not the prospect of free instruction so tempting.

She came to regret not choosing an easy early escape. Henrietta was a relentless schoolmistress, not given to coating her criticisms with sugar. The play was a simple enough piece, a one-act curtain-raiser titled *A Fair Encounter* with but two characters engaged in a dialogue, but the clever lines were hard to remember, and Lillie despaired of calling them to mind without delivering them in an unconvincing monotone. She lacked sympathy for the character of Lady Clara, a silly aristocrat who cared more for floral arrangements than people, and so was unable to bring her to life. Henrietta refused to accept this as an excuse: "What you think doesn't matter, dear. It's what Clara thinks. Once again, now; from your entrance."

They rehearsed in the drawing room and on the lawn sloping toward the river, for hours at a time. She had not only to memorize her lines, but keep track of where she was supposed to stand, when to move from this spot to that, and never to turn her back to the audience, imaginary though it was. She remembered Wallack's disparaging remarks upon the British custom of addressing the spectators instead of the person to whom the words were directed, and thought it as artificial as the paste jewelry Henrietta supplied from her seemingly inexhaustible store of properties and costumes, the odd detritus from dozens of productions from times past; why, she inquired, could she not wear her own brilliants?

"Because they would look cheap and false. In the theater, nothing is so real as pretense."

They haven't seen my *jewels,* she almost retorted, before reminding herself she no longer had any, only her wedding set and family trinkets.

The play took place in the Twickenham Town Hall, nearly without its leading lady. It all became real and ghastly as Henrietta helped her with her makeup, thick as Jimmy Whistler's oils and fully as overpowering to her nostrils. "I'm unwell," she said. "You know my part as well as yours. Can't you do them both?"

"I'm not in the habit of talking to myself except when M. Lebouchere is pretending to be listening. There's no escape for you, my girl. It's sink or swim."

She swam. She foundered at the start, completely forgetting her opening speech in the flicker of the footlights with the great dark gulf of dimly seen faces beyond—smiling, she fancied, in smug anticipation of seeing her in the pillory. She felt deathly pale beneath all the greasepaint. Clothing rustled. Someone coughed nervously.

Then, suddenly, the words came; not from memory, but from the other side of the thin corkwood door behind which Henrietta was awaiting her cue: Her coach was feeding them to her in a harsh whisper. Thus prompted, Lillie began—and almost before she knew it, her ordeal was over. Applause burst forth like grouse from a bush, an explosion that deafened her to the beating of her own heart.

"You did well," Henrietta shouted in her ear during the curtain call.

An enormous bouquet of white roses awaited her in the dressing room, tied with ribbons in the Prince of Wales's own racing colors. Her fingers fumbled opening the envelope:

I know you're going to be a tremendous success, and I wish I were there to congratulate you properly.

Albert Edward

Another benefit followed, for the Royal General Theatrical Fund. She played Kate Hardcastle in *She Stoops to Conquer*. Reading the script reminded her of her time of confinement, when she had first discovered it in the pile created by her eager suitors in the London theater. She cooed the lines to little Jeanne in her crib. The child seemed to be listening critically. How long would so intelligent a creature accept Lillie as her Aunt Emilie? She left money with her mother for the child's care and left off crying until she was out of sight of the house.

Money was the subject of most of her discussions with George Lewis, the lawyer who had helped her arrange her separation from Edward. He reported that Mr. Langtry was pressing for reconciliation; divorce was out of the question, considering the delicate situation involving a daughter of whom her husband remained unaware. Lewis hinted discreetly that he could not represent her indefinitely without some form of retainer. From there he slid smoothly into an account of a recent chance meeting with John Hollingshead, manager of the Gaiety Theatre. "He heard of your triumph in Twickenham."

"Hardly a triumph, Mr. Lewis. A new kitten in the house is always good for five minutes' conversation."

"You underestimate yourself, I think. Hollingshead made an offer of a hundred a night for three months."

"*Pounds?*"

"Pounds, certainly. Far from forgetting you, it seems your public is all the more keen for you for your mysterious absence. Shall I tell him you accept?"

"Not just yet. You've been the soul of patience, and I hesitate to ask yet another favor—"

"Ask away, Lillie. You must know I adore you."

"That's why I hesitate; but it has everything to do with whether I am to take to the stage. Edward has a low opinion of performers, and is certain to raise a scandal that would poison any debut. Do you think—"

"An injunction? I'm afraid that would have the same—"

"Nothing so public. Perhaps you could find him a position of some kind, something that would take him out of London? A client whose affairs need tending? He kept a weather eye on our finances when we were first married. I wore the same black dress until it practically fell off my back."

Lewis frowned, bent a horsehair pen between his palms. "Supervision would be required. I'm sorry to say he'd been drinking heavily when we spoke."

"It's an imposition, I know." Her smile was beseeching.

"Well, I can't make promises. I'll enquire around."

"Thank you, dear George. I'll consider Hollingshead's offer."

Lewis represented a number of people in the theater. The sudden unexpected death of Adelaide Neilson, a Shakespearean actress, had left her American interests in disarray. As a recognized figure in society and a member of a good family, Edward agreed to travel abroad and look over the estate. Visiting his wife for the first time in nearly a year, he preened a bit. "This could be the beginning of great things, Lillie. With me providing for you, there will be no nonsense of your becoming an actress. Yes, I hear these things. I'm not quite the pariah you imagined." The plosive on *pariah* released a touch of juniper into her parlor; he'd stepped down from brandy to gin.

"I'm very glad for you, Edward, but I need money now. My situation is desperate."

"But it's no profession for a lady."

"Yes. Well, being a lady doesn't pay the rent. It's a long time between race horses."

Hollingshead and the Gaiety were disappointed. She opened instead in Tom Robertson's *Ours* at the Haymarket in January 1882. Bertie and his charming wife, Princess Alexandra (who quite approved of her husband's choice in mistresses), were in the Royal Box, an event that never failed to fill every seat. All Lillie's friends were in the audience; her old nightmare forgotten, she seized the play—a crude thing it was, tiresome and stiff, contrived from start to finish, but lusciously staged, with a wardrobe to match the sets—and made of it a showcase for the Jersey Lily. Petals were heaped at her feet. No less a light than Henry Irving expressed compliments, and dear Ellen advised her to pay no more attention to advice from Ellen Terry. Oscar took both her hands in his. "I shall write all my plays for you when I return from America. I've been invited to lecture there on the science of aesthetics."

"And what is that?"

"I'm not entirely certain, though I suspect it will place me deeper in my tailor's debt. Shall I look in upon Edward?"

"That won't be necessary," she said. "I'm going there myself."

It was true. Prompted, as it turned out, by the ever-enterprising Henrietta Hodson, Henry E. Abbey, a producer from New York, had offered to sponsor an American tour for Lillie and promised her 60 percent of the profits. Henrietta assembled a company with the aid of her sister, with whom she had once gotten the better of W.S. Gilbert (pre–Gilbert and Sullivan) in a booking dispute, and lined up three plays beginning with *As You Like It*, to try out at the Imperial Theatre before the troupe set sail.

"That white elephant," said Oscar. "However, you're certain to fill it, and settle whatever qualms Abbey may have about divvying the proceeds. Good Lord, Lillie, is that *you*?"

They were strolling down Knightsbridge, where a middle-aged man in a tweed cap stood on the corner wearing a sandwich board bearing her profile four times life-size and the legend, addressed to the makers of Pears' Soap: "I have much pleasure in stating that I have used your soap for some time and *prefer it to any other*. (signed) Lillie Langtry."

"You've been neglecting your reading, Oscar. It's in every journal in town. The Pears people paid me a hundred thirty-two pounds for the endorsement."

"An odd figure. How did you arrive at it?"

"One hundred thirty-two pounds is exactly what I weigh.

Need I say it was Henrietta's idea? She never overlooks an opportunity to put me in the public eye."

"Your weight in gold. A wonder I didn't think of it myself; although I should no doubt swindle myself through my own vanity. Has the soap a pleasant scent, at least? I'm bound to detect it everywhere I go, even Cleveland, Ohio, on the banks of the mighty Cuyahoga."

"You'll have to ask my maid. They gave me a case, but I passed it on to her. I use cold cream."

"Let me know what brand, and whether you intend to endorse it. I shall tell my broker to buy up every available share."

She quite enjoyed the crossing aboard the S.S. *Arizona*; Henrietta did not, and secretly Lillie enjoyed the discomfiture of her stern headmistress. *Mal de mer* was the complaint, rats also; despite its station as flagship of the Guion Line, this loudly trumpeted "Greyhound of the Sea" invited vermin like any tramp steamer. One did not, for example, venture beyond one's stateroom without a lamp, the better to warn them to scurry for cover. They seemed to share the discretion of old family retainers, trained from youth to perform their duties unseen. The Jersey Lilly saw to it that her companion partook of thin broth, which seemed to stay down long enough to keep up her strength, and when sleep came, fled to the chattery sanctum of the captain's table and the attentions of Frederick Gebhard. Freddie was the heir to a New York dry-goods empire (all Americans, it seemed, were wealthy) and her first ardent suitor to belong to a generation behind her own. She treated him with the genial condescension of a young aunt, and was pleased to note that he returned the courtesy in a manner distinctly un-nephewlike.

When the weather calmed, Henrietta recovered herself sufficiently to join Lillie in entertaining their fellow passengers with *A Fair Encounter*. Lillie marveled that the dialogue that had caused her so much distress only months ago now came to her as easily as drawing-room conversation. She knew she would never be Sarah Bernhardt, but in certain circles a light *aperitif* was if anything preferable to strong wine.

Oscar Wilde, she learned upon disembarking in New York, had paved the way. "Nothing on earth," he told the grubby little reporters in their hard hats weeks before in dour January, "would have prevented me from welcoming the Jersey Lily to these shores. She will brighten this gloom with a radiance that only the sun can match and warm the chillness of the coming dawn with the divine glow of her gorgeous presence." Now he greeted her to the strains of "God Save the Queen" blared by a brass band, dressed in the velvet suit and cape he'd worn to San Francisco and back, and presented her with the now-standard tribute of a lavish bouquet ordered all the way from her native island; had it passed the *Arizona* aboard a swift cutter?

The Yankee press was as eager to embrace the mythos of pre-announced beauty as it was to tear down the divine right of kings. "One may see a hundred as pretty on Fifth Avenue at any time," sniffed the man from *The New York Times*, "but if they could carry themselves with the ease, grace, and self-possession of Mrs. Langtry, they are to be envied."

It was her first successful London season all over again. Her photographs blossomed in shop windows overnight, her face smiled out from posters plastered on every vertical surface, music sheets issued from a place called "Tin-Pan Alley" superimposing new lyrics on old tunes under titles like "The Langtry March" and "The Jersey Lily Waltz." Emerging from Lord &

Taylor on Broadway, she had to leap into a horsedrawn cab to avoid being manhandled by an adoring mob. Competing piano manufacturers sent huge packing cases containing their instruments to the Albemarle Hotel, insisting upon obtaining her endorsement, and security had to be summoned to eject a representative of Bongo Beer from her suite; the five hundred dollars he offered in return for her permission to use her name surpassed her arrangement with Pears' Soap, but it was obvious her pandering days were past. J. Pierpont Morgan, the richest man in the world, bought tickets to a charity event in which she was involved.

The "Langtry Panic," as it was called, aroused attention on both sides of the Atlantic. The editor of a Tory publication on Fleet Street lamented the fact that she had not been present with Cornwallis at Yorktown, else America would still be part of England.

It was a tragedy, amid so much positive publicity, with its salubrious effect on box-office receipts at Abbey's Park Theatre, that the place should catch fire and burn almost to the ground.

She could see the flames from her window at the Albemarle, clawing at her name on the roof in letters visible as far as Atlantic City. The pump wagons had arrived in time to save the sign—there was symbolic comfort in that—but anyone could see the place was a blackened shell.

It was a disaster, but not unmitigated. The sets and properties were gone, along with the costumes of the rest of the company; but Lillie, who had chosen to pay attention to Ellen Terry's first piece of advice and ignore the last (to pay no more attention to her advice), had had all her own costumes sent to the hotel and not to the theater. From that tiny acorn of fortune grew an oak from dead ashes. New Yorkers had paid to see her, after all; it scarcely mattered whether the other members of the troupe appeared in codpieces or plus-fours. All she needed was a stage.

"We're ruined," Henrietta said.

"Save your tears for Mr. Shakespeare. Hand me my address book, will you, dear?"

The answer to Lillie's wire arrived within the hour:

MRS LANGTRY

DELIGHTED EVICT EDWIN BOOTH AND OFFER YOU
HOSPITALITY OF MY THEATER STOP NEVER LOST
HOPE WOULD PLUCK THE JERSEY LILY

LESTER WALLACK

"A person could take that two ways," Henrietta said.

Lillie folded the telegram. "I'm sure he only meant it one way."

Her Rosalind was a success everywhere but in the notices. Audiences queued round the block, "stage-door johnnies"—a phrase coined on the spot by a reporter for James Gordon Bennett's *Herald*—stood hours in the rain to open her carriage door, the florists for blocks were denuded of lilies and roses delivered to her dressing room. Henry Abbey dickered with theaters in Boston, Philadelphia, and Chicago to send *As You Like It* on the road. The *New York Post*, meanwhile, declared her performance the "work of a clever amateur subjected to a brief course of intelligent training," and the man from *Music and Drama* damned her with faint praise: "She is always the beautiful Mrs. Langtry, playing a parroted part to make money out of foolish Americans."

Oscar sought to comfort her. "Mr. Pulitzer's *World* will set things straight. My review marshals all the might of the Greeks, the Romans, and the Pre-Raphaelites in your defense. Do you know, when I was in St. Joseph, Missouri, the notorious train robber and murderer Jesse James was shot down the road, and a parade of his neighbors passed my door carrying shutters and other souvenirs from his house? Who but an American would choose his holy relics from among the criminal classes?"

"I doubt even Jesse James was denounced on the floor of Congress."

The Honorable Richelieu Robinson had entered the following remarks in the *Congressional Record*:

> This is only one of the follies which indicate the poison, the pyaemia, the malaria that are dosing our American manhood to death. This worship of everything English is a new and dangerous disease. . . . Republicanism can be preserved only by preserving that healthy hatred of everything English, and all her ways. . . .

Asked to comment, Abbey countered with Mrs. Langtry's modesty as both a great beauty and a successful actress, while gloating inwardly over the spike in interest in the Chicago opening.

"What's Gebhard say?" asked the man from the *Times*. "Robinson did all but mention him by name."

"Frederick Gebhard is a respected member of society, a man of good family, and a pillar of the community. He has offered his services as Mrs. Langtry's companion. I need hardly remind you that it's inappropriate for a lady to venture out into the streets unescorted."

The *Telegram* reporter mentioned that her husband was in America and might accept that responsibility.

"I understand Mr. Langtry is busy organizing Adelaide Neilson's estate."

"My editor says Neilson's a better actress dead than Lillie Langtry alive," said the representative of the *Tribune.*

The *Times* returned to the original subject. "Why won't Gebhard comment, if everything's open and above board? Every time the press approaches him, he threatens us with his stick."

"Mr. Gebhard can say and do as he pleases," Abbey said. "That's the privilege of having plenty of money. Gentlemen, I have nothing more to say on the subject."

In private, Henrietta lectured Lillie on the importance of appearances.

"He's seven years younger than you. Once you have a reputation as a cradle robber, it's difficult to lose, especially if you're a woman."

"Perhaps. But the biography you wrote for me shaved three years off my age, and Freddie could pass for three years older than he is. Really, dear, we're talking about a difference of a few months." She twisted her wrist this way and that, reflecting light off the opals—her birthstone—in the bracelet Freddie had given her.

"You have a husband. You can't afford any entanglements."

"It's hardly that, merely an infatuation. We're going home in the spring; that will be the end of it."

Lillie's involvement with Gebhard would continue for eight years.

III

THE CROW AND THE FOX

A starving crow perched itself on a fig tree and waited for the figs to grow ripe enough to eat. A fox watched him for a time, then said, "Sir, you are tragically deceived, for you are encouraging an anticipation that will never bring you joy."

—AESOP

FIFTEEN

He arrived tentatively, initially recoiling from the first loosening of the shell. This was no disgrace; the world was not a place to enter blindly and without caution. He would be aggressive about everything else from then on.

Roy was there when that first flap quivered, and he was present also when the chick pecked one of its nest-mates to death in a dispute over a cracked kernel of corn. After that the others kept their distance. He grew at twice their rate.

Roy named him Stonewall Jackson.

When Stonewall was fighting size, the Judge took personal charge of his training. He killed a retired cock named El Mercador two minutes into his first trial. The old veteran was slow and scarred from comb to tail, but it knew all the tricks and had slain three younger opponents before being put out to stud; Stonewall appeared to have hatched knowing all the tricks.

Moreover he enjoyed fighting. When a jealous competitor released a weasel into the coop late one night, Roy rushed to the sound of the squawking with his shotgun, jumping when the intruder made a panicky exit over his bare foot. He found Stonewall standing spread-legged at the top of the ramp, a piece of bloody fur in its beak and a glitter in its eye. Mexican residents of Langtry were convinced the bird belonged to the devil, exiled to earth for raising too much hell in Hell.

Roy's love of the sport had been unrequited before this. He reckoned that he'd lost a dollar on his first cockfight and spent a thousand trying to win it back, but for the first time since he'd moved to the Pecos country, his pockets clanked with silver. Challengers came from all over, each eager to be the one who broke Stonewall's string. They buried their champions and returned home poorer than when they'd left.

When the Judge could no longer find acceptable odds in Val Verde County, he put on the Confederate uniform he wore when he performed weddings and took Stonewall to San Antonio, where he was celebrated after the fashion of Lillie Langtry when she played Chicago and St. Louis. Roy charged a nickel a head just to uncover his cage and let him strut back and forth for the entertainment of his admirers. The cock had developed a taste for dried chili peppers, just like his master, and grew fat and sleek on them. (Witnesses swore he shat blue fire; certainly Roy's son Sam, who had the honor of cleaning out the cage, complained that the fumes from the droppings made his eyes water and his nose run.)

A Yankee named Slauson challenged Stonewall to fight a mean little bantam named General Hooker. The general had taken on all comers in old Mexico, and it was whispered that the pair had been forced to flee following the grisly death of a fighter belonging to President Porfirio Díaz. Roy put off the suggestion, calling the bantam a runt and no fit opponent for an American champion; everyone knew the cockfighters below the border adulterated their birds' feed with sand and could only fire them up for battle by mixing it with tequila. Slauson dismissed such talk as cowardice. "Trust a Johnny Reb to crawfish."

Roy would have none of that. A man might call him yellow and get away with it because Roy was too lazy to give him satisfaction, and the War for Southern Independence was getting to be a long time in the past, but Stonewall's reputation was another thing. He agreed to the contest.

The match was billed throughout the city as the Second Battle of Chancellorsville. (It was a bad omen, but Roy's historical memory was spotty.) Because of Stonewall's size advantage, Roy magnanimously offered to fight him without steel spurs. He never forgave himself. Stonewall's San Antonio diet had made him sluggish, and he was unaccustomed to fighting without armor; his balance and timing were affected. Although he managed to puncture one of General Hooker's lungs, ending the contest victoriously, he lost an eye, and despite the best efforts of the finest veterinarian in town, died that night of blood poisoning.

Roy wanted to invest his winnings in a monument and plot in the Catholic cemetery, but the padre told him that was impossible. "Why not?" Roy asked. "He's as Catholic as you are. His father's name was Jesus and I never fed him meat on Friday."

"It isn't a matter of faith. Chickens cannot be buried in consecrated ground. They have no souls."

Whereupon Little Roy and Sam restrained their father from assaulting the priest. They recognized that Roy's grief had separated him from his normal good sense. "Stonewall had more soul than this place has candles!" he said as they escorted him from the church.

The man who had lent the alley behind his cantina to the cockfight agreed to give the rooster a proper burial. The next day, when the Beans were safely on the way back to Langtry, he stewed and served it to customers. When Roy got wind of this years later, he was briefly angry, then philosophical. "I reckon a good part of San Antone went home with a little bit of Stonewall in 'em," he said.

That wasn't the end of the affair. Several months after the fight, Slauson, owner of the late General Hooker, was arrested south of the border and charged with fraud. Standard procedure in cockfighting called for each owner to hold down his bird while the other's pecked at its head in order to ensure a lively display of martial spirit. Unfortunately for Slauson in Mexico, the roosters were still circling for advantage when his champion's opponent collapsed suddenly and died. A bottle of strychnine crystals was found on his person, and an examination of his cock's beak revealed that a notch had been filed on top of it, suitable for introducing the poison without harming the carrier. The defendant was suffered to pay a substantial fine to avoid serving a year in the mines.

The news troubled Roy, but because of the time factor he dismissed his suspicions about the tragedy in San Antonio. He might not have been so quick to do so had he known that strychnine is an unpredictable agent that affects some victims more slowly than others, and that several of the cantina's patrons fell ill within hours of dining on Stonewall stew.

By then, however, the Judge had acquired another pet that occupied the same place in his affections.

Consistent with custom, there are a number of stories that seek to explain Bruno's presence in Langtry. The one most tempting to tell is that the bear broke loose from a traveling circus after eating its trainer and terrorized the local citizenry for half an hour before Roy tired of the spectacle and stepped down from his front porch to deal it an eye-crossing blow to the snout. But the Judge was approaching sixty at the time and was less disposed than ever to leave the comfort of his rocking chair for anything so strenuous, and the widely held belief that a good punch in the nose is an adequate remedy for a bruin in full charge has spiked the population of a number of cemeteries.

The likeliest account is almost as good, and consistent with the rule of happenstance that governed most of the turns in Roy's life. Bruno came to town along the old coach road, sharing his cage-on-wheels with the inventory of a man who advertised himself as Major Edgar G. Howe, chief distribution agent throughout the Southwestern states and territories of the U.S. for the chemical firm of Baxter and Baker of Chicago, makers of Dr. Jules Fordham's Miracle Cure. Howe claimed kinship with Elias Howe, inventor of the cotton gin, and explained that he'd earned an honorary commission in the Confederate Army in return for his services as a cloth merchant: "Not cheap shoddy, gentlemen, I assure you. No Southern boy ever went naked for wearing out a uniform manufactured by E.G. Howe and Company of Memphis, Tennessee. I'll stand my cotton drawers beside anyone's." He blamed carpetbaggers for his company's bankruptcy after the defeat, but owned that without it, he would never have had opportunity to educate the public about the scourges of Ague, Catarrh, Night-Sweats, Halitosis, Testicular Itch, Boils, Toe Rot, Women's Complaints, and La Grippe, or the properties of Dr. Fordham's elixir that effected their solution. Lecturing from the platform of his wagon, he extolled his product's success when applied either topically or internally, and to demonstrate its pleasing flavor rolled up the side-curtains to reveal the six-hundred-pound black bear seated in its cage and passed a bottle between the bars; the beast took it between its great leather-padded paws, pried the top off with its teeth, and downed the contents in one gulp.

"Witness, ladies and gentlemen, Bruno's luxurious coat. Six months ago he was diagnosed with mange. Baldness was his fate."

Roy, who had resented having to rise from his chair to see above the heads of the crowd that had gathered in front of his porch, had until that moment contemplated arresting the major and fining him for creating a public nuisance. The gasp that accompanied the bear's appearance amused him, as he was too old and fat to recoil from common mortal fear, and the pleasant low rumble that issued from the animal following its dram, ending in a loud belch, was so much like his own reaction to a well-earned drink that he chuckled in recognition and ordered a case.

"Judge, I never knew you suffered from any of them things." Phil Forrest, who had been elected constable to replace Sergeant Tom Carson after the Rangers camp broke up, was a sad sack who always assumed the worst.

"I don't, but I can charge two dollars a bottle after all these folks drink up what they bought direct from the underwear drummer. Tell him to deliver it inside."

Major Howe hesitated when he found the Judge stationed behind his bar, bung-starter at hand and the *Revised Statutes* resting in front of him with his yellow-handled Colt on top. At every stop on his way through Roy's county he'd heard stories about the Law West of the Pecos and his ingenuity for discovering infractions in every situation. He set the case of bottles on a table and hoped the fine wouldn't obliterate his profits.

"How much for the bear?" Roy asked.

The patent-medicine man misunderstood. "He's old and slow, Your Honor. He lives on dried apples and Dr. Fordham's. I doubt he's et a man in years. If it's a matter of keeping a wild animal in town—"

"I wasn't asking how much you'd pay to keep him. I'm asking how much you want to take him off your hands."

"Oh, I'd never sell Bruno. He's the best salesman I ever had. God's honest truth, Judge, this stuff wouldn't cure a ham. It's pure grain alcohol with a little paragoric for taste. There ain't a bear living can resist cherries."

Roy picked up the bung-starter and banged it on the bar. "By your own admission I find you guilty of selling liquor without a license. Fine's fifty dollars."

"You know how many bottles I got to sell to make fifty dollars?"

Bang! "Make it sixty. You want to try for seventy?"

Howe's shoulders sagged. "How's twenty sound for the bear?"

"Throw in the cage and another case of that Miracle Cure and I'll suspend the fine. I got a bear to shelter and feed."

After a few days, Roy got to thinking how unfair it was to ask a wild creature to confine itself to a space the size of a cloak-room in a place as big as Texas. He commissioned an iron collar and chain from the local blacksmith with plenty of length for roaming and had Bruno shackled to the pecan tree to serve as a kind of bailiff when court was in session. Since some customers discovered they weren't thirsty enough to walk past a bear, par-ticularly one that was still getting used to its collar and spent hours on end swinging its great barrel-size head back and forth and clanking the chain, he had a stake driven behind the build-ing and moved it there during business hours. The bear had by this time acclimated to its new situation and responded posi-tively to being able to stretch its limbs after so many years cooped up in an enclosure; it allowed itself to be led as docilely as a milch-cow. When the weather was hot and it shed fur in clumps, Roy moved his chair to the backyard and scratched its back with a rake, drawing sawmill cries of ecstasy from deep in its chest.

How the animal gained the reputation of Bruno, Bean's beer-drinking bear, came about a week after the last of Dr. Fordham's elixir was gone. As it turned out, Bruno had been pleasantly inebriated on a constant basis since the beginning of his travels with Edgar G. Howe, and when the effects wore off, the size of the hangover that followed was scaled precisely to his physical dimensions. The bawling kept the town awake for days, and brought a disgruntlement on the part of the sufferer that made the process of feeding it its daily meal of dried apples a dump-and-run affair, and hang the bushel basket; by the end of the week the yard was littered with them and Roy had run out of spares. The Judge himself was so deprived of sleep that he briefly considered fining himself for disturbing the peace. Even Phil Forrest, normally the most stoic of creatures, said he would resign his office and take a job tending bar in raucous San Antonio for the rest. Clearly, this could not be allowed to happen, as it was Phil's prowess with the Winchester he carried everywhere that kept order in court now that the Rangers were busy chasing Mexican rustlers back across the Rio Grande.

Bruno himself provided a solution to the problem. Roy had had a falling out with A.B. Frank and Company in connection with an account long overdue, and had decided to brew his own beer on the premises and eliminate the middle man. The results so far were less than successful, as he was impatient with the process of fermentation and insisted on serving the beer green, with hops and the odd drunken spider floating on top and a taste bitter enough to cause lockjaw. (It was said that a horse thief on trial for his life asked to dispense with jury deliberation and go directly to the hanging, because the wait came with the offer of a beer.) Bruno, plagued with a thumping head and visions of pink bats nipping at his hide, clawed a couple of boards off the lean-to where the latest batch was curing in a crock and drank it down to the bottom. When Roy went out to investigate why the bawling had stopped, he found the bear lying with its front legs curled around the crock, snoring like a bishop. Long after the Judge patched up his differences with Frank, he continued to make home brew for the bear, bottling it to give pilgrims the pleasure of watching the beast pry off the top and drink it like a six-hundred-pound baby sucking on a bottle of warm milk.

It was at this time that Roy received a warm letter of response from Lillie Langtry (written in the Palmer Method by a secretary), to his announcement of the naming of the town in her honor. Being too excited and impatient to sound out all the syllables himself, he handed it to Zulema to read aloud while he sat raking Bruno's back. Mrs. Langtry thanked him graciously, regretfully declining his invitation to visit, as the journey was at the moment impossible, but offering to present the community through her American agents with an ornamental drinking fountain for the use of its citizens.

Roy studied on the matter for days, arriving at a decision when Bruno was tethered out front and the children were busy collecting his empty beer bottles strewn out back to return for the deposit. He called to Zulema, relieving her of the chore and telling her to fetch her writing block. When the child was ready, he asked her to reply that Mrs. Langtry should save her money for more useful things, as the only thing the citizens of Langtry did not drink was water.

SIXTEEN

Lillie laughed. Her voice, which even the most disapproving drama critics had compared to the mellow strains of a golden flute, was at its most pleasing when she was amused. "You're not serious! He said that?"

"*Oui*, madame." Her new secretary was from Lyons, and came recommended by Bernhardt, who went through them the way they said Napoleon used to; the Divine Sarah's fame now was global, with letters of deathless admiration arriving at her Paris flat on wooden pallets. Lillie's own correspondence was not much less demanding, although Lillie herself was. The French actress charged her amanuensis with all manner of responsibilities, including seeing to it that her custom-made coffin was not left behind when she went on tour; Adelaide Neilson's death at a young age had inspired in her a morbid dread of dying before her time, and being interred in a cheap box of provincial construction. The Lyonnaise was devoted to her new employer for her lack of pretense, and performed numerous tasks for her that were not part of her *spécialité*. Lillie's enemies and some of her friends said she spoiled her servants ("Poor dear, she's unaccustomed to them, growing up as she did scrubbing the floor of her father's country church"), but they tended to remain with her whatever the status of her finances.

At the moment, that status was more than respectable. She was planning another American tour, this time for an even larger percentage of the profits, and Freddie Gebhard's generosity had forced her to the novel expedient of hiring a bank box to protect her jewelry from footpads. As she listened to the letter that had come all the way from Texas, stopping at every place Lillie had stopped over the past year, acquiring cancelation marks the way a steamer trunk acquired labels (all for the price of a penny!), she tried on tiaras, necklaces, and bracelets before her vanity mirror, deciding which to take with her on the trip. Gossip had reached her—as it always did its subject—that while men purchased tickets to see her face and figure in plays they would normally have fled from like pestilence, women came to admire the brilliants she wore, understanding them to belong to her own collection. If, as she had heard said of that stiff old bear J.P. Morgan, the appearance of his roseate nose on Wall Street had the same effect as a major foreign investment in American goods, the glitter of Lillie's adornments onstage was the saving grace of the theater.

Some called her vain, acquisitive, and worse, she knew; but she knew also that she would never cast spells like Bernhardt and Ellen Terry with just her acting ability. She remembered her lines and delivered them with adequate conviction, but her two nearest rivals had been thespians since childhood, and moreover were born with talent. Lillie was a journeywoman, nothing more; she would live a hand-to-mouth existence playing second leads in curtain-raisers and third-rate, failure-proof ancient chestnuts if it weren't for her storied beauty. It was a commodity that spoiled quickly. The mirror was a critical friend, pointing out every tiny crease and sag. Paint and powder could do only so much. The discriminating eye must be blinded by light reflected from precious stones.

"Shall I compose a response, madame?"

"Hm? Oh, yes, the sweet old Judge. Tell him I admired his candor and wit. The latter would be quite popular in London circles, but the former should certainly banish him from the island."

"I think he would appreciate it more if it came from you."

"No time. I should think he'd be too busy himself, rounding up cattle rustlers and fighting red Indians, to bother with someone as unimportant as an actress."

"Perhaps you're right."

"Yes, dear?" Lillie paused in the midst of fastening a clasp, smiling in the mirror.

The young woman colored. "I meant about his being too busy to write himself. It is a schoolgirl's hand."

Lillie finished with the clasp and picked up a hand mirror to study her profile. "What else is there?"

"A letter bearing the seal of the Prince of Wales."

"I've been expecting that. It's an invitation to a reception for some dreary visiting Hohenzollern or other. It can wait."

"Monsieur Langtry has written."

"How much does he want this time?"

Edward had returned from America in a darker humor than he had left in, complaining that he had settled the Neilson estate in five hours but that George Lewis's conflicting instructions sent by cable had kept him there five months. During that period, news of his intemperance had reached his father in Belfast, and a chilly letter had come from the elder Langtry's solicitor, informing him that his allowance had been discontinued pending evidence of an improvement in his behavior. Simultaneously, the success of Lillie's own American adventure had rekindled interest in her worldwide, with the additional novelty that she was now recognized as an astute businesswoman; negotiations made on behalf of her company by Henrietta Hodson and her even more ruthless sister Kate had made Lillie look very good at the expense of the hard-nosed Yankee entrepreneurs on the other side of the bargaining table. Edward had come to her in London asking for money, and she had agreed to provide him with a monthly stipend in return for his promise—in writing, composed by Lewis—to stay away. But money was a slippery commodity in his hands, finding its way swiftly into the pockets of distillers and gaming operators. He made regular requests for advances.

His latest supplication having been dealt with (to the disadvantage of her bank balance; really, the man required more maintenance than a racehorse), she listened to a lovely letter from Jeanne to her *Tante* Emilie, written in rudimentary French with the help of the tutor her mother had hired for her in Jersey. Lillie missed the child sorely, although they had spent much time together on her last visit, and had asked Lewis if it would be practical for mother and daughter to sail together to New York.

"I shouldn't recommend it, darling. She could not help being photographed and interviewed. Even if nothing slipped out, Edward would certainly learn of the existence of a Langtry niece no one ever told him about. He's a buffoon, but not so foolish he wouldn't put two and two together. You've only just recovered from the Freddie Gebhard business; a scandal hinting at a lovechild would ruin you, especially over there. It's a puritan country, as I'm sure you'll remember."

She'd closed her eyes, as against a murderous headache. An arrogant St. Louis newspaperman had barged in on Lillie and Freddie at breakfast in her suite at the Southern Hotel during the *As You Like It* tour, and had sparked a firestorm of outrage in the press beginning in his own columns, leading to a physical encounter with Freddie in that same hotel and a challenge to a duel. The fellow was a former Confederate officer and a crack pistol shot. With great difficulty and not a little tact, Lillie had persuaded Freddy not to accept. The couple was forced to part in Memphis for the sake of the western box office receipts.

"Very well, George. I shan't press you on the subject." Every time she was forced to leave Jeanne in the shadows she felt as if she were abandoning her all over again. She would not be four years old forever, and the more time they spent apart the less time Lillie had to exert a mother's influence over her reception to whispers and innuendo.

It was 1885. America and England were in mourning, the former for the death of Ulysses S. Grant, the great Union general and eighteenth President, the latter for the slaughter of General Chinese Gordon and his forces at Khartoum. But she had done with wearing black. In Paris, preparing for her western excursion she chose bright colors and smart fashions—blue pleated skirt, snug bodice, and scarlet sash to wear to the races, deep jeweled hues for evening, piratical hats and silver-handled parasols for carriage rides in Central Park. She commissioned costumes from the same source for the play—*Peril*, a perennial favorite of audiences, and the subject of a bold new experiment, to tour with a single piece constructed around its star—and selected larger-than-life styles and patterns that would register in the balconies. The House of Worth, directed by Charles Frederick Worth and his son Jean Phillipe, created the designs in close conference with their client and saw them through from the first cut to the final fitting.

Lillie tried on her new reputation for business. "I assure you, messieurs, your name will be in every programme. I am not your usual languid patron. When I appear in public wearing your designs, your orders will increase many times from both sides of the Atlantic. You are entitled to the amount you charge, but I ask you to bear these things in mind when you submit your bill."

After conferring with his father, Jean Phillipe took advantage of the publicity for the fall line to tear up the Jersey Lily's bill in front of reporters. Accommodating a celebrated lady free of charge in return for the honor of dressing her was without precedent, and drew attention from all the House of Worth's competitors. (A reduced bill was sent to her by private messenger, with the unspoken understanding that it would not be mentioned by either party.)

New York was ecstatic to welcome her back; Freddie was more so, causing the old sensation to be revived when he insisted upon kissing her in public. Harriet Hubbard Ayer, wife of a prominent manufacturer of cosmetics in Chicago, leased a luxurious flat for her on West 13th Street in return for endorsing Herbert Hubbard's products; Bernhardt and Lillian Russell, Lillie's counterpart in the Manhattan theater, were already onboard. The apartment was served by a hydraulic elevator whose operator had strict instructions to bring no one to that floor who wasn't invited. She could share the place with Freddie with no fear that the St. Louis affair would be repeated.

Reviewers were critical of the play—it was more of the same, they said, only got up in more outlandish costumes, with Mrs. Langtry's thespian inadequacies all the more prominent for her central appearance in every scene—but the Lyceum was sold out for its entire run, with standees crowded shoulder-to-shoulder at the rail like patrons at the bar in Delmonico's Restaurant. Obsessed with her as they were, the critics failed to take much notice of the fact that her leading man, Arthur Elwood, forgot most of his lines. The company knew, which the writers of the notices did not, that Elwood was in love with Lillie, resented Gebhard's presence, and spent more time drinking and muttering in saloons than he did in rehearsal.

The situation was not much better in Boston, and in Cleveland, following the tensions caused by sharing close quarters on a long-distance train, Lillie spent much of her free time drawing Freddie off to avoid confrontations with Elwood. The pair strolled down Euclid Avenue, looking in shop windows and pausing for Lillie to sign autographs: an elegant, quiet young woman sharply at odds with her unconventional image, walking chastely arm-in-arm with a well-built gentleman who conducted himself with charming reserve. Observers assumed that this was not the same spoiled son of wealth who had nearly slain or been slain for protecting the honor of a married woman.

In St. Louis of troubling memory, Freddie and Elwood nearly came to blows. This time, it was Elwood she led away, calming him with cool logic and reassurances. She felt that had she been present at the time of the fight with the St. Louis newspaperman, she could have defused that situation similarly and avoided all the fuss. But Elwood's performances didn't improve, and after he appeared drunk onstage in Chicago, she informed him that his contract had expired and that she was discharging him. Elwood sued, claiming he'd been told his contract would be extended for an additional ten weeks if the tour was successful.

"Your courts are not unlike our own," she wrote Roy years later, "equal parts decorous and savage. One wonders that all judges are not as practical as you, and arm themselves beneath their robes of office."

The case was heard in New York's Third District Civil Court. Reporters accustomed to that beat were vexed to find their usual seats occupied and themselves forced to stand in the back of the courtroom. The gallery resembled the auditorium of the Lyceum; some of the spectators came with opera glasses to see what Lillie was wearing and whether it included her jewels.

They were somewhat disappointed when she arrived in a conservative suit with a quiet check, a hat with a veil, and just her wedding set.

"I wish you'd cabled Lewis for a recommendation," Freddie murmured as he escorted her to their seats. "You know nothing about American justice."

"It's based on ours. I don't need an attorney."

Elwood testified that he had entered into an oral agreement with Mrs. Langtry to extend his contract in Boston and that she had reaffirmed it in St. Louis. His lawyer, a sharp-faced forty with mariner's whiskers circling the lower half of his face, called the defendant to the stand. A rumble of surprise passed through the gallery when she confirmed that she had agreed to keep Elwood with the company if the receipts justified a longer tour.

"And did they?"

"Yes. Much better than any of us had hoped."

"Then you admit you violated your agreement."

"I do not. The play was a success in spite of Mr. Elwood's performance, not because of it. I discharged him for incompetency when it developed that I was delivering nearly as many of his lines as my own. It was either that or stand on stage waiting forever for my cue while he stammered incomprehensibly."

"Is it not true that you had a romantic relationship with my client onboard your ship from England, only to break it off when you were reunited with a certain party known to many of those present?"

"It is not. The infatuation was entirely on his side. I did nothing to encourage it." Here she adjusted her veil, catching the light on the stones in her wedding set.

"I submit that you did, and when the situation became awkward, you fired Mr. Elwood for no cause." The attorney straightened, hooking his thumbs inside the armholes of his waistcoat. "Did you chaperone Mr. Elwood on the occasion of a certain St. Louis walk?"

"No. There was no chaperone."

"Then *he* was the chaperone?"

She colored slightly. "Put it any way you like."

She was dismissed, but all eyes remained on her as she passed the plaintiff's table. Their gazes met briefly and she walked on without expression. One journalist noted for his editors that the caliber of Mrs. Langtry's acting had improved greatly; in any case it was a crowd pleaser, as the jury found in her favor after an hour's deliberation.

The company, minus Elwood, left for the West. The *Spirit of the Times*, whose circulation improved whenever Lillie's name or likeness appeared in its pages, engaged her as an unofficial (meaning unpaid, but, oh, the advertising!) correspondent, providing a European's view of North America: "Sort of an *Innocents Abroad*, only in reverse," the editor explained. She purchased a copy of Mark Twain's book and read it on the train. From Denver she wired: "Arrived safely thus far on my journey. Have seen buffaloes and prairie dogs."

In truth, she loved the mountains and deserts, the incredible expanses of tall grass, and the cowboys in their quaint raiment galloping alongside her day coach astride their small tough ponies hoping to catch a glimpse of its celebrated passenger. She regretted she had no time to include West Texas in her itinerary and visit the town that had been named for her—Ellen Terry hadn't such a thing, neither did Bernhardt—and drink a glass of champagne in the Jersey Lilly Saloon (the American obsession with freedom seemed to encompass the spelling of proper nouns). Her thoughts were involved with securing a new leading man and assembling an experienced company back home, an enterprise that required supervision, and since the contretemps in St. Louis during the previous tour had left a sour taste in Henrietta's mouth, Lillie would have to take charge. London did not sway as easily as Sioux City, where any gaseous politician could pother on about free silver (whatever that meant) before a rapt crowd on a dusty street; the city on the Thames had cut its teeth on Garrick and Irving, and had much more to divert it. Lillie didn't quail at the notion of being shown up by actors of greater skill and talent. She may not have been a "force of nature" (Bernhardt, always Bernhardt, until the end), but the fact that she had so easily picked up where she had left off after bankruptcy and confinement, just as if she had never been gone, convinced her that her momentum had taken on a life of its own.

This acknowledgment, this new conviction that she was no longer Emilie LeBreton, the country girl shambling about a ball-room floor in a dowdy dress, but Lillie Langtry, an attraction as dependable as the crown jewels, was the beginning of her descent; but so steep and swift had been her climb that it would be a long time before she noticed, and longer still before the world caught on.

SEVENTEEN

In 1886, the world slipped clean off its axis and Val Verde County failed to re-elect Roy Bean Justice of the Peace.

When he sobered up, he held himself partly at fault. Little Roy had tried to get him to campaign. Since that meant saddling up old Bayo and tramping from door to door, pressing the flesh and handing out complimentary cigars, Roy had refused. "If a man won't vote for me on the strength of a free beer, I don't want his vote." He'd overlooked the fact that the ballot boxes had been moved from the Jersey Lilly to Del Rio, or that a man traveling the sixty miles in between could change his mind more often than his shirt.

There were other factors to consider. The county was changing, the population growing, its personality shifting. The pioneers who had fought Comanches and outlaws for the land were fading into the background, and with them the attitude that the law was a pliable thing that had to be stretched and molded to accommodate the special needs of a place so close to the international border and so far from traditional authority. Already the six-hundred-mile trek poor old Tom Carson had made with a small group of Rangers to bring prisoners to justice in Fort Stockton was generally looked upon as part of the local mythology by those who knew the story at all, and Roy's legendarily creative methods in enforcing order met with glum faces and shaking heads instead of knowing laughter.

He reckoned it was the Eldridge train wreck that precipitated this turn of events. A passenger train had collided into the rear of a train carrying freight across the line in Pecos County a hundred miles west of Langtry, killing the engineer of the passenger train. When news reached Roy, he boarded an express for Eldridge, arriving with his coroner's credentials before a Pecos official could be summoned, and in the interest of expediency (with a nudge from the Southern Pacific, which wanted the matter dispensed with before it festered in the press), he was installed to direct the inquest. There was a five-dollar fee involved, and since he had a lifetime pass to ride the train free of charge, the trip was 100 percent profit.

The proceedings took place in a turpentiney new public meeting hall with a monster gas-powered fan suspended from the ceiling to stir the air and dust, and brass spittoons placed strategically about the floor. He sat behind a long golden-oak table rescued from a Masonic Temple fire, holding a proper gavel, and heard testimony that the freight had pulled onto a siding to let the passenger train go by, but that for some reason the switch was not closed afterward, causing the second train to enter the side track and slam into the freight. He dozed off during the technical details, but came awake and alert when the brakeman who'd been assigned to the freight acknowledged that he had not been aboard at the time of the accident, having stepped off in Dryden and missed the departure. The Judge hammered him with questions until the brakeman admitted he'd stopped for a short beer, and that when the whistle blew to announce the train was pulling out, he'd been too distracted to notice.

"I know a thing or two about beer," Roy said. "They all run about the same height, and I never drunk just one that stopped my ears to a blast from a steam whistle."

"Well, it might could've been two."

"Let's split the difference and say it was three. Whose responsibility is it to hop off a sidetracked train and throw the switch back the other way?"

The brakeman answered in a low tone. Roy smacked the gavel, which he thought made a pathetic shallow clack inferior to the vengeful boom of his bung-starter. "Speak up!"

"Mine, Judge. I wasn't there to do it."

Roy ruled that the engineer had come to his death through criminal neglect and found the brakeman guilty of murder.

"Hang on! I ain't alone in this. What about that whistle?"

"You said you was too drunk to pay it any attention."

"I don't mean the one that blew in Dryden. I mean the one that didn't blow in Eldridge."

It happened that this morsel had surfaced while Roy was nodding off. In conference with his bailiff, a Pecos County sheriff's deputy with an old powder burn on one cheek, he learned that two witnesses swore that the doomed engineer of the passenger train had failed to blow his whistle as he approached the siding, as required by law. Roy scratched his whiskers, then declared the engineer an accessory before the fact in his own murder.

The Judge allowed now as how that last example of Bean logic may have turned the tide in his opponent's favor on Election

Day. "This country's lost its appreciation of a good yarn since Garfield was cut down."

Phil Forrest, who had been swept out of office on Roy's soiled coattails, demurred. "It was hogging the Pecos coroner's job done it. Folks take it bad when they think a fellow's throwing a wide loop."

Roy bit into an apple, lost a tooth in it, and threw it, tooth and all, to Bruno, scratching a great shoulder against the post he was chained to. The bear sniffed at the apple and disposed of it without condescending to chew. "Well, I don't propose to sit here while somebody else fills my boots."

"There's nothing you can do, Judge. The people done spoke."

"We'll see what the *Revised Statutes* has to say. It's in a way of being Dr. Fordham's Miracle Cure, only one that works."

On February 18, 1887, the Commissioner's court in Del Rio reviewed a letter of petition written in Zulema Bean's round hand and bearing Roy's seismographic signature. It stressed the need for a new Justice Court precinct to represent the increased population in the county, citing a section in the 1879 edition of the statutes addressing the issue. Finding that no changes had been made in that section, the commissioners voted to establish Precinct No. 5 in a slice of land between the Pecos River and the western county line. They appointed Roy Bean Justice of the Peace there and directed him to post bond to qualify for the position.

He did so immediately, if ruefully; his fiefdom was shrinking, to a space hardly the size of the State of Rhode Island. He could still call himself "Law West of the Pecos," sparing the ignominy of taking down the sign (especially important now that he'd dropped and shattered his faithful lump of glass, putting the lie to "Cold Beer"), but it grieved him that in conversation he could not preface it with "The" as long as there was another such office within a hard day's ride. The difference to him was the same as the one between a steer and a bull.

Educated enemies referred to the three months that followed as the time of the Unholy Schism. The overlapping nature of the redistricting plan had resulted in two J.P.s holding equal jurisdiction over the same electorate. Roy, who didn't count educated men among his friends, cleared up the matter—and eliminated his personal dilemma over semantics—with a demijohn of whiskey.

John Gilcrease, the man who had nudged him out of office, was a florid-faced jack-of-all-trades whose residence in West Texas predated Roy's by several years. He excavated wells, repaired roofs, and ran errands for the Southern Pacific, a powerful ally that kept close tabs on the market value of its various friends and servants. Moreover, he had no issues with Jesus Torres, who was still Val Verde's biggest landowner and who had never forgiven Roy for outmaneuvering him in the 1884 election. Gilcrease had himself gone unpaid for installing a cistern behind the Jersey Lilly until his creditors had taken him to court for the price of his building materials—Roy heard the case and found for the plaintiffs, heaping insult upon injury—and when Torres offered to back him in a campaign for the office, he'd laid aside his reservations about working indoors and agreed, just to make Roy squirm. He'd never expected to win.

When the impossible came to pass—twenty-five votes to seventeen—he'd shuddered, briefly entertaining forfeiting the position. But Torres convinced him that if that fat old soak could do the job, anyone could; "and, seriously, Señor Jefe, how long can it be before the filthy reprobate is forced to stand before you, and taste the bitter fruit of retribution?" Gilcrease shrugged. He was not a vindictive man, but he decided there were no holes in the legal system so large that a good man with tools couldn't patch them. He told the commissioners where he could be reached and went home to chop wood.

He hadn't stacked half a cord when duty called. The county paid him to conduct an inquest into the death of a local Mexican day laborer; five dollars for two hours' work. His axe could rust while he earned wages like that.

Roy got a dose of the blue devils upon hearing of this unprecedented bounty, which would have fallen his way back when he was the only J.P. for six hundred miles. His dark humor boded ill for the unfortunates who appeared before him requesting the mercy of his truncated court. A string of onerous judgments in cases of minor infraction led to a long dry spell; litigants, it turned out, were taking their business to Gilcrease for better rulings, just as customers had gone to Torres's saloon and ice cream parlor when Roy was manufacturing his undrinkable beer.

The Judge's level of tolerance regarding competition was low as always. He toyed with the idea of loading Bruno into a spring wagon and letting him loose in the Del Rio hall, but some fool might panic and shoot his pet. And stubborn though he was, Roy knew the day had passed when he could go to his rival's camp and run him out by brute force.

Clearly, however, the *status* could not remain *quo* if Roy were to avoid tending bar and butchering the occasional goat for his principal income. He'd been in Langtry too long to steal a horse and light a shuck for greener pastures. That was a young man's game, and the pastures weren't as green as they had once been.

But what age took away in initiative it made up for in insight.

Pioneers fell into two categories: those who sought survival under the vast open ceiling of the sky, and those who made their living from those who did. The latter performed services for the former in enclosed spaces, entering figures in ledgers and sliding spectacles up and down their noses like trombones; decidedly, John Gilcrease was not one of them. Roy's ingrained indolence had provided him with a system that divided his responsibilities between the cool, fermenting shade of the Jersey Lilly barroom and the fresh air and sunshine of the porch out front. Gilcrease was cursed with industry, and would regard the paperwork Roy largely ignored as a mountain that needed to be scaled. It was no work for an outdoorsman. Time would eat away at his sense of duty; time and the tedious nature of the job, until all that would be required to bust him loose was a kick.

Roy could wait. Waiting was one of the things he was best at. In San Antonio, he'd done nothing long enough for nothing to be expected of him, then struck, driving away in broad daylight the wagons and teams his enemies had claimed as their own. He was like old Bruno when it came to patience: seated in the same spot day after day sunk in his folds of fat, too lazy even to brush away the bluebottles clustered around his nostrils and in the moist corners of his eyes, but always ready to lash out with a paw the size of a pitchfork and take all the flesh off a man's face. It was no wonder bear and judge got along.

Roy told the story to his daughter, counting on her to straighten out the grammar when she wrote to Lillie.

"I'm the only man that could ever make anything out of the office. Winter passed, and the Hon. John Gilcrease started thinking about all them fences needed mending and wells that wasn't dug, and here he was burning coal oil in the middle of the day, getting purple ink on his fingers. He stuffed all his papers into a rucksack, his commission too, and took them over to the Jersey Lilly, where we dickered a spell. He left after an hour with a couple of old bear skins and a tame coon he got fond of, but I think it was the jug of whiskey I threw in that cinched the knot. On May 11, 1887, he resigned his commission and his jurisdiction was annexed to mine."

Roy, swigging from a demijohn during dictation, swallowed a dram and directed Zulema to scratch out the whiskey part. He'd already written Mrs. Langtry about the bibulous local situation, and didn't want to leave her with the wrong impression of him in case she was temperate in her habits.

At this point in their association, the jurist knew little about the actress (and Lillie rather less about Roy). The drummer who kept him supplied with the material for what the Judge's acquaintances called "Roy's wallpaper" cut her likenesses out of the journals that advertised and reviewed her American theatrical tours, mounted them in pasteboard frames, and sold them to Roy for several times his investment, discarding the accompanying text in hotel and depot wastebaskets from Chicago to Denver. He did this not to spare his best customer the shabby speculation about her personal life, but because he'd never seen Roy read anything but the labels on the sample bottles of fine sipping whiskey he tried to interest him in carrying, and assumed he wouldn't waste time on anything that appeared in print. The drummer himself spoke English far better than he read it, and was little aware of what he was throwing away.

The walls of the Jersey Lilly were a patchwork quilt of Lillie close up, full length, smiling, pouting, sitting, standing, walking, Lillie reproduced from paintings, photographed (in black-and-white and sepia, and tinted in coral, russet, and turquoise like the girl on the Angel Blanca cigar box), sketched in charcoal, pen-and-ink, and pastels, holding bouquets of Jersey lilies and leaning on an arm in a seersucker sleeve belonging to some anonymous gentleman who had been amputated with scissors from the tableau. A daring shot of her with her lovely limbs exposed in tights as Rosalind in *As You Like It* was juxtaposed with her demure black-bonneted profile as rendered in oils by George Frederic Watts, and first-time visitors gave a start when her full-size portrait from a color lithograph poster stirred its skirts and stepped away from the wall; it was pasted to a door, and came alive whenever someone entered from the storeroom. Beside these legitimate representations, those of imposters stood out like steel washers in a pile of double-eagles, but they were useful space-holders for more of the real thing, as Roy was running short of walls; as it was, a man was challenged to find his own reflection in the advertising mirror behind the bar among the cabinet photos and cigarette cards featuring Lillie in every pose crowding the surface.

But the image Roy prized most was the ectoplasmic, pale-skinned creature burned onto a square of glass a man could conceal in his palm, before which burned a goose-tallow candle day and night on its own shelf above the beer pulls. It was the loose pebble that had started the avalanche that had swept him off his feet, and the only thing he didn't allow the mestizo woman he paid to tidy up the place to touch. He dusted it himself whenever he passed it, with a turkey feather he kept handy in a shot glass.

"Ambrotype." He pronounced the strange word with the same wonder of discovery that had introduced him to the phenomenon that was Lillie Langtry. He could not accept that there were others who did not share it, and often took it upon himself to convert the heathen. He was inclined, he knew, to be a bore on the subject, but it was worth being dismissed as a tedious old man if it brought enlightenment.

Pallid, imperfect reproductions he was sure they were; but a man could imagine the spirit that had inspired them. Pictures of her at every angle in every mood, but always mute, left their owner with the impression of a lovely, mysterious woman who never opened her mouth except to recite the lyrics of great playwrights and poets. This made her a being of an entirely different creation from all the women he'd met in the flesh, conjured from golden smoke and silver fog in a place as unlike Texas as the craters of the moon.

EIGHTEEN

To reduce Oscar Wilde to a state of shock was a major social coup, rather like dumping ice down inside the starched collar of the Prince of Wales and getting away with it, and Lillie had done both.

True, Oscar was a married man now (as if that gulled any of his friends), and would only be his usual inquisitive self if he tried on the manners of the respectably wedded gentleman, even in that tiger-striped waistcoat. But she giggled when he opened his ormulu case and she snatched an ovoid Egyptian cigarette for herself, watching his brows climb toward his hairline.

"I smoke onstage," she said, embroidering the air with it. "The habit appears to make no distinction between art and life."

"How can a habit truly be bad, when it's so easy to acquire?" He struck a match for her and watched her draw the smoke deep into her lungs. "How very American. D'you know, cigarettes are considered effeminate in Boston, whereas in Prairie Hole, Nebraska, the cowboys consume ten to every one of Bertie's cigars?

They purchase the paper and tobacco separately and roll them the way a Parisian chef rolls crêpes."

"Yes, I know. I've seen them."

"I almost forgot. You're a U.S. citizen now."

"Not quite. I've only made enquiries through Abe Hummell, my Yankee attorney. The laws regarding grounds for divorce are less medieval there."

"Edward remains obdurate?"

"He means to keep me on a golden chain; the gold to be supplied by me. What did you think of the play?" There was finality in the abrupt change of subject.

They were at a reception in Jimmy Whistler's new digs to celebrate the successful opening of *As in a Looking Glass*, which compelled Lillie to stretch her dramatic talents to portray a wicked woman opposite Maurice Barrymore, whose small son John was an unnerving presence during rehearsals, always staring at the actors. But the play was an excuse; Jimmy was announcing his return from exile after paying off his creditors.

Oscar blew smoke toward the drawing-room ceiling. "Lena Despard is thoroughly despicable; and now that I've said it aloud I know where our modern playwrights get the names of their characters. You underrate yourself as an actress, Lillie. You are day to her night."

"It's all in the hand properties." She gestured with the cigarette. "If I were a man, I should have been called upon to kick a dog upon entering. You needn't try to get on my good side with flattery, dear. You're there already."

"I'm quite serious." He reached inside his preposterous waistcoat and brought out a roll of foolscap secured with a yellow ribbon.

"A diploma? Has Oxford decided to forgive you at last?"

He frowned; had it been anyone else, she would have thought he was offended. "Do not try to out-Wilde Wilde. As you well know, I passed with honors—a part of my past I shall never live down. It's a play, you goose."

"Not *Vera*."

"A most successful failure, that. One day the British will observe the anniversary of its premiere with fireworks, like Guy Fawkes's. I do not delude myself that *Lady Windermere's Fan* will ever ascend to so lofty a depth."

"It sounds frothy."

"It is a bubble. Only you could breathe upon it without causing it to burst."

"Which do I play, the lady or the fan?"

"You play a woman with a past."

"I'm playing one now. Were you taking notes in the orchestra?"

"*This* past comes back to haunt you in the person of an adult illegitimate daughter."

Some biographers who have attempted to rescue Lillie from the historical ash heap have stated, astonishingly, that the irony of this statement flew right over her feathered hairdress. Others maintain that her failure to connect the description to her own situation is proof that Jeanne was in fact Edward Langtry's child. Scholars in between insist that she missed nothing and that it was the irony that led to the rift between Oscar and Lillie; but Oscar was the one who took offense and began their estrangement. The mundane truth is her mind was diverted by the insertion of the word "adult" into the phrase.

"You don't intend to suggest that the public would accept me as the mother of a grown woman. How old do you think I am? How old do I look?"

He pivoted deftly around this tiger trap. "It will accept you precisely as you portray yourself. You are a great actress. The critics who condemned you in the past have acknowledged that, based upon your performance in *Looking Glass*." He began to undo the ribbon.

She touched the back of his hand, stopping him. "Don't open it and don't read it to me. Take it out in twenty years."

"But I wrote it with you in mind." His tone went up a full octave; the only time she disliked him was when he acted the part of a spoiled child. "Read it. If you don't like it, there's the end of the matter."

"I'm sure it's good. I'm just not interested in playing character roles."

"It's the lead!"

She didn't want to hurt him. She knew he was a clever poet, and he had raised the practice of drawing-room conversation to the level of art—one of the lighter ones, like Sunday painting and lawn bowling—but she simply could not perceive of him as a playwright of any sort. *Vera* had closed so quickly, appearing and disappearing while she was on tour in America, that she had been unable to see it and form an opinion. The critics, whom he had roasted with devastating wit over their reception of Lillie onstage, had made use of the opportunity to hold him up to public ridicule. In her heart of hearts she knew they were right about the smallness of her own talent, and so could not dismiss them entirely. Better to let him think she was more put out about the question of age than she actually was than to tell him what she saw as the unvarnished truth. "Really, dear, you should offer it to Ellen. She's a professional and wouldn't let vanity interfere with her judgment." Let her be the one to take the wind from his sails. (Was she never to be free of making nautical analogies, so long after the *Red Gauntlet* had cruised beyond ken?)

But he was obstinate. She had never known him not to let go of a trifle. He plucked again at the ribbon. "It's filled with poetry and paradox. The lines are as buoyant as spun sugar. You won't even realize you're acting. Listen to one scene."

"I don't know any other way to tell you the answer is no."

Jimmy Whistler leapt into their midst. "Love letters, from a newlywed? What will your bride think?" He was cinched tight in his corset and counterfeit French tailoring; he clung to his fiction of a romantic Parisian banishment, when everyone knew he'd been leaning upon the hospitality of friends in the country, drifting from one guest suite to the next, uncannily on the last day before he wore out his welcome. He had reached that state of inebriation where the coarsest insult seemed to him the soul of banter. How she loathed him; and how she loathed herself for her inability to break away from his glittering orbit.

Oscar, the six-footer, hoisted the cylinder of paper above Whistler's reach, like a schoolyard bully taunting a lowly underclassman. His petulance was flagrantly out of character. "It's private, dear fellow—as I suppose it is to be from Lillie as well."

"Don't leave," she said. "You haven't even had tea."

"Or wine, either. I daresay I have a port that will—" Jimmy hovered in mid-sentence as Oscar collected his cape, hat, and stick and left, clutching his manuscript in one fist.

The painter fiddled with the stem of his glass, his color coming and going. "I warned him marriage wouldn't agree with him. I suppose it's a case of shooting the messenger."

"Oh, Jimmy, you are not the core of everyone's apple. There are things on heaven and earth that have nothing to do with you."

"I beg to differ. Everywhere I go, there I am." And he wandered off to tug on Bernard Shaw's red beard.

Lillie had only a moment to eulogize before she became the center of another chattering circle (whenever Oscar Wilde detached himself from someone, her in particular, the season was declared open), but she felt strongly that some kind of Rubicon had been crossed. She and Oscar would not speak again for a very long time.

She was pleased to see that the slightest ripple in her life could fan up a tidal wave on the other side of the world—in her case, the side that lined the pavement on Rotten Row when she went out for air. When word leaked out that the revival of *As You Like It* was canceled because she had contracted a case of measles that developed into complications of influenza, the journals issued daily updates on her condition as if the Queen herself had been stricken (how the old dragon must have broiled over that!), and when, still a bit pale under her powder and more dependent than usual upon the strong masculine arm of her escort, she reappeared in public, the reaction in the foreign markets heaped another couple of hundred thousand on the fortunes of Morgan and the Astors. Her recovery was not complete until Freddie Gebhard cabled that he was on his way across the pond to escort her back to America.

His immaculate good looks, hair parted just right of center and pomaded, moustaches waxed at the tips, and a brilliant sapphire stud in his cravat, delighted journalists who hinted at his infatuation with the married queen of international society. Edward Langtry, that gray mouse, had seemed to fade away in photographs directly as they came from the developing agent, and the Official Secrets Act was pliant enough to enforce a blackout upon her relationship with the Heir Apparent, but an American sportsman of a respectably wealthy family was fair game. He deflected reporters' questions in New York harbor and before boarding the boat train to London, politely but firmly, and slid into town a little before the beacon of notoriety could catch Lillie's eye. She'd underestimated both his eagerness for a reunion and the speed of his crossing.

Beverly, her new butler and a treasure, managed to dissemble his distress when Gebhard arrived at his mistress's flat unannounced. "I'm afraid Mrs. Langtry is occupied, sir. She can receive no one this afternoon."

"She's not still sick, is she? All the papers say she is quite recovered. If it's a relapse, I can have an American specialist here in—"

"She is well, sir; she is otherwise indisposed."

"Well, you can jolly well un-indispose her; how's that for assimilating to the language of the natives?" The American was boisterous after the confinement of travel. "Just tell her Freddie's here."

"If you would care to leave your card, I shall see she receives it."

Gebhard hesitated, searched the retainer's slack features for an answer to his next question. "There's a fancy rig hitched out front. I thought it had to do with a neighbor. Who's her visitor?"

Lillie's laughter tumbled down the stairs from her first-floor parlor. It was answered by a measured male tone. She laughed again.

The American shoved aside the butler and charged up the steps. Lillie appeared on the landing, arm-in-arm with a tall, thickset man with silver in his whiskers, morning dress extremely well pressed and brushed, and gaiters as white as milk. They stopped speaking abruptly when Gebhard confronted them.

"Lillie, who is this fellow?" he asked.

After a brief silence, the pair passed Gebhard and descended the stairs. "I'm immensely relieved to find you looking so well," said the man. "If anything, you're lovelier than ever. The Princess will want to know what you were prescribed."

"Rest and darkness, and thin broth to maintain strength. Without illness as justification, I cannot recommend it." She did not so much as glance at her American visitor.

"Alexandra and I are looking forward to attending when *As You Like It* opens at last."

"I'm so pleased. After so much delay I'm not sure I can fill more than half the seats on my own."

"You're modest as always."

They were at the door. Beverly helped him into a satin-lined overcoat and handed him a silk hat and a stick with a gold top the size of a cricket ball. He took Lillie's hand gently, patted it, popped the top of his hat, and departed without his gaze ever having met Gebhard's; but it had not been an evasion by any means. He simply had not existed in the gentleman's universe.

"I call this a fine welcome." Gebhard's voice shook—whether with rage or premonition, he wasn't certain. "All these months you've been begging me—"

She looked at him for the first time. Her own voice was deadly level. "This is intolerable. You've disgraced me in front of the Prince of Wales."

"The—I didn't recognize him. His face looks different on currency."

"Beverly, show the gentleman to the door."

"Lillie, I'm sorry. I had no idea. Don't you know what it does to me to come all this way and find you—"

"Get out."

He straightened, feeling foolish to find he was holding one of his gloves, stripped off when he'd entered. He'd completely forgotten the other. He felt half-dressed for the occasion. "I'll go only if you'll come with me. I've traveled more than three thousand miles to bring you back."

"Back to what? You?" Dry laughter rustled in her throat. "You talk as if you'd walked the whole way. I've seen your accommodations, don't forget. We shared a private train as far as St. Louis."

"We shall again. You're an American now, or almost. It's your country. You belong there with me."

"I'm Lillie Langtry. I belong to no one but myself."

The butler's hand was on his elbow. He shook it off.

"Do you realize how you sound? You talk as if your lines were written for you. Sometimes I think you no longer know when you're onstage and when you're not. I'm your lover, not your leading man."

"You're padding your part. There is no leading man in my life."

"Certainly not that prig who just left."

"You're talking about our future king."

"Not mine. He's grown old and fat, that's why I didn't recognize him. He'd have to pay a woman to be with him if he weren't going to run this filthy empire one day."

"Beverly."

The servant cleared his throat. "Sir."

"I'll throw myself out when I'm good and ready. This isn't the sixteenth century, Lillie. It's 1890. King's just a title you give to someone whose blood has become so corrupted by incest he can't get along on his own. You needn't lie down and roll over for his like."

The report of her palm striking his cheek made his ears ring.

He put his own hand to it. It felt hot. Then he worked his fingers into his glove. "That's just what the scene required," he said, "a dash of melodrama. Dear fat old Bertie was right about one thing. You're too modest."

Lillie felt faint; she had not recovered completely after all. As the sensation passed, calm took its place. She unclasped the necklace she was wearing and held it out. The stones were the opals he'd given her shortly after they began their affair. She'd taken them from her bank box to wear when she greeted him, before Albert Edward had surprised her by dropping in.

"I'm sorry you came all this way for nothing, Freddie. It must have been very inconvenient. These should more than compensate you for the fare."

His face darkened. Then he snatched the necklace from her hand and dashed it to the floor. The stones scattered like children's marbles. The door slammed behind him, ringing the chimes in the tall clock in the entryway.

"Cheap theater," she whispered, too low for even Beverly to hear.

And then there was just Jeanne.

NINETEEN

"Cockfighting's good so far as it goes, but one match is pretty much like all the rest," Tom Carson said. "Ever consider prizefighting?"

Roy said, "Don't you reckon seventy's a little late to be taking it up?"

"I mean promoting. That's the money end."

They were leaning over the wire fence that enclosed the chicken yard, the retired Ranger sergeant and the Justice of the Peace he'd served so long before progress broke them up. Carson drove out now and again from his piddling horse ranch outside Del Rio to share a chaw and a jug of busthead, stepping down from his doctor-type buggy and hobbling about on the outer edges of his feet to avoid putting weight on the ulcerated soles; he'd contracted an undiagnosed disease that slowed the flow of blood to his extremities, causing the flesh to putrefy. Whiskey seemed to deaden the discomfort while making the condition worse, a fact unprecedented in the experience of both men, who set it down as one more of the injustices of advancing age. The former sentinel of order, tough as the hickory stump he'd resembled, had grown white-haired and fat and inclined to dribble brown juice down his stubble.

Roy studied on what he'd said, tossing fistfuls of cracked corn from a gunnysack at the sorry substitutes for Stonewall Jackson that squawked and fluttered their stubby wings when he pelted them but didn't let it stop them from pecking at the kernels where they landed. Roosters in captivity had much in common with civilized men.

"I ain't tetched just yet, Sergeant. You mean to mix me in with that hornet's nest in Austin."

"I never knowed you to walk past one without poking it with a stick."

"They've went and outlawed bullfights and prizefights and even drinking, some places," Roy said. "They say you can't get a beer or a hand of poker in Dodge City. I'll warrant cockfights are next to go. This country sure ain't what it was when I come to it."

"Well, Kansas is Yankee country and I say to hell with it, but as to Texas we got nobody to fix it on but ourselves. We made it safe for preachers and women. What do you say, Judge? It's been dead around here since you fed that drunk to old Bruno."

"That might've been a miscalculation. He got a taste for pullets after I threw him a dead'un, and now I have to clip their wings to keep them from flying inside his reach. If he takes a liking for drunks I'll have to keep him out back or lose my business."

The incident had had to do with a Mexican woman who came to the Judge with the sad tale of an unproviding Anglo husband with a weakness for skullbender. She was done with the marriage, but lacked the stake to return to Old Mexico and buy her way back into her parents' good graces and the hospitality of their home. Strictly speaking, the situation didn't fall within the jurisdiction of his court, but when Roy found out the husband was doing his drinking at Jesus Torres's establishment north of the tracks, he sent Phil Forrest, who was back in office as constable, to collect him and told his boy Sam to fetch a set of manacles from the back room. They'd lain in disuse for a long time, as dangerous felons no longer decorated the base of the old pecan tree out front as often as they used to. Roy hadn't hanged a man since Benjamin Harrison left office.

When Forrest frog-marched the befuddled husband across the tracks and dumped him on the floor of the Jersey Lilly, the Judge asked the defendant if it was his intention to sober up and attend to his domestic duties. Roy was a great believer in the sacred institution in spite of his own experience.

"Go to hell, you old bastard. I do as I like."

Forrest swung his Winchester, catching the prisoner on the side of the head with the buttstock.

"Not so hard, Phil. I ain't found him guilty yet."

The constable pulled him back up onto his knees.

Roy drummed his fingers on the *Statutes*. "Will you sign over your house and chattel to your wife to dispose of as she sees fit?"

"Chattel, what the hell's that?"

"Pots and pans, some sticks of furniture, and that burro she says her father put up as her dowry."

"Hell, no! She'd just cook it and make a bad job of it at that."

"You leave me no choice but to find you guilty of desertion and hand you over to the custody of an officer of this court."

"I been in jail before, in San Antone. The food's better'n the slop I get from that old hag at home."

"Who the hell said anything about feeding *you*?" The Judge directed Forrest to turn the man over to his custodian and banged his bung-starter.

The constable dragged him outside and shackled him to a porch post. Bruno sat chained to his post nearby, licking chicken blood off his paws and watching the operation with post-prandial curiosity. The Judge passed around the beers and sat down with Sam and Forrest to watch the show.

The prisoner blinked in the harsh sunlight, legs sprawled out in front of him, too drunk to stand or show any reaction when the bear finished its ablutions and lumbered over for a sniff. Apparently the stench of ferment and vomit reminded Bruno of his own agonizing hangover after consuming the last of Dr. Fordham's Cure, because he made a grunt of distaste and cuffed the man hard enough to turn him head over heels.

This had a sobering effect. The man scrambled on hands and knees to the end of his chain. Bruno, however, had thoroughly explored the limits of his range and circled around to bat him again. By now it had become a game, and his master threw him a bottle of beer whenever he connected.

Forrester said, "I don't reckon it's his wife's plan to make her a widow."

"Bruno knows what he's about. He could take apart a watch and put it back together if he had thumbs."

But when after a half hour the bear showed its great pink palate in a mighty yawn, indicating that it was ready to put the sport to rest, possibly with blood involved, Roy ruled the prisoner sufficiently in possession of his faculties to hear the sentence of the law, and had Sam throw out a bushel of dried apples to distract Bruno while Phil Forrest unshackled the shaken defendant. "Just because a bear shows his playful side don't mean he forgot he's a bear," he wrote Lillie, somewhat to her confusion; although when she applied it to her friends in the salon she thought it appropriate.

"This court rules in favor of the plaintiff, and orders the defendant to turn over to her the family burro and household effects, in return for which it awards him fifteen minutes to get out of town." The bung-starter struck. From that day to this, it remains the only documented case in which a human being was placed in the custodial care of a lesser animal.

"This Fitzsimmons business shapes up to trouble all the way to Washington City," Roy said, with a twinkle in his moist-plum eyes that said that wasn't altogether a tragedy. "Arizona's got the cavalry out to keep him and Corbett from crossing the border into Mexico, as if that makes any sense. The governor of Arkansas put them under arrest for conspiracy to assault each other. I reckon that leaves them with no choice but to shoot it out with six-guns." He put down the gunnysack, swilled from the jug of Old Johnston, and handed it to Carson, who paid him the supreme tribute of not wiping the mouth with the heel of his hand before he tipped it up.

Carson swallowed and swept his sleeve across his lips. "Corbett don't enter into it. He's gone from beating the stuffings out of John L. Sullivan to prancing on Broadway like Lillie Langtry and letting this fellow Maher split his lip in his place. That 'Gentleman Jim' moniker's got him putting on airs."

Roy scowled. Like most good Americans he laid the great John L.'s defeat by the dandified Corbett to chicanery and fancy footwork, and like Roy Bean he didn't cotton to people comparing the Jersey Lily to anyone. "I reckon anybody's got the right to beat the brains out of anybody else in a free country. Robert E. Lee didn't die for anything less." His interpretation of American history defied all arguments based on anything so suspect as logic. "What's the name of this fellow's so hot on putting Maher and Fitzsimmons to the test?"

"Dan Stuart. He's in El Paso just now, but it don't look like he'll get his match there either. Our governor's a married man, and you know how much a woman thinks she's got the exclusive right to batter a man into insensibility."

Carson knew his man. Roy bore the mark of Maria Virginia's baking pan as indelibly as the rope burn around his neck, and the sergeant was a veteran of the matrimonial wars himself; no wife born to woman would understand a Ranger's vow to uphold the glory of Texas before his responsibilities to the household. There was also the possibility of a commission for himself if he managed to arrange a venue for the Fight of the Century, but that was hardly a consideration when the manly virtues were at stake. He rolled good busthead around his mouth and waited for the decision he knew was coming.

"Wire him in the name of the Law West of the Pecos. The leather ain't been cured that can hobble Roy Bean."

The controversy had become international. The governor of Arizona had placed the territorial militia on high alert in case Stuart, a veteran promoter who'd been in the fight game since he was thrown out of an arena at age eight for the unauthorized sale of peanuts, tried to gather a crowd for his exhibition there, and in Chihuahua the Mexican cavalry detached itself from the brewing revolution to prevent the *Norteamericanos* from exporting their decadent ways across the border: "*Mexico para corridas; no para hombres luchas,*" rose the cry in city and pueblo ("Mexico for bullfights, not man fights!") Stuart had himself sown rumors of an Arizona venue to keep the authorities from stopping the trains carrying his combatants to Texas, feinting with his left while connecting with his right and hoping to pull off the event and scatter his people before the politicians could regroup; but he'd underestimated the delicate condition of men trained to batter out one another's brains. Peter Maher, who'd stepped in to take Jim Corbett's place, developed a severe case of redeye from alkali dust encountered between Las Cruces and El Paso, and was ordered by the physician traveling with his party to rest. "Sand in the eyes is a mighty poor substitute for sand in the craw," wrote one disappointed newsman. But no one was more impatient than Stuart. The businessmen of El Paso had offered him six thousand dollars cash to mount his exhibition in their city, but under official pressure the promise began to evaporate in inverse proportion to his increasing expenses. Fighters, trainers, doctors, sparring partners, cut men, runners, and publicity flacks had to be fed—Bob Fitzsimmons himself consumed three steaks and a dozen eggs a day in his training camp outside the city limits—and the printers had to be paid regardless of the fact that the Valentine's Day date they had advertised on posters and in programmes and handbills had come and gone. He'd considered hiring a barge and holding the fight on a sandbar halfway between the U.S. and Mexico, but he'd been informed the bar was barely large enough for the athletes to maneuver without falling into the river. His people had been holed up across from Ciudad Juarez since Christmas 1895 and running up hotel bills well into the new year. The sheriff awaited a court order to seize the cash box and equipment for sale at auction to satisfy the growing list of creditors. Roy knew a thing or two about that situation. His telegram could not have been better timed.

"Langtry? What's Langtry?" Stuart is reported to have asked his good right hand, a Texas native and a former contender who'd been spared for better things by a shattered thumb.

"Little-bitty place halfway between San Antone and hell. This Bean fellow's been running the show there since Quanah was a pup."

"Can he deliver what he says?"

"He's got space to burn and even the governor leaves him be."

"He won't get religion at the last minute?"

"Dan, he's crooked as a dog's hind leg. God couldn't straighten him out with a hammer and forge."

"How soon can we get this bunch aboard a train?"

Things moved fast after that; faster than anything that had ever happened in Val Verde County, and before federal troops could be dispatched or Maher or Fitzsimmons got a hangnail. The eastbound put into Langtry at 1:32 P.M. the day of the fight, carrying Stuart's whole circus and a couple of dozen cars filled with spectators, and two hours later the westbound disgorged another load of enthusiasts and press. A freight pulled in with lumber for the ring and bleachers and Thomas A. Edison's Kinetoscope, a sorcerer's arrangement of moving-picture cameras, acetylene lights, reflectors, and a gasoline-powered generator packed into a carnival wagon the Wizard of Menlo Park had christened the Black Mariah, having traveled all the way from New Jersey and been sidetracked in San Antonio to await word of the time and location of the latest Fight of the Century (there had been one already, and there would be two more before the Turn); it would be one of the first public exhibitions of any kind to be captured in motion and preserved for the ages, or until the reels of celluloid and silver nitrate turned the color of vinegar and dissolved into goo, then yellow dust as combustible as magnesium powder.

Close on the heels of the freight followed a passenger train bearing two Texas Rangers, under orders from Austin to stop the fight at all costs. Governor Culberson had been in office just over a year, long enough to tot up the married men who had voted him in and balance them against Roy Bean on the opposite side of the ledger. He was also determined, like all the chief executives of the Lone Star State that had gone before him all the way back to Sam Houston, to succeed where all the other states and territories and Washington had failed.

Ed Aten and his partner had hung behind in San Antonio while their fellow Rangers divided forces to cover the various locations that had been suggested for the spectacle, some of them by Dan Stuart's people themselves to confuse the authorities. Some rowed out to the aforementioned sandbar, where they spent a miserable night swatting mosquitoes of both nationalities (all agreed the Texas variety was the more aggressive); others trekked as far as Palo Duro Canyon in the panhandle, and one remained in Guadalajara to marry a local widow after the rest of his company returned to the States. Aten, whose father had served with the U.S. Cavalry against the Comanches, and whose uncle had been one of the Rangers who ran Wes Hardin to ground in 1877, was an experienced hunter of men and animals who reasoned that a public entertainment traveled heavy, and that where the bulk of its equipment went, so went the rest. When the laden freight pulled out, he and his companion swung aboard the engine slick as Jesse James. The engineer was waiting for them with his fireman's shovel in hand.

"You ain't riding up here. Jump off or I'll knock you off."

Aten was not a man to bother with cumbersome things like proper identification. He shoved his uncle's Paterson revolver into the man's belly and told him to keep the freight's caboose in sight.

The freight was checked through to Strauss, Texas, well past Langtry and the last stop before El Paso; the Ranger suspected subterfuge, even when it continued west after a brief stop in Langtry to take on water, and rode on through to Strauss, where flatcars covered in canvas were transferred to an eastbound freight. There he and his partners boarded a passenger train headed in the same direction. To their surprise and satisfaction, they found themselves in the company of men in overalls; Stuart's carpenters, commissioned to build the boxing ring and seats for the spectators. Back in Langtry, the men got busy with hammers and saws while Ed Aten wired his captain in El Paso.

The Rangers arrived in plenty of time to stop the proceedings, but cooler heads prevailed in the face of the size of the crowd that had turned out, liquored up from pocket flasks and demijohns of Old Johnston set out on pallets with Little Roy and Sam collecting fistfuls of cash. Crowd control took precedence; the Fitzsimmons-Maher fight went down as one of the more orderly displays of fisticuffs in that period when five-ounce gloves had just begun to edge out the bare-knuckled confrontations reminiscent of the raw mining camps of Colorado and Arizona. Three skulls were fractured, a half-dozen drunks rolled for their pokes, and nineteen pockets were picked. Judge Bean processed all the Rangers' arrests with Industrial-Age efficiency, and the proprietor of the Jersey Lilly charged pilgrims a dime a bottle to watch Bruno pry off the top and drink and lick the froth off his muzzle.

With so much color, does it matter who won the fight? Perhaps so. Fitzsimmons, who recovered from a series of combinations to flatten Maher with a short right hook that connected with the crack of a pistol shot. All America and England talked of the match; until Fitzsimmons lost out to Tom Sharkey by a foul in San Francisco later that year, and then referee Wyatt Earp drew more column inches than both combatants combined when he took off his coat in the ring and revealed he'd forgotten to take off the big Smith & Wesson revolver he'd carried into the O.K. Corral gunfight in Tombstone fifteen years earlier. Lillie wrote Roy to congratulate him for making Langtry, Texas, more famous than its namesake, if only for a week or two.

All that remains, now that all the witnesses are dead and buried and time and the elements have eaten away most of the filmic record, are a few dozen jerky frames of a pair of ant-size belligerents grappling in a roped-off square surrounded by characters in squashed hats and ill-fitting overcoats pumping their arms overhead. If you look closely you may spot a portly, white-bearded figure in one shot off to the far left with his waistcoat unbuttoned except at the top and a broad sombrero on his head. It might be Roy; then again, it might be Santa Claus.

TWENTY

The revival of *As You Like It* was a success, financially and critically. Lillie's reputation, and the opening-night presence of the Prince and Princess of Wales and their daughters, ensured the first, and most critics agreed that the Jersey Lily had learned a great deal about her adopted profession since her first attempt at Rosalind. It was a particularly glittering London theatrical season, with Irving and Terry rotating *Hamlet*, *Othello*, and *Henry VII* at the Lyceum, young Bernard Shaw's inaugural play *Widowers' Houses* skewering the upper class at the Haymarket, and *Lady Windermere's Fan* obliterating all memory of Wilde's disastrous *Vera* at the St. James.

Lillie and Oscar had patched up their difference over the proposed casting for his Mrs. Erlynne, without apology or even reference to that conversation, by the simple expedient of attending each other's opening, and raising glasses backstage to its success. Oscar, however, was changing. His sudden notoriety outside the salons of the West End had gathered round him a simpering entourage of boys from Eton and Cambridge who giggled at every one of his *bon mots* and even at perfectly straight responses to remarks directed at him; their reaction assured, his wit became labored and wan. Worse, to Lillie, he'd begun to take on weight. She, whose slender grace in middle age had sparked rumors of a spartan diet and marathon sessions with dumbbells (fictions both), despaired to see her friend grow sleek with so many eager disciples at hand to fetch him champagne and paté while he stood rooted in one spot. He resembled a stuffed sausage in his snug waistcoats and tapered trouser-legs and his new short hairstyle exposed a roll of fat at the base of his skull. "*Burgermeister* Wilde," he was now addressed by Jimmy Whistler, whose own wit had acquired a waspish sting.

The faces in this sycophantic circle shifted, but one was always present, that of Lord Alfred Douglas, a beautiful creature, fair-haired and sparrowlike. He was the unlikely son of the Marquis of Queensberry, whose rules of the ring had raised the practice of fisticuffs from the fish-slimed docks of Liverpool to the gymnasia of the gentlemen's clubs. Upon those rare occasions when Oscar appeared without his shadow in tow, "Where's Bosie?" was his immediate greeting from acquaintances. Just what had inspired Oscar's affectionate nickname for his companion was as much a mystery as the attraction, for the boy was dull, his attempts at verse derivative and weak.

Sudden fame and wealth had upset the fine balance of Oscar's discretion. His friends had approved of his marriage, and his enemies had been placated by it, and silenced by the birth of his two sons; surely, then, his effeteness was the pose of a man secure in his masculinity. But Lillie, who had taken pains most of her adult life to resist narcissism and its perils, had been among the first to take alarm when her friend began showing up more often in Bosie's company and almost never with Constance. She wanted to draw him aside and tell him that notice and acclaim did not make one invincible, rather less so than when he was known only to a few, but from the time the curtain went up on *Windermere* until it closed on the tragedy of Oscar Wilde, he was never alone, and she would not open herself up to the ridicule of his court by offering anything so earnest as advice, and so she kept silent, and never forgave herself for not coming forward when he was still in a position to consider it.

Indeed, even the word "earnest" would descend into mockery when Oscar followed his triumph with *The Importance of Being Earnest*, a farcical comedy of errors that would outstrip *Windermere* and cause him to scatter all caution to the wind. This was no longer the canny word-wizard who had concealed all his demons in plain sight in *The Picture of Dorian Gray*, that scandalous novel about the pleasures of the flesh that had been censored in America, and caused customs officials there to seize and destroy every copy that washed up on its shores. He seemed bound and determined to advertise to the world that he *was* that libertine Gray, and to strip himself of even the doubtful subterfuge of a portrait decrepitating in a shut-up room while its subject presented a face to society unmarred by so much as a wicked thought.

Certainly it was more as Gray than as Wilde that he walked square into the clutches of so bestial a character as John Sholto Douglas, the Marquis of Queensberry and (said some wags later, attracting threats both legal and physical from their subject) Wilde's father-in-law, through the unofficial match of his son Alfred with the poet and playwright.

An ardent atheist (he had been voted out of the House of Lords for referring to God as "the Inscrutable") and failed poet (he demonstrated a genius for plagiarism by cribbing boldly from Christina Rossetti), he had transformed the sport of boxing and been divorced by his wife for battery. He left his children to be raised by governesses, paraded his mistresses in public, and had once horse-whipped the Foreign Secretary for elevating his eldest son, Lord Drumlanrig, to the Peerage in his place. He spent as much time defending himself in court as pressing suit against those he accused of maligning him, a company which seemed to encompass half of London. Only a fool would provoke such a creature; at the height of the scandal Lillie was reminded of Roy Bean's comment in a letter about the obstinate nature of bears.

In 1894, suspecting his third son Alfred's preference for male companionship, Queensberry threatened to discontinue his allowance if he refused to sever his relationships.

"My dear fellow," said Oscar, when Bosie complained to him, "who needs money? Credit is the capital of a younger son." Then he advanced him part of the royalties from *Windermere* to satisfy the young man's landlord. It was the first of many crucial mistakes he would make in connection with the affair, for it put it on the standard of the British pound sterling.

When Lord Drumlanrig chose to eject himself from the House of Lords by putting a pistol ball in his brain, it came to his father's attention that he had been paying blackmail to keep secret his correspondence with Lord Roseberry, clerk to the Foreign Secretary (of the horse-whipping incident); at that point the circumstances of his firstborn's rise in politics became plain. The Marquis was in no fit place to brook young Alfred's dalliance with the flamboyant—and monstrously more successful, poetically—Oscar Wilde; and then following a series of postal ripostes between them (pugilistic on Queensberry's side, piquant on Oscar's), the outraged father left a card for Oscar at the Albemarle Club with a message scribbled on the back:

To Oscar Wilde, posing as Somdomite.

When the club porter delivered it, Oscar deciphered the scrawl as referring to him as "ponce and Somdomite," and engaged a solicitor to sue the author for criminal libel.

No costlier misreading had ever taken place. When the action turned horribly wrong, Oscar's concerns had less to do with terminology. "In retrospect, I should have challenged him to a spelling contest."

The crux of the problem, for him, had to do with the fundaments of the English Rule of Law. In matters involving slander and libel, the burden of proof fell upon the accused. In order to clear himself of the charge, the Marquis of Queensberry was called upon to establish the truth behind his accusation.

"But who could bear witness against you?" asked one Wilde confederate whose naïveté had earned him a temporary vogue in sardonic cliques.

"Oh, who could not? I have cast my bread upon waters near and far. I shall find it before many days have passed."

The acquittal by weight of evidence of John Sholto Douglas, ninth Marquis of Queensberry, was followed in close order by the trial of Oscar Wilde for the crime of sodomy. On the day prosecution was posted, Lillie found Oscar in his elegant study on the first floor of a house shrouded in funereal silence. He was surrounded by the works of the pre-Raphaelites he professed so to admire, some in frames, some stacked unadorned like folding card-tables against the walls, and not a tooled Morocco binding or a mother-of-pearl jewelry box without a tray of cigarette stubs balanced upon it, and rows of them burning gutters on the Wells, Fargo box he had brought from America to store his nonseasonal wardrobe. His visitor threw open purple velvet curtains and flung up sashes to let out the murk of tobacco smoke. "Really, Oscar, you are not Sherlock Holmes, resolving the iniquities of society with cheap shag."

"This fellow Doyle may be on to something," said he. "His superhuman genius is a cocaine fiend, you know. I am currently exploring the mysteries of absinthe, which truly does make the heart grow fonder."

He was sprawled upon a tuffeted chaise of a shocking shade of tangerine, sipping from a tall glass filled with a jade-green liquid, with his collar sprung and his shirt untucked. A cigarette smoldered perilously close to flesh between the first and second fingers of his right hand. She had never seen a pair of eyes so shot with blood, and she had toured American mining camps where the men brushed their teeth with Kentucky rye to avoid typhus. His chin was stubbled and there was a grossness about his meaty lips, which had frequently been compared to those of a voluptuary, that repelled Lillie.

"Oscar, Oscar; get thee to Paris, where all things are forgiven short of murder."

"I should not like that. If ever a fellow were ripe for justifiable homicide, it should be Lord Alfred Douglas."

"You mean John Sholto Douglas. Bosie isn't your tormentor."

"But he is. He encouraged me to press a suit that he himself has evidence was false, and now that it has fallen apart he's left me. I won't bore you with a list of his pettier cruelties. His debts to me would buy a favorable verdict from the jury, but they are uncollectable. He should be beaten to death by this fine fellow

Fitzhugh; or is it Fitzroy? I am woefully ignorant upon the subject of the descendants of the bastards of aristocracy."

"Fitzsimmons, Judge Bean informs me; by default. It seems a shameful way of resolving a dispute between champions."

"We have the good Queensberry to thank for that. In the old days, the fellow who beat out the other fellow's brains was clearly the victor. Now it all comes down to blows delivered below the belt." He ignited a fresh Egyptian off the butt of the last with fingers stained gold from nicotine. "What do you hear from Roy Bean, that great jurist of rustic Americana? You must know that I hang upon his every rough-hewn word. I would write a play around him, but I simply cannot bring myself to drop my *gs*."

She plucked the cigarette from his hand, placed it between her lips, drew in a deep draught of smoke, and blew it out her nostrils, like Fafnir in one of the late Herr Wagner's Germanic operas. She herself had been approached with the prospect of playing Brunhilde, but had thought herself far too slight for the role, and a better mediocrity as an actress than as a singer. "He's unregenerate. The governor of Texas stripped him of his authority—something to do with placing a defendant in the custody of a bear, a real bear, with claws and fangs—but he refused to vacate the office. The locals kept coming to him with their complaints out of habit, until he was reinstated through sheer volume of popular opinion. A generation of Texans has come to maturity knowing no law but his."

"The situation is much the same with the Queen."

"Nothing so royal, I fear. I would compare it with a vote of confidence in Parliament."

"Would that he were hearing my case. I should be exonerated

or hanged from a handy limb. Mercy would be served in either event."

"It isn't like you to wallow in self-pity."

"And yet it is the most sincere kind. No, dear, I shan't flee across the Channel like a dishonest bookkeeper. Perhaps I shall reunite with my muse in prison. She is dividing her residence at present between Shaw's digs and Whistler's studio. Jimmy cut me cold in the street the other day, did you hear?"

"He is a vile man and a false friend. I'm done with him."

"I shouldn't burn any bridges were I you. You are running out of friends, false and otherwise. Edward, Freddie Gebhard, Henrietta Hodson, that blighter who sued you in America. One must always have at least one friend in reserve for emergencies, like a fire axe."

"I have you."

He shook his head. "You shall have none if you insist upon having me. Don't be so hard on Jimmy; he should have no commissions if his sitters suspect we are friendly, and he is quite unequipped to starve in a garret. It's only romantic if you possess the temperament."

"Don't talk nonsense, Oscar. You're not convicted yet."

"Must I cut you cold in the street to get my point across?" His tone was bitter.

She changed the subject. "I'm an American citizen now, have you heard? My solicitor there, Abe Hummel, thinks I have a better chance there of divorcing Edward. I have property in California, a state that doesn't require proof of infidelity in order to grant a decree."

"That's fortunate. There are too many distillers of gin in Britain to name them all as co-respondents."

"Desertion is the charge, although I can't help feeling I'm the guilty one."

"What does Jeanne say?"

She studied him closely. Drunk or sober, Oscar was a difficult man to read. He wrapped himself like an onion in layers of cynicism and irony so thoroughly that even he might not have been able to tell what he suspected from what he knew was true. "My niece is but fifteen. She has time enough to learn on her own how complex a thing is life."

"What is the time?" he asked abruptly. "I seem to have forgotten to wind my watch."

"Half-past one."

"I have an appointment with Sherard at two. He's writing my biography, you know. I have just time to change my collar and my story."

She thought this a fiction. Robert Sherard had suspended his work on Oscar's life for the very good reason that no publisher in England or America would touch it. *Windermere* and *Earnest* had been pulled from theaters and all his published works were out of print. From Buckingham to Burma, the empire seemed to have entered a conspiracy to erase Oscar Wilde from the face of the earth. It was all so predictable, and in every way consistent with her opinion of the ephemeral nature of fame. She touched the back of one of Oscar's large flaccid hands and let herself out.

Oscar was released from Reading Prison in May 1897, his health broken and in constant pain from a punctured eardrum suffered in a fall in his cell. His name was whispered now, like the love that dare not speak its name (Oscar's words, read aloud in court from a letter to Bosie), and it was said that he had formed an addiction to absinthe to deaden the ache. In any case he was unavailable to confirm or deny the rumor, as he had taken up residence in Paris directly upon his release. There he was said to exist in seclusion, penning unprintable verse like de Sade.

Lillie, meanwhile, had troubles of her own, some financial, some—more seriously—social. Both received great play in the press.

GREAT ROBBERY OF MRS. LANGTRY'S JEWELS

She was not long back from appearing in *Gossip* in New York when a gentleman friend invited her to attend the opera. Since her collection of jewelry was nearly as celebrated as she was, she could not appear in a box without wearing some of it, and sent Beverly, her butler, to the Union Bank with a slip signed by her, authorizing him to bring the tin box that contained them. He was informed by a clerk that the box had been given to her representative on August 18 and had not been returned.

She presented herself to the bank and confronted a pale-faced clerk, who confirmed what Beverly had said.

"I was in America on that date," she said. "Show me the order."

He called for it from the file. "There, madam. The signature matches the one we have on record."

"It's a forgery." Although it looked genuine enough. "Describe the man."

But a month had passed since the incident. His face had been lost in the traffic that traveled through the establishment.

Scotland Yard was more helpful, but not in regard to recovering her property. The inspector conducting the investigation appeared at her flat with an advertising tearsheet from a popular publication:

> I have much pleasure in stating that I have used your soap for some time and *prefer it to any other.*
>
> (Signed)
>
> *Lillie Langtry*

"That damned Pears' Soap," said she.

"Yes, Mrs. Langtry. I rather think I could reproduce the signature myself."

"Can the stones be traced?"

"Not if they were pried loose and disposed of a few at a time, possibly on the Continent. This fellow has had quite a head start."

She instructed her attorney, George Lewis—Sir George, now, thanks in part to his reputation as her representative—to sue the Union Bank for negligence in the amount of forty thousand pounds, a sum that staggered London.

Things evolved. An anonymous letter arrived offering to sell her back her property for five thousand pounds. Bank representatives met with a rodent-faced party in Dieppe on the coast of France, but were unable to obtain proof that he had the jewels. A great deal of speculation followed in the columns. Dr. Arthur Conan Doyle, riding the crest of Sherlock Holmes's popularity through his stories in *The Strand*, suggested that it was an inside job. James McNeill Whistler, now thoroughly estranged from Lillie, accused her of colluding with the bank for free publicity. "Faded beauty has no other recourse."

The Union Bank was anxious to put the matter behind it, but

forty thousand pounds was out of the question; since the jewelry had not been inventoried, Lillie's word alone as to its worth was inadequate. Had she kept receipts?

She replied coldly. "Every piece was a gift, gentlemen. A lady doesn't ask for receipts, nor is she in the habit of buying brilliants for herself."

She accepted a settlement in the amount of ten thousand pounds. Sir George insisted that he could get twenty-five, if she gave him time.

"I'm as short on time as I am on jewelry. That box contained my net worth."

"You have no investments?"

"I have my property in California, which I intend to keep. Then there is the *White Lady*, which I cannot afford to keep. This year's slip fee alone would put a roof over my head for two years; and not a common shake-shingle roof, when you factor in maintenance. It's expensive being rich." This suggestion was less casual than she had managed to make it sound; she adored the great oceangoing yacht, both because it reminded her of the glittering first weeks of her marriage to Edward, and because it was the only trophy she still had from her tempestuous affair with George Alexander Baird, a man drenched in wealth and cruelty, who had sent her to hospital over a silly little flirtation with a man whose name and features she could no longer call to mind. It had set him back a great deal during the Panic of 1893, and was her pound of flesh and bear's hide, claimed as spoils after mortal combat.

Why, she asked herself, this late preoccupation with bruins? She had never seen one outside the steelpoint engravings in the American periodicals in John Millais's studio, where they were always slavering over the supine figures of determined frontiersmen armed only with fierce knives. It seemed she had come to look forward to the rude wisdom of the Judge who lived in faraway Texas, a land that seemed so much more distant than California, despite the discrepancy in mileage. She *must* make time to stop in Langtry on her next tour, and pose for a photograph with Bruno, that loyal ursine officer of the court. It must be quite the metropolis by now.

"It's a grand vessel," said Sir George, "but the market in pleasure craft is depressed just now. The brokers who rented her will know how best to proceed."

"No. I know them. They'll dilly-dally for months while she eats me out of house and home. The only way is to put her up for auction and advertise widely. Will you take that up with them?"

There was no question but that he would. A K.B.E. had not been sufficient to free Lewis from the gravitational pull of the Jersey Lily.

"They said it isn't done," he reported later. "A yacht isn't a houseful of used furniture."

"That's repressive, Old-World thinking. We're three years away from the twentieth century. Instruct them to auction the boat and submit the text of their advertisement. They can blame me if the thing falls on its face."

"Sinks, don't you mean?"

"I am done with nautical metaphors. My marriage fairly dripped with them."

She spoke as if the union with Edward was ancient history; but he was contesting her American divorce. That was the social trouble that would plague her for years to come.

"A California divorce has no standing in England," he told the press, when the delivery of the documents had become public record. "She cannot remarry here without committing the crime of bigamy. I threw the decree in the fire, and it gave as little heat as you may imagine."

"What about the charge of desertion?" inquired the man from the *Times.*

"I never left home. It was she who pranced about the globe in the company of all sorts of fellows."

A defiant speech, lapped up by the journals that had built their circulations on the cynicism of the lower classes as regarded their social betters; but one without teeth. That was, of course, unless they reached the ears of Jeanne, who as the age of majority approached would soon enter a society that was no friend of actresses and adventuresses.

TWENTY-ONE

He appeared in Langtry suddenly full-grown, just under six feet and 120 pounds and most of it bone, with a whomp jaw covered with pimples and a lazy eyelid that made him look half asleep if you saw him from just the one side. He was so loose when he moved, Roy thought his bones were connected with silver wire, like an anatomy-class skeleton he'd bought from a surgical-supplies drummer and then sold to someone else when it frightened Zulema. He had no hips at all and held up his pants with a rope tied to his belt and slung over one shoulder so that they drooped on the side opposite. Folks figured he was trouble on the hoof.

He said his name was John, and he reckoned he was seventeen or thereabouts. He told some people his parents were slain by Comanches, others they had left him at a train station with a stack of nickel novels to keep him entertained while they took off East, or maybe up toward Canada. He didn't know what name he'd been born with and had been drifting along under a variety of them since running away from an orphanage, or a foster home where he was abused and forced to perform slave labor, or a work farm he'd been sentenced to for stealing chickens. (Roy sensed a kindred spirit behind the inventions.) He came in with the crowd to see the big fight and had stayed behind when it was over.

Roy met him over the barrel of his yellow-handled Colt when a window broke in his storeroom and he went in to find the youth stuffing a gunnysack with tins of food; even the sack belonged to Roy. The Judge convened court on the spot and found him guilty of petty theft and fined him fifty dollars. The boy skinned his lips back in a lopsided grin and said if he had fifty dollars he wouldn't be stealing food and when Roy agreed with his logic he ruled him a ward of the court and said he could work it off in six months.

"I'd druther you hung me."

"Son, that was my first choice. I ain't so old and set in my ways I can't change my mind twicet."

When after six months John informed him his debt was paid, Roy reviewed his case and said he owed him another ninety days. "I forgot about that busted window."

That's the story that was told most often. Another said he was brought before the bench by Phil Forrest, who'd braced him on suspicion of vagrancy and turned a lot of other men's pokes out of his pockets. That would explain his interest in the sporting life, but however the relationship came about, Roy called him "son" from the start. He later claimed to have adopted him, and made up a story about John following Little Roy home one day and Roy telling Little Roy he could keep him. This version was probably to spare him the stigma of being considered a thief. But it was wasted effort on the Judge's part, because John Bean proved himself a thief every chance he got.

Little Roy was seldom at home these days, but Sam, Zulema,

and Laura resented this new addition to the family and tried to frame him for infractions in which he'd taken no part, to diminish him in their father's eyes. They should have known, however, that he was blind to faults he himself possessed. If anything, each fresh evidence of youthful rebellion only proved that John might as well have sprouted from the same patch as all the other Beans.

Everyone in town, with the Judge's exception, expected the boy to wind up at the end of a rope, even John himself; but when the worst seemed to be coming to pass, it was Sam Bean headed for the noose, and John who saved the day.

Little Roy's kid brother was as loud as his family namesake, but lacked his Uncle Sam's gentle nature. He got into a disturbance with a dangerous man named Upshaw over a saddle blanket—the details were unclear, but as a symbol of trouble that blanket remained as vivid as the day the yarn was dyed—threats were exchanged, but Sam was quicker to respond, and when it was over Upshaw pumped out his life through two holes in his back from a 45–70 rifle.

The young man's timing could not have been worse. This was late in 1896, when Roy had been removed from office by the governor over the matter of Bruno's punishment of the drunken husband, and holding an inquest into a death in which his own son was involved was not something he could get away with, no matter how loyal were the locals who continued to come to him with their complaints. It also happened that in his place, Austin had established Val Verde County's most prominent citizen: Jesus Torres, Roy's sworn enemy of many years.

Torres, to his credit, was reluctant, not only because this wasn't one of those confrontations Roy would laugh off in the expectation of being able to even the score later; true, the prospect of violence slumbered but lightly beneath Roy's folds of fat, but the

Spaniard was more concerned with his own reputation if he agreed to shoot this particular fish in a barrel. But there was nothing for it but to question the witnesses and reach the inescapable conclusion. He ruled Upshaw's death a homicide and recommended Sam's indictment. Immediately thereafter he departed for Old Mexico to attend to legal problems with family property there.

Roy was for arming himself and Little Roy and going to Del Rio, where the trial was to take place, to make a show of paternal and fraternal devotion whose significance judge and jury could not fail to grasp. John explained to him that this would only harm Sam's chances. Force of that kind was no longer condoned in near-twentieth-century Texas, and Roy's own influence cast no shadow beyond Langtry.

"Well, I sure as hell don't figure to roll over while they railroad my boy. There's people all over this country been waiting for years to give me a taste of my own hemp, and'd just as soon it be my own flesh and blood as me."

"We got a week till the trial," John said. "There'll be time enough to show your teeth if things don't go Sam's way, and I'll be standing right next to you showing my own."

Little Roy, who had inherited his uncle's quiet side, was inclined to agree; and Roy, who considered John's rangy vulpine build and whomp jaw a decided asset in a war of intimidation, backed off. He locked himself up in the Jersey Lilly with a season's inventory of busthead, where no one attempted to disturb him in his reverie, mean as he was as old Bruno on the water wagon.

John quit town right after. Zulema and Laura were sure he'd lit out in the face of certain disaster. They were young women now, with their mother and grandmother's aristocratic beauty, their haughtiness also, seasoned with their father's native disregard for appearances and probity; suitors had dashed themselves to pieces against their iron cynicism long before they could be introduced to Roy. The sisters pleaded with Little Roy to intervene with the Judge and persuade him to adopt his earlier plan for action. But their brother was loath to attempt to change the old man's mind in his present condition, and told them to be patient.

John appeared rested and well-pressed when he greeted Roy and Little Roy in the Del Rio courtroom, and younger than when he had come into their lives only three years before. It wasn't a good sign. Roy, hung over and red-eyed, snarls in his beard, equated genuine concern with dissipation, and felt that a man who had been doing all he could for his adopted brother should look as badly used as he. Little Roy was worried as well, but before they could confer the bailiff entered, calling for all those present to rise for the judge.

They found no comfort when the prosecution's first witness testified that Upshaw's killer had taken time to sink down on one knee, shoulder his rifle, take careful aim, and place two slugs in the victim's back at a distance of less than fifty yards. John patted back a yawn. Roy, observing it, wondered if he'd reared a weasel in his chicken yard. But when the man on the stand was asked to identify the rifleman, he squinted at Sam, fidgeting behind the defense table and said he didn't recollect the fellow's features; the sun had been in his eyes and, truth to tell, Your Honor, he'd been drinking.

A parade of witnesses followed. The incident had taken place at the town's central four corners near the end of siesta, with loafers all about; Roy had been as disappointed by his son's choice of time and place as by the crime itself. Their accounts matched their predecessor's in every detail, including confusion over the identity of the man who had pulled the trigger. The prosecutor, a private attorney retained by the dead man's widow, reminded them of the penalty of giving false evidence, and repeated himself upon the point until the judge threatened to hold him in contempt for attempting to prejudice the jury.

John yawned again. He was more tired than he looked.

"The prosecution calls Mrs. Josiah Trent."

Mrs. Trent was married to the agent who managed the train station in Langtry. She had seen the shooting through the station window, and her husband had gone out to comfort the victim until he expired in his arms. She had no particular animosity toward any of the Beans, but no particular liking for them either, and was moreover a member of the First Baptist Church and the Grand Army of the Republic. She was unlikely to be suborned or her testimony to be ignored.

But as that lady was rising from the gallery, the man behind the bench announced that the hour was late, and adjourned until the following morning.

Sam was returned to his cell. John, Roy, and Little Roy shared boardinghouse accommodations, but when asked what he'd been about, John pleaded exhaustion and retired. Very soon he was snoring. Over an enormous breakfast of eggs, ham, biscuits, and gravy an hour after dawn, he refused to be drawn out. He was superstitious, he said, and considered it bad luck to discuss the details of a plan before it had run its course. Little Roy was unsatisfied, but munched a piece of dry toast in moody silence. Roy broke his fast from a glass flask.

Mrs. Trent was among the first to arrive in court, but her testimony was postponed. Sam's attorney, a former Confederate officer who had represented defendants and the State of Texas in the Jersey Lilly (and had remained after session to drink and play cards with Roy), argued that evidence obtained through the barrier of a window was not eyewitness evidence by definition. Over objections by the prosecution he pressed that the language of the law excluded evidence obtained from an obstructed point of view, and that a person or object was defined as an obstruction that stood between the so-called eyewitness and the event under examination.

The prosecutor leapt up from his chair. "That's preposterous! A window is transparent."

"Your Honor, the *Statutes* say nothing about transparency."

The judge motioned both counselors to approach the bench. While they were conversing in low voices, the prosecutor's laced with sharp sibilants, John shifted in his seat, as if his limbs had gone to sleep, then resumed his recumbent position. He really was just a collection of loose bones.

Mrs. Trent was not heard. Sam's lawyer moved for a directed acquittal because the state had failed to make its case. The prosecutor's objection was overruled. The judge dismissed the jury and ordered Sam's release.

Throughout the rest of Roy's life, John Bean turned away questions about his involvement in the decision. Naturally he would be self-protective, but as he kept his own counsel in most things, the simple conclusion remained inadequate. Roy was deeply impressed; the handful of old-timers who could claim they really knew him were aware of a closeness between the Judge and his stray that had not existed before. The rest of the family resisted forming any such affection, but they stopped complaining about him. Roy was gone, and his children preparing to drift in opposite directions from the Langtry center, when John relented.

It was Sam who brought up the subject. "That horseshit about windows sounds like something Pa might've come up with."

"I reckon anyone could read that book of his. That Johnny Reb he hired for you was ready to throw in his hand when I brung it to him."

"How'd you get to the other witnesses? You only had a week."

"Hell, Sam, they wasn't worth the time. Don't you think they knew they couldn't come back to town if they stuck to their story? I figured the judge in Del Rio would take a mite longer to convince." He showed that slipjaw grin. "Didn't Pa say it a hundred times? 'There's more ways than one of doing business.' "

Sam Bean kept gunpowder out of all his battles after that. There is absolutely no truth to the story that he came before his father in the matter of a Chinese shot to death in a saloon brawl and that Roy released him on the grounds that there was nothing in his book about it being against the law to kill a Chinaman. The defendant in that case was a friend of the Judge's and no blood kin.

But on the day of Sam's victory, the Beans' celebratory mood evaporated when the train slowed for the station and a smudge of black smoke sagged low over the tracks. The Jersey Lilly was no more, burned to the ground by one of Upshaw's friends, who had wisely not remained long enough to see the flames take hold. When they did, the barrels of Old Johnston had gone up like a powder magazine, raining bits of shingle and Lillie Langtry all over town.

The 1879 *Statutes* and Roy's yellow-handled Colt were spared, because he never left town for any length of time without bringing along those loyal companions; but as for everything else—the bar, the stock, Roy's bung-starter, a pet raccoon he was teaching to work the beer pulls, and the shrine to the Jersey Lily—all was gone. Stirring through the ashes days later, he lifted out a square of glass and passed his fingers over the cracked surface; the heat had erased the spectral features from the image, leaving only a halo of shimmering hair and a slender shoulder clad in black. He wept.

IV

THE ROSE AND
THE AMARANTH

An Amaranth growing near a Rose-Tree said, "I am jealous of your beauty and fine scent, which pleases gods and men equally." Replied the Rose: "Envy me not, dear Amaranth, for I bloom but briefly, while thou art deathless, and bloomest always."

—Aesop

TWENTY-TWO

A likeness broken is a trust betrayed.

She was unaware that her image had been shattered thousands of miles away, but Lillie was as superstitious as any other country girl and might have been prepared for what was to come had she known. She was about to lose her public.

Querulous and annoying as his comments read in the press, Edward Langtry had succeeded where he had failed in the past, winning sympathy from those to whom he turned for support. The American divorce, he announced, had broken his heart, as much by the callous way in which it had been brought to his attention—he'd read about it in the agony columns before the documents were delivered to him by messenger—as by the underhanded manner in which his wife had obtained it, six thousand miles away from London in the sinful goldfields of California. He repeated that it was she who had deserted him, and claimed that before leaving for New York in connection with the Neilson estate farce he had settled upon her the sum of ten thousand pounds for living expenses. As the informal press conference wore on and he fortified himself from the decanter at his elbow, he said he was considering a countersuit for alienation of affections and including a certain member of the royal family in the action.

"However seemingly cruel it may be," he continued, slurring his way through *seemingly*, "I affirm that I never heard that my wife gave birth to a child of which I am reputed to be the father, until I received the divorce citation." He would not gratify the reporters with further explanation.

Lillie saw herself portrayed as a calculating wench who, bent on wealth and fame, had attached herself to the first eligible bachelor who came along, then abandoned him once she had what she wanted. It was at this time she was quoted as saying that she'd fallen in love with a boat and married the man—and by denying she'd said it, convinced many that she had. Now the smutty word "adultress" had gurgled up from the murk, and with it the suggestion that she had stepped up yet again by dint of wile. What must Bertie think? It must be kept from Jeanne.

Before her legal statement was read in the San Francisco courtroom, she had asked for custody of her daughter, Jeanne Marie Langtry, and in so doing revealed to the world that she was the mother of a grown woman. (How Oscar must have been amused by that, in spite of his own ordeal.) Jeanne herself, informed by Lillie in private, had taken the news calmly; she had always felt a closer bond with her *Tante* Emilie than her friends at school had seemed to have with their aunts, and at age sixteen, when a girl began to consider herself on the verge of young womanhood, she was delighted to learn that she was the child of the most beautiful woman on two continents. Although the reasoning behind the subterfuge was cloudy—something to do with a brutish, unreliable father in Edward and a mother concerned with her daughter's safety—she'd found the news less sensational than did the public once it broke.

Then, too, there was the distraction of an anticipated voyage to America with Lillie. A tour was planned for a new troupe, and it was time her adopted country met the next Langtry. Trunks of clothes were commissioned from Madame Nicolle, that funny, affected old woman who had dressed *Maman* (she must get used to calling her that!) all those years ago when she first went to London. For Lillie, the consultations and sketches and fittings kept Jeanne too busy to pay attention to what was being said in the journals and whispered in drawing rooms. Reporters knocking at Mrs. LeBreton's door were turned away with dotty non sequiturs, untainted by deceit; Lillie's mother was a widow now, elderly, and the world was inclined to forgive her for explanations that didn't explain anything. Her famous daughter's adventures had demonstrated to her the advantages of public perception, and the lessons had taken.

But that perception, which had gone Lillie's way for so long, was turning.

Whistler's accusation that the theft of her jewels was a ploy for attention had been reported as fact in several newspapers. She had wanted to take them to court for libel, but Sir George Lewis had counseled her against attracting more notice than the calumnies warranted. However, her silence was treated as an admission that there was truth behind them.

When her gamble to put up the *White Lady* for auction brought her two hundred eighty thousand pounds for a yacht that had cost her nothing (nothing, that is, save a week in hospital recovering from injuries dealt her by its original owner), editorials appeared holding her to account for the sins of greed and lust, for profiting from a gift from a lover; the impression they created was of a common prostitute. ("Hardly common," remarked Oscar, who in his Parisian exile had yet to receive so much as a line of comfort from Lillie. "There isn't a dressing table in London that would support such a sum in cash.")

She was branded an interloper when it was revealed that the mysterious "Mr. Jersey" who had run a horse at Nottingham, where women were discouraged from competing, was in fact the Jersey Lily; ladies of society denounced her as a suffragette—a creature whose overtures she herself had discouraged, as the movement was held in low esteem for its headline-grabbing practice of knocking the phalluses off statues in public places—and an enquiry was opened into whether the animal should be disqualified if indeed it ever won.

She ignored the controversy and entered the horse for the Liverpool Cup. It finished first. At the height of the debate over whether she should be allowed to keep the trophy, she set it in a new direction by announcing that the horse would compete in the long-distance handicap at Cesarewitch, one of the most important races of the season. She would win the world back through audacity, where before it had admired her for restraint.

It was October 6, 1897. Her birthday was approaching, and it was as good a time as any to reinvent herself. She gave a lavish reception for the gentlemen from the sporting press to declare her Cesarewitch intentions. When she called for questions, she was asked to comment upon her husband's commitment to an asylum for the insane.

Much later, when the thing had run its sad course and she could look back on it with more philosophy than pain, she wrote Roy, in her own hand: "You are too modest to make mention of the fact, but I am certain a man of your exploits and standing is familiar with fame and its bleaker aspects. Revelations of the most personal nature come to you by way of the public forum, and your unguarded reaction placed immediately beneath a strong lens for all to witness; and you are reminded all over again that to be well known carries the conviction (frequently reconfirmed) that in some distant province, someone you have never met, toward whom you bear no ill will, wishes daily upon you all the miseries of Job."

(Roy, who just then had been spending a fair amount of time with the Word—studying it, as he did the *Statutes*, for a ruling in his favor—replied: "You won't see it writ, but it's d—n plain to me that when God throwed Adam and Eve out of the Garden He told them to take the snake with them.")

The early reports were as disoriented as Edward was most days. Because "the former Mr. Lillie Langtry" was discovered stumbling along the railway tracks near the coastal village of Chester, muttering to himself, it was assumed he'd fallen off a train; not an uncommon fate among men who traveled with pocket flasks. His clothes were torn and soiled and he smelled strongly of spirits. But passengers who had shared the Irish Channel crossing with him reported he'd lost his footing on a companionway ladder and crashed to the deck, striking his head but angrily refusing medical attention. Having apparently missed the boat train to London, he was hustled off the tracks by yard men for his own safety, but was unable to provide a coherent explanation of his presence there, or even of his identity. The police were summoned, and noting his condition and finding only a few coins in his pockets (speculation was he'd been robbed by toughs who preyed on drunkards) arrested him for vagrancy and drunk and disorderly conduct. The magistrate before whom he was brought saw at once that this was no matter for overnight incarceration or thirty days in a workhouse. He ordered the prisoner to be held for examination in the County Asylum at Upton.

It was a hideous disgrace. In that age of scientific enlighten-ment, madness was widely regarded as an affliction connected with gonorrhea and syphilis, diseases too sordid to appear in print. Respectable men who suffered from them were treated in private with doses of mercury, and declared cured long before the decay reached the brain; in advanced cases, the victim was placed in a private institution under the strictest confidence. Public commitment was for the working classes. When it hap-pened to a man of good family, the conclusion was that he'd been abandoned by those close to him. When it happened to the husband of the most famous woman in England apart from the Queen, all the dark imprecations that had been whispered against her came out into the light of day. It mattered not at all that they were no longer bound legally; if anything, Edward's fall was traced directly to that action on Lillie's part. She had torn his heart, then taken away his reason.

She found it difficult to defend herself because some part of her agreed with this assessment. All Edward had ever been guilty of was weakness. To rid herself of him she had painted him, first to her parents, then to her daughter, as a drunken brute. She had accused him of common procurement, when he was not present to speak in his own defense, conspired to deceive him, and when he came to her asking for a reconciliation, she had held him off with money. She remembered those early days aboard the *Red Gauntlet*, the handsome young man at the helm with his scarf flying in the wind, and wondered if she was as wicked as the things that were written about her. Yes, Edward had changed, but it was she who had changed first; they'd been drawn together by a mutual distrust of salon society, and it had taken only an afternoon at Lady Sebright's (whatever *had* become of that waxworks of a woman?) to persuade her to break their pact.

At the same time, she resented him for the very weakness that had allowed her to separate herself from him with so little effort, only money; for his smallness, his niggardliness, his stubborn blindness. Of all the men in England, France, and America, royals and squires, day-laborers, cowboys—and, yes, an iron-fisted judge in remote Texas—Edward alone had been constitutionally unable to grasp the significance of Lillie Langtry. The magistrate was right. The man was insane.

She was left with no choice but to lift her chin (she was in the habit anyway, to avoid showing a sag) and plunge into the racing scene at Cesarewitch. She chose turquoise and fawn as her jockey's colors and wore a straw hat with flowers of those hues sewn to it, and placed twenty thousand pounds on her horse, Merman, with a fat little bookmaker.

"It was Merman, by a neck," wrote one reporter in a racing journal. "And what a neck! For it belonged to none other than 'Mr. Jersey,' better known as Lillie Langtry."

She wondered if the compliment was double-edged. She examined her neck every day in the mirror and was aware that beauty, like wealth, was fleeting. But not wealth at the moment. The horse paid eight to one. She nuzzled the panting chestnut in the winner's circle, clad even more ornamentally than she in a floral horseshoe, and felt an iron grip on her arm.

"I'm so proud of you, Lillie." Albert Edward, grayer and more portly than ever, beamed at her through his silver whiskers. "Come with me to the Jockey Club and we'll celebrate."

"They won't let me in, Bertie, even as your guest. Women are restricted."

"I wouldn't dream of breaching their policy. I've been told that Mr. Jersey will be most welcome."

She drank too much champagne, and the party that evening at Regal Lodge, her country house, was more dizzying yet, with a grand birthday cake iced in her racing colors and showing Merman pulling ahead of the favorite at the finish, the work of the bakers to the royal family. She had struck a blow for her sex, re-established herself as one of the richest women in Britain, and turned forty-four, all on the same day. Surely she had redeemed herself in the eyes of the world.

Two days later, Edward Langtry died in the Upton asylum, aged fifty. Pneumonia and the shock from his fall aboard ship were listed as the causes. Comparisons were made in the press between his grim final hours and the grand party at Regal Lodge taking place at the same time. *The Times* reported that his widow had had the shocking bad taste to send a wreath to the funeral made of turquoise and fawn blossoms, her winning colors. She had not; but what was truth once the bear had turned?

TWENTY-THREE

The twentieth century. The phrase staggered off the tongue like a drunk falling off the Pecos high bridge, but apart from feeling strange in the mouth it had no effect on West Texas at the start. Back East, illustrated newspapers were predicting a future filled with personal Zeppelins and tall buildings shaped like corkscrews, while along the Rio Grande the Rangers were stringing up Mexican bandits like Christmas balls, using nineteenth-century ropes. Progress crept across that scrub country slow as the sun; but like the sun it didn't stand still. If you sat on your front porch long enough you could see it approaching.

In 1902, Val Verde County commemorated the twentieth anniversary of Roy Bean's first appointment to the bench with a group photograph followed by three days of fiesta. All the surviving Rangers who had served with him and could be found—those who had parted with him amicably—came in by train and buckboard and one sputtery Oldsmobile with a gushing radiator, drank complimentary glasses of beer in the New Jersey Lilly

("Hey, Judge, got any ice cold?" Brays of laughter), and posed in front of the saloon for a panoramic camera that looked like an artillery piece mounted on a tripod. Gun battles, bad whiskey, and years of the type peculiar to Texas had whittled down the ranks, but there were more than enough rough customers to tree a town twice the size of Langtry.

It started out exclusive to past and present officers of the court, but as word got around the event grew like Roy's own legend. Farmers and small ranchers packed their families onto spring wagons and came from sixty miles in every direction to see history before it dried up and blew away like Russian thistle. No crowd that large had gathered there since the Fitzsimmons fight, or ever would again.

The new saloon stood on the spot where the original had burned. It was smaller, built on the cheap by carpenters who lacked the skill of the Southern Pacific men who'd been involved the first time; fire buckets, spittoons, and empty powder kegs collected water from the leaky roof and when the wind blew, which was practically all the time, dust came in through gaps in the siding and turned a man's beer to mud if he didn't drink it fast enough. (Fortunately, that wasn't a serious problem.)

They said the fire that had destroyed the first Jersey Lilly had broken the Judge's spirit. Partially that was true, for he wasn't the same man afterward. But lumber was still a costly commodity in that baked-over land, and the court wasn't taking in as much as when Roy was the only Law West of the Pecos. Neither was his saloon now that younger citizens were flocking to Jesus Torres's place to see and hear his new disk-operated music box. There wasn't enough in the till to hire a man who knew a level from his liver. The owner paid his crew in busthead, and allowed as how he should have kept the cork in the jug until after the day's work was done.

Architecturally, however, the place resembled its predecessor, a simple frame lodge with a stovepipe piercing the roof, and all the signs had been repainted. The unobservant visitor, returning after an absence of several years, might have noted no change except for the loss of the storied pecan tree to the fire. Although the little drummer who'd helped Roy decorate the walls had retired, Roy had managed to restore a semblance of the shrine with ornamental handbills, posters, and a cabinet photograph purchased for a highwayman's price from a studio in San Antonio on one wall. (They helped cut down on drafts.) The last was a rather awkward pose of Lillie reclining in a beaded satin gown on a chaise, hands behind her head. It was a bridal shot, taken on the occasion of her wedding to Sir Hugo de Bathe in 1899; she was Lady de Bathe now. Her hair looked dyed and she appeared horse-faced in the picture, but Roy seemed not to notice and no one pointed it out to him.

The court, too, proceeded according to form, if only sporadically. In the autumn of '96, Torres had managed to bump him from office for deputizing Bruno, but the Judge simply had refused to acknowledge the order. Loyal customers who had been coming to him for justice all their lives continued to do so, and he dispensed it almost without interruption until the next election restored his authority. Nothing short of his younger son's involvement in a murder had compelled him to recognize any other state of affairs. When that business was discharged he had a new bung-starter and the old *Statutes* and a bar to rest them on, and that was all the law required.

The prissy little photographer from Little Rock set his camera working. The lens rotated from left to right, burning images of

Roy straddling old Bayo in a sombrero and the waistcoat he buttoned only at the top, two rows of Anglos and Mexicans standing and kneeling in front of the porch with their hats on the backs of their heads, some with their old Colts and Winchesters down from their parlor walls, and old Tom Carson, the stumps of his amputated legs poking out from the seat of his wicker armchair.

The oblong photo, as long as an oxenbrace and mounted in a copper frame made especially for it, hung behind the bar for years after Roy's death, then disappeared. The theft was blamed on an anonymous souvenir hunter. When the state bought the property and established the Judge Roy Bean Visitor Center, a reward was offered for the picture's return, no questions asked, but it never materialized. (Rascals from Roy's time would sense a trap.) In its place, the man appointed as curator hung a scowling picture of Roy surrounded by his four children, looking respectable with a heavy watch chain stretched across his middle. A coat of paint was added to the dilapidated building, and picture-postcards glorifying the old days were made available for purchase in a wire rack.

The fiesta that followed the photographic session busted out windows and lit a mule on fire, but only for a minute before someone put it out with a bucket of slops from the saloon. (Roy had splurged on fireworks, borrowed from a wedding in Old Mexico, but no one was trained in their proper employment. Punctured eardrums and missing fingers identified veterans of the celebration for several years afterward.) One former Ranger accepted a dare to leap his horse over a flatbed railroad car on a siding, but failed to consult the horse; it put on the brakes and the Ranger completed the stunt alone, breaking his leg in three places ("the car, the ground, and the hitch rail," Roy wrote Lillie).

Torres discovered a powder charge fizzled out against the north wall of his saloon. His competitor said it was probably a protest against his decision to hike the price of beer for the fiesta. For seventy-two hours it was like Vinegarroon days.

And then it ended. The old warriors went home to their families, the broken automobile was towed away by horses, the rubberneckers struck their tents and pulled out, the Mexicans swept up, and Langtry settled back into a state of somnolence. Roy treated his thumping head with hair of the dog and fanned away blowflies with a paper frond advertising a local mortuary. From his front porch he looked out on the welcome banner hanging in tatters (the winner of a horse race had tried to cap his victory by standing in the saddle and swinging from it when his mount passed underneath; he was in traction in Del Rio) and felt old.

Bruno was gone. No one knew his age when he'd come to town aboard Edgar G. Howe's medicine wagon, but his muzzle had grown white and in his last months he'd failed to stir himself even to snatch an airborne pullet from above his head, showing no interest in dried apples and subsisting entirely on beer. Roy found him one morning gone to his ancestors in a scatter of empties.

That's one version. There is a shameful story about a whiskey drummer named Betters who tricked Roy into ordering the bear's execution, but it's too sad to repeat. Better to remember Bruno lying at peace beneath the fine granite monument his master had had made for him in San Antonio. For a time his shaggy hide graced the floor of the old Jersey Lilly, but it had gone up in the fire.

A bad-tempered bear took his place in the cage, but Roy had it put down with buckshot after it got loose and broke a burro's back, and bought a mountain lion he charged visitors to watch tear chickens apart. It wasn't the same, and so he tried to plug the hole left by Bruno with plenty.

Historians differ over whether Judge Bean pioneered the concept of the roadside zoo or borrowed it from someone else. Certainly he was among the first to collect admission from pilgrims for a peek at the lion, a three-legged timber wolf chained to Bruno's old post, and a two-headed goat he sent Little Roy to fetch back from Juarez when he read about it in the *El Paso Times*. A thirty-pound orange cat waddled between sightseers' legs, frightening them into thinking the bobcat had escaped from its wire pen. There were chickens everywhere, hogs the size of hippos, raccoons, and a Brazilian monkey that climbed up onto Roy's lap when he passed out and stole his reading glasses from his waistcoat pocket. He advertised a Burro With Its Tail Where Its Head Should Be, but people caught on quickly to the fact that he had simply put the animal in a corncrib head first, and he discontinued the attraction as too obvious. A deal to purchase a captured buffalo fell through when the bull broke out of its cattle car during a stopover in Denver and stomped three people to death before it was dispatched with a Henry rifle.

"Damn shame," said Phil Forrest, when the word came. "There ain't many of them critters still walking about."

Roy said, "I reckon I'll have to take its place."

He flattered himself that he was as much of an attraction as a freak goat, with justification. Passengers traveling West sat up straight when they crossed the high bridge, then saw the big water tank and the little frame shack on the plot of ground where so much justice had been laid down and so much whiskey sold. They knew about the lump of glass, the dead men fined for carrying concealed weapons, and the beer-drinking bear from newspaper fillers and word-of-mouth, and when they saw the source of so much entertainment seated big as life in his rocking chair on the front porch, they could barely wait their turn to step down and pay too much for a dollop of Old Johnston in a glass of Pecos water and ask the Judge if it was true he'd once had a tramp's leg cut off when the man tricked him into giving him money to set a leg that wasn't broken.

"That's a damn lie," Roy said. "We took a little hide off with a rusty saw is all. He stepped right lively out the door when he got loose. I call that a miracle of healing."

But placing himself on exhibit got old sometimes, and he disappointed tourists who found him passed out with flies busy in the fresh tobacco staining his whiskers. They concluded he was as much a fake as his backwards burro. One of them gave up trying to get a rise out of him, drank a bottle of beer in the Jersey Lilly, and got back aboard the train without paying. Awakened by the Mexican tending bar, Roy scooped up his yellow-handled Colt, told the conductor to hold the train, and dragging the bartender along marched through the cars, turning some male passengers pale at the sight of the hogleg and his bloodshot eyes inches from their faces, his breath curdled with Levi Garrett's and sour grain.

At length the Mexican grunted and pointed. Roy cocked the Colt and barked the man's teeth with the muzzle. "Thirty-five cents or I press the button."

A cartwheel dollar surfaced in a shaking hand. Roy made change and left.

"You never worried about short-changing a customer in your life," said Forrest, when the full account was reported by the Associated Press. "Why start now?"

"I'm extra scrupulous with cheats and drunks."

But this was reaching into the past. John Bean had left—to

fight the Spaniards in Cuba, some said, others to dig for gold in Alaska, or to try his hand in moving pictures; there are always three stories connected with John, half again more than with Roy. Little Roy got a job with the railroad, throwing tramps off the cars. Laura and Zulema married and moved away. Sam hung around to take his turn behind the bar and help keep order when court was in session, but he got bored often with the sleepy Langtry life and spent a lot of time in jail in San Antonio for busting up places and being drunk in general. Roy did all his drinking at home now, telling the same old stories to whoever would listen, and more or less just sat around waiting. He was in his seventy-eighth year.

In December 1902, everything changed.

One of the Roys who had resulted from the Judge's shuffling of married couples snared a wild turkey and brought it to him for Christmas. It shaped up to be a lonely meal, but Roy had a brainstorm and made detailed arrangements with the railroad to ship the bird live to Lillie Langtry, who was dividing her time between an apartment in New York and her horse ranch in California; he'd read that she was in the East just then, in rehearsals for *Mrs. Deering's Divorce*. Since the play represented her return to the stage after a brief retirement (she was in financial straits again, having invested heavily in South African securities just before the Boer War), all her appearances were sold out, and she was encouraged to expand the North American tour.

She responded within a week:

My dear Judge Bean,
    I wish you could have seen the expression on the concierge's face when he came to my suite to report that a <u>creature</u> had arrived for me by

*special messenger. I had it sent round to Delmonico's, where some
friends and I enjoyed an elegant American Christmas Eve dinner,
which was so much less heavy than our English fare of greasy goose and
dense plum pudding. We drank to your health, and as for myself, I can
never thank you sufficiently, my fellow U. S. citizen, for this Yankee
feast.*

    And now to my news! . . .

Yours most cordially,
Lillie (Langtry) de Bathe

Roy's Mexican bartender heard him cry out, found the old man suffering from an apparent fit of apoplexy, and ran for help. But the Judge had not been stricken at all, except with ecstasy. The Jersey Lily's 1903–04 tour now included San Antonio and El Paso; her route would take her directly past Langtry.

"She's coming!"

"Lillie!"

"In the flesh, by God!"

"*Dío mío, la liria de Jersey!*"

Jesus Torres accepted the news in bitter stride. "Sooner or later, everything turns the old son of a bitch's way."

Roy convened the welcoming committee inside the saloon, banging it into silence with his bung-starter. "We got a year to get ready, so keep your steam down. First thing we need's lumber."

"I reckon I'm getting on," Phil Forrester said. "In my day it was flowers."

"To hell with flowers. She's got enough of them to plant the desert sixteen times over. She's the first woman to have a saloon and a town named after her, and she'll be the first actress to have a dad-gum opera house built just for her."

The structure rose from the site of the coop where Stonewall Jackson had pecked his way out of his shell so many years before, and where Bruno had left his empties, with a covered dogwalk to connect it to the Jersey Lilly. The town had a professional sign-painter now, and he set aside the project he was working on for Torres (a roller-skating rink, of all things) to letter ROY BEAN'S OPERA HOUSE TOWN HALL AND SEAT OF JUSTICE on a board six feet long, which Roy leaned against the wall under the panoramic picture for customers to admire while construction continued. He took up a collection and sent all the way to San Francisco for a fey decorator who had done over the famous Bella Union to see to the interior details. Even Torres chipped in, in return for the ice-cream concession.

Forrest, ever the voice of simple reason, asked the Judge how he expected Mrs. Langtry to shoehorn a local performance into her crowded schedule. Roy scowled over a blueprint of which he could make neither head nor tail. "Phil, I swear you let that Winchester of yours do all your thinking. I sent her a turkey, for chrissake. You ever hear of singing for your supper? Read your Bible."

Christians thought this blasphemy, and blamed Roy's heathen nature for what befell him. Medical professionals said it had more likely to do with sleepless nights planning Lillie's reception and hours frying under the Texas sun making sure the carpenters didn't scrimp on nails and pegs to spare Lady de Bathe incontinent creaks and groans while she was treading his boards; such a thing would reflect badly upon an infatuation of twenty years, longer than most marriages, and with all the early fancies intact. Men and women of temperance insisted it was his bibulous and libertine ways that led to the inevitable collapse. The only thing everyone agreed on was that he woke up one morning with a hangover that wouldn't go away, and that he was still complaining about it when life left him, ten months before Mrs. Langtry came to pay her respects. Roy, in almost his dying breath, said that he'd succeeded at least in horse-trading Jesus Torres out of some profit in that damn ice-cream business of his. To the end he persisted in putting a positive spin on things.

TWENTY-FOUR

The Sunset Limited thundered through sagebrush and tumbleweed, between rows of gigantic silver pines and towering cliffs where the right-of-way had been blasted through solid rock; through the continent's spine. Over the muscular land the private car rolled, paneled in rosewood and mahogany and upholstered in mohair dyed the color of Jersey lilies. (She would have preferred turquoise and fawn, but the directors of the Southern Pacific had been so accommodating she wouldn't dream of the imposition.) It was a vast place, encompassing all climates, an adolescent still, but showing its sinews now that it had flung the last of the Old World from its hemisphere, the once-mighty Spain of the Armada and Cortez; a world power, this, with a cowboy in the saddle. She had not been introduced to President Roosevelt, but what she'd read of him put the late Mr. Disraeli and the late Sir William Gladstone thoroughly in mothballs. The Queen was dead (it seemed so strange to address Bertie now as Your Majesty), so was the Empire, having taken its own life in savage Africa: Long live the Empire. Lillie had bet on the right horse when she'd sworn allegiance to the Stars and Stripes, even if the wager had been made on credit.

What a slippery thing was fortune, easily obtained and even more easily relinquished. One invested in one's reputation, but it was backed with nothing. Jewelry came next, solid things one could hold in one's hand, but they fell so easily into the hands of others, so one turned to one's native country, but even that was built on shifting pebbles, piles of slag mined by the Boers. How silly Shuggy (Sir Hugo de Bathe) had been, trying to recoup his famous wife's investment by enlisting in that futile conflict. But then he was a boy, too young for her by an age, and determined to prove himself a man in her eyes. They hadn't seen each other in months, which was just as well. In America, it wouldn't do to prance around with a title. It was January 1904, a new year in a new century, and it was already shaping up to belong to the Yankees.

He lay on his cornshuck mattress by a window looking out on blackness, with a coal-oil lamp making a mountainous shadow of his belly on the wall, reflected in the glass as in a mirror. They had carried the bed down from the sleeping loft to avoid having to hoist him up the ladder when his legs failed him. It was March 1903, iron cold when the heat of day had drained away into the sand, and he could barely stir beneath the weight of quilts smelling of rancid bacon and unwashed flesh. He heard the slithering of playing cards, the clink of a bottle against a glass, Jesus Torres conversing in low tones with Billy Dodd, an old friend and likely Roy's successor.

Torres was being magnanimous in his survival, placing his saloon in the hands of employees while he stood vigil on the enemy of his entire adult life. For years now their feud had simmered only.

Over a generation the relationship had acquired the comforting consistency of a sturdy friendship. Roy had known the spoiled Spaniard as long as he'd admired Lillie.

Thinking of her brought a sharp pain that made him groan and brought Doc Ross out of the rocking chair to check his pulse, pressing cold fingers against the old rope-burn on his neck beneath his whiskers. That a man should come so near the light of his days only to be forced to watch those days run out first was monstrous unfair. He asked, without opening his eyes, when Sam was coming.

"I'm right here, Pa."

"It's good you came," the doc told Sam. "Family's important."

"It was a far piece. I rode that borrowed horse plumb into the ground."

Roy smiled weakly. No true Bean ruined his own horse.

The train seemed to be slowing. Was she there? She opened her reticule and examined her face in the mirror in its ormulu case, a gift from poor Oscar, dead these four years. (His last words, reported in the press: "Either that wallpaper goes or I do." Oscar, dear Oscar, to the last. She had intended to visit him when she was in Paris, but cowardice had kept her away; another bitter and useless regret. She'd heard he was depressing to see, obese and jaundiced.) Beauty was gone, the mirror confirmed; artifice alone remained. When she had been photographed with Jeanne the one time they had traveled together to New York, people had said they looked like sisters. Now she was about to become a grandmother, and she seemed perfectly cast for the role. It seemed strange that anyone could ever have believed she'd been offended to be asked to play a middle-aged woman.

Not that she would ever be allowed to portray a grandmother except onstage. The announcement of the impending birth had come to her by way of reporters. She and Jeanne had had no contact since the young woman's marriage into an upper-class family with a distaste for all things theatrical and a horror of infamous women. Considering that, it really had been most democratic of them to take a bastard into the fold.

She'd powdered over the last trace of tears when the conductor knocked and entered to tell her they were stopping for water. No, missus, they were still several hours from Langtry. He hesitated, concern showing on his kind, pudgy, clean-shaven face. "I'm afraid you'll be disappointed, as there isn't much to the place. The Sunset don't stop there usually."

"Yes, your employers were most gracious to agree to let me have thirty minutes there. I'm so looking forward to meeting the funny old man who's been writing to me all these years. Do you know Judge Bean?"

"Well, now, you *will* be disappointed. I'm sorry to tell you he died last spring."

"Oh." Suddenly she was devastated. Oscar gone, Mother and Father, Jimmy Whistler (how she'd despised him, and enjoyed his company, his ludicrous monocle and corsets; how she missed his chirp), most of her brothers. Roy Bean had remained the one constant, and now he, too, had left. She felt an odd sensation of widowhood. It was as if Edward's death had affected her finally.

The conductor apologized again, touched his visor, and hobbled back out on bad feet, a hazard of the profession that came from walking many times across that enormous continent. She herself had crossed it more times than she could count, but her first experience of Texas, the bottom third anyway, flat and without feature, created no sensation of movement. The parlor car might have been standing still, with someone shaking it to deceive her, as when those boys had unhitched her carriage the night of her London debut in *She Stoops to Conquer* and carried it on their shoulders with her inside like a maharani in a sedan chair, all those years ago. Had anyone ever been so young? Had she? Poor Judge Bean.

"When did you say it happened?" Sam asked Billy Dodd.

Talking about him as if he was dead already.

"Day before yesterday. Some of the boys found him wandering around the saloon like he didn't know where he was. He couldn't talk so they sent for me and I had his bed brought down. I wired the doc in Del Rio and you right after."

"I seen him in San Antone last week. He seemed all right then. It was at a cockfight." Sam's voice cracked. "He liked cockfights for as long as I can remember."

Stonewall Jackson, that was some game rooster. He never should've risen to Slauson's bait, or volunteered to let him fight without spurs. Roy didn't believe that poisoning story. A real champion went down fighting a clean fight. He reckoned a good part of San Antone went home with a little bit of Stonewall in 'em.

"He's smiling," Billy said. "I think he heard you."

Roy licked his lips. They were as dry as buffalo chips. "Sam here yet?"

"Right here, Pa. Don't you hear me?"

"When he gets here, tell him he's got a hiding coming. You don't bushwhack a man downtown in broad daylight."

John; there was a Bean and it don't matter what names he used before he came. That business with the window in the train station was pure-dee something from the Revised Statutes. Roy knew him for family from the start; he'd have come up with something else to keep the boy around if he hadn't thought of that busted window. Maybe that's what put windows in John's mind. Damn funny coincidence, him breaking into the storeroom when everybody in town knew the Judge took his siesta at the same time every day, just on the other side of the partition. Roy allowed as how he'd left unfinished business when he pulled up stakes in San Antone to find his destiny in Vinegarroon. So many pretty señoritas about in them days, and there was something Mexican in the boy's face, and something of Roy, too, back when he used to raise hell.

"They hung me, but it didn't take. I calculate it was all them chilis I et, curing my neck from the inside."

"What'd you say, Pa?"

"I don't think he's here, Sam." This was Doc Ross.

"Well, where the hell else'd he be? This here's the Jersey Lily."

She must have dozed, because suddenly there was a porter pouring tea, using a silver service on a butler's table. He worked silently. It was the change in the sound of the wheels that had awakened her. They thudded hollowly on a wooden trestle.

"That's the high bridge over the Pecos River, ma'am," said the porter, a fine-featured Negro in an impeccable white jacket and cotton gloves, with a beautiful command of English. "It won't be long now."

"I suppose not." She had butterflies, of all things; it was *A Fair Encounter* all over again.

"There's a funny story about this bridge, if you don't mind them a bit morbid. An experienced actress might appreciate it."

She smiled, training a loose dyed curl behind her ear. "The Judge wrote me about it, and I've heard it twice since I left Louisiana. Is it really legal to fine a dead man for a civil infraction?"

"I don't suppose he'd raise an objection. Will that be all, ma'am?"

"Please stay a bit. I find myself growing more nervous by the minute. They may decide that I don't measure up, and change the name back to—what was it? Something like Rangoon."

"Vinegarroon. All the Southern Pacific employees on this route are well-versed in its history: A.B., that is. After Bean. I used to see him when I was on the local. He had a lifetime pass, but I think he lost it years ago. But everyone knew who he was, so he always rode free. He was drunker when he came back from San Antonio than he was going out, but I don't believe I ever saw him sober. He smelled."

"I understand he was quite a character."

"There are some who say that. Just as many if not more say he was a bad man who hid behind the trappings of his office."

"I daresay the Union Bank of London would find a place for such a man on its staff."

"Ma'am?"

"Nothing. Just a bitter old woman reflecting upon the dead past. What do *you* say?"

"I have no opinion, ma'am; but then I never appeared before him. I don't know where he stood on Negroes, but I'm told it was unfortunate for a Chinaman to ask for justice in his court."

She sipped tea. It was perfect. "I must say I'm pleasantly surprised by Texas. If all you knew of it was what I read long ago in a friend's collection of American publications—giant bears, red savages, and road agents—you'd understand why it's taken me so long to make the journey. I thought it wise to leave my jewels in New Orleans. That's one reason I'm afraid I'll disappoint Langtry. Sometimes I've wondered if I'd be better off staying behind and sending my jewelry on tour."

"It wouldn't satisfy them, Mrs. Langtry. I doubt they'd know a diamond from a doorknob, but they'll certainly know the Jersey Lily from looking at the Judge's pictures all these years. If they were somehow to treat you ungraciously, he just might climb out of his grave and fine them all for contempt. Or worse."

"*That sure is one beer-drinking bear. You'd swear it's old Tom Carson when he burps.*"

"*That's Bruno he's talking about,*" Sam said. "*That bear's been dead for years. He's out of his head.*"

"*More likely in it,*" said Doc Ross.

"*A hundred pesos for Joaquin's head.*"

There was something about this dying jag that cut a man loose. He didn't have to just sit and rock and tip a warm jug and wait for the train to pick him up and take him someplace lively. He could be young and gristly or old and fat, whoring around Los Angeles, deliberating over the ownership of a horse in Langtry, hauling a billiard table up to Pinos Altos, fishing off somebody else's back porch in San Antone with a demijohn of good busthead chilling in the current. If he missed Old Mesilla, well, there he was with one arm around the waist of a pretty black-eyed girl and the other busting caps at the stars on a street where the air was thick with the sweet smell of tortillas sizzling in pans of lard. Instead of laying about in long-handles under a pile of stinking quilts he could be galloping around and around the Presidio in Frisco, dressed like a torreador with a silver-embroidered sombrero on the back of his head, baying at the moon. So this was what heaven was; he always sort of figured.

"*What's keeping Sam? I swear if that boy moved any slower he'd be going backwards.*"

"*Pa, I been here right along.*"

"*Fetch Torres over here pronto.*"

That fellow came into the lamplight. He was thick through the waist now and balding, but he had the longest, prettiest eyelashes Roy had ever seen apart from the young things of New Mexico and

California. The dignity of age had dressed him in sober brown broad-cloth, but his shoulders sagged beneath years of domestic abuse. His German wife was more autocratic than ever, and even in death old Don Cesario remained in charge of his son.

"Yes, Judge."

"You might want to reconsider making extra ice cream."

"What do you care? For all I know you planned it this way just to inconvenience me."

"Just don't hold it against Lillie when she comes or I'll kick your brown ass back across the Rio Grande where it belongs."

"Vaya con díos, *you old bastard.*"

Roy turned his head toward the window, and the world turned with it.

"Is anything wrong?" Lillie asked.

She had dismissed the porter, but now here was the kind-faced conductor, walking like a man picking his way through cactus, or whatever it was that grew in scattered ocher clumps outside the window. The train had stopped in a patch of desert identical to what it had been chugging through for hours.

"We're here, missus. Langtry."

She was heartsick. It was one thing to be moving across desolation, another to be stopped in the middle of it with no escape in any direction. The land stretched in monochrome, flat as tin right up until it touched merciless blue-steel sky in a line straighter than anything Jimmy Whistler could have drawn. A jackrabbit the size of a French poodle, with great paddle-shaped feet, appeared from behind a clump of vegetation, took three hops, then spun on some hidden pivot and raced back the way it had come; toward what? What could a creature possibly have had to forget and go back for in the desert? Lillie finished her tea in one draught and gathered her things. If she were to be marooned like a heroine in a melodramatic novel, she would at least have her parasol to use for a weapon.

"There she is!" A bawling, burly voice, accustomed to shouting into the wind.

And there was plenty of wind, flapping her skirts, tugging at her hat, and doing its best to lift her by the parasol. She held onto it with one hand and gave the other to the conductor, who helped her down the steps of the platform and from his stout little stool to the ground.

She saw then that there was a town; albeit one so brief that her coach at the end of the train had been too far back to parallel the station. A great wooden water tank on four timber legs groaned and grumbled against the pressure from the wind, sounding like an old man struggling to get up from a chair, and a station overhang bore her name on a sign. It was real enough, if small. But who could boast of a similar tribute? All Henry Irving had was his knighthood, and such a fuss some other K.B.E.s had made when the lists were posted, turning in their orders in protest. Thank God she was no longer a British subject.

She was engulfed. The town numbered some one hundred residents, and no one appeared to have stayed indoors. She shook hands with piny-smelling cowboys, women in gingham and calico, children, a handsome large Spanish gentleman with thick luxurious lashes, a postmaster, the station agent; it was all so democratic. She smiled, met their greetings with sentence fragments ("I'm so—" "Of course—" "You're very—" "Yes, it's—"), and fought that damn stray curl lashing in the wind. It was like Rotten Row in the '70s, without the class barrier.

At length the crowd parted—guided, it seemed, by a Moses-like gesture on the part of the fine Spanish gentleman, who took the hand of a young black-haired girl dressed in communion white with a red sash around her waist. Something about the tenderness of the offering suggested she was his daughter.

The girl folded her hands beneath her budding breasts and cleared her throat. She spoke in a strong, clear contralto, surprisingly rich and not unlike Lillie's own. "Mrs. Langtry, ladies and gentlemen, in the name of my schoolmates and all the citizens I beg leave to address a few words of welcome to our fair English lady, the Jersey Lily. We all feel proud indeed to have the honor of greeting and shaking hands with the talented lady whose name our town bears."

So much poise, thought Lillie, and so young. Envy ran through her like a lance.

Another speech followed by W.D. Dodd, who had been appointed by the governor to fill out Roy Bean's term of office as Justice of the Peace. He wore a bowler hat, Prince Albert striped trousers, and stovepipe boots polished to a liquid shine, breaded slightly with blowing sand. He seemed a quiet contrast to everything she had heard about his predecessor, and many of his words were lost in the wind. He lifted his arm. She saw that she was to take it, and they proceeded toward a homely shanty facing the tracks. A cowboy flamboyantly attired in flannel, bandanna, chaparajos, and a hat with a great swooping brim unholstered a long-barreled pistol and fired it skyward. It made a disappointing plop in the open air and smoke tore away from its muzzle. Evidently the race was on; they had but twenty minutes, with the conductor smoking a pipe, watch in hand, by the champing locomotive.

On the way, Judge Dodd stammered an apology for the absence of Roy's eldest son, whom railroad business had called away from a prominent part in the welcoming ceremony. Lillie, who knew stage fright in whatever terms it was couched, made murmurs of sympathy.

The Jersey Lilly, which swayed with each gust and seemed to be held together chiefly with signs, sported a long, shady front porch with a splayed chair moving rhythmically on its rockers and a chained monkey watching her with bright eyes in its old-crone's face. (Next door stood unfinished construction, its naked framework bleaching in the sun.) Inside, the saloon assumed the proportions of a railway car, with a bar to one side, solid tables to the other, and a ladder shaggy with splinters separating them in the middle, providing access to a loft. Generations of hieroglyphs had been carved into the tables and a bloated deck of playing cards rested on each. The rounds of the Windsor chairs were scarred all over from the rowels of many spurs. The air was redolent of tobacco, sour mash, and border justice.

Observed from windows and the open doorway, she lifted her skirts clear of a floor strewn with peanut shells and packing straw and strolled among the spittoons and buckets, looking at faded images of herself around a three-sheet poster for *The Lady of Lyons* pasted on a wall (her Pauline smiling at her across the decades), touching the cold steel of a great gaunt revolver lying atop a tattered book the size of a Gutenberg Bible on the bar; one worn smooth, the other rough.

She was aware of someone standing too close behind her. Americans had difficulty keeping a respectful distance, native curiosity getting the better of indigenous reserve. This one smelled as pungent as a Kansas City stagehand. She turned, wearing the polite but firm smile she kept for such moments.

No one was near. Judge Dodd stood four yards away, unobtrusively blocking the packed entrance with his thumbs in his waistcoat pockets, exposing the gutta-percha handle of a pistol stuck in his belt. He returned the smile with a tentative tug at the corners of his mouth.

The train whistle blew, straight up her spine.

Mrs. Deering's *Divorce* was a success with critics and the public. Such had not always been the case in that solidly Christian country when it came to lampooning the marital bed. In 1899, *The Degenerates* had been banned in Pittsburgh, Cleveland, Detroit, and Washington, D.C.; but in this new Edwardian world (Bertie had jettisoned his first name upon his succession, along with much of his sense of irony), all the old bets were off. She did notice that the audiences were growing older, their sticks more utilitarian than ornamental.

The tour ended in Toronto and Lillie returned to New York to find a package waiting. It contained a heavy revolver with a yellowed bone handle in a custom cherrywood case. An engraved brass plaque on the lid read:

> PRESENTED BY W.D. DODD OF LANGTRY, TEXAS, TO MRS. LILLIE LANGTRY IN HONOR OF HER VISIT TO OUR TOWN. THIS PISTOL WAS FORMERLY THE PROPERTY OF JUDGE ROY BEAN. IT AIDED IN FINDING SOME OF HIS FAMOUS DECISIONS AND KEEPING ORDER WEST OF THE PECOS. IT ALSO KEPT ORDER IN THE JERSEY LILLY SALOON. KINDLY ACCEPT THIS AS A SMALL TOKEN OF OUR REGARDS.

She would not trust it to a bank or out of her sight for any extended period; it was not jewelry or a husband, something that could be replaced, but unlike kings and princes and daughters, it was built to last, by Samuel Colt's Patent Firearms Manufacturing Company of Paterson, New Jersey. When Langtry blew away, when Roy Bean was just a handful of tall tales, what else was there to prove that Emilie LeBreton had ever existed? Certainly not her name etched in glass. The revolver traveled with her all over the world, she would take no price for it, not in rubies or shares in American Telephone & Telegraph or a custom-built sixteen-cylinder Bugatti, and when she died in Monaco in 1929 at the age of seventy-seven, it was found where she'd displayed it, propped in its open case on her mantel, a kind of shrine.

ROY & LILLIE:
LOVE, AMERICAN STYLE

The bizarre, largely one-sided love affair that took place for twenty years between Roy Bean and Lillie Langtry could only have started in America. No other society on earth encouraged casual communication across classes, and had he lived in any other country, Roy would probably have wound up at the end of a rope, and the Law West of the Pecos would have been very different indeed.

The westward expansion after the Civil War progressed so rapidly it outdistanced the United States' system of justice. Not only was the law nearly impossible to enforce with the existing courts often several hundred miles removed from the scene of the crime; there was serious disagreement over whether their officers had jurisdiction. It wasn't uncommon, as late as the 1880s, for deputized authority to pack a felon several days' ride to civilization, only to see the man set free because of a disagreement over just what that authority entailed. Under such circumstances, lynch law appears less a symptom of mass hysteria and more a matter of practical self-defense. As Owen Wister so eloquently stated the case through Judge Henry in *The Virginian* (1902):

> . . . We are in a very bad way, and we are trying to make that way a little better until civilization can reach us. At present we lie beyond its pale. The courts, or rather the juries, into hands we put the law, are not dealing the law. . . . And so when your ordinary citizen sees this, and sees that he has placed justice in a dead hand, he must take justice back into his own hands where it was once at the beginning of all things.

Before Roy Bean came to Vinegarroon, Texas, suspected criminals were either marched six hundred miles to Fort Davis by Texas Rangers—leaving their part of the country at the mercy of bandits—or strung from the nearest tree by concerned citizens (who may or may not have included Rangers). After his appointment, defendants were tried and either acquitted and released, or convicted and fined or hanged. The difference was the presence of a third party behind the bench, and the very fact that a verdict of not guilty was an option argues in favor of even so doubtful a champion of justice as he was.

Why Bean? One might as well ask, "Why Earp?" or "Why Hickok?" Keeping the peace in the cattle towns and mining camps frequently involved experience in breaking it. Like Wyatt and Wild Bill, Roy was the hell-raiser the directors of the Southern Pacific Railroad needed to protect its construction crews in the Pecos River country, often from themselves, and he delivered quickly and colorfully. (The railroads, it should be noted, exercised an iron control through lobbying and bribery over the state, territorial, and federal governments that would not be seen again until the rise of the banking institutions in twenty-first-century Washington.) The Texas Rangers, who had never hesitated to make their own law wherever they went, had little incentive to make another six-hundred-mile trek over a matter of legal principles, and so with their reputation and support, the title "Law West of the Pecos" was no empty boast.

For a time, it was in justice's best interest that Roy's more outrageous rulings were widely reported; the sharps and thimbleriggers who brought so much unrest to the cramped conditions in the workers' camps, and the thieves and murderers who preyed upon the track gangs, were likely to ride a hundred miles out of their way to avoid sure and swift punishment at the end of his bung-starter. But just as it was with all the other desperate men pressed into office in desperate times, the very progress he made possible made his methods obsolete, and dangerous to maintain. Hickok lost his position in Abilene when he shot one of his own deputies during a firefight; Earp was run out of Arizona for the bloodbath that began near the O.K. Corral. The question is not how Roy Bean came to be Justice of the Peace, but how he managed to remain in office, with only two brief interruptions, for twenty-one years.

To begin with, he was a tricky old devil who knew how to manipulate the unique legal situation of his time and place for his own benefit. Second, and more important as the frontier faded into history, he was (wait for it) a man of vision. Fifty years before Tombstone and Deadwood learned that the key to their survival lay in exploiting the very things that had threatened their existence in the early days, Roy Bean grasped the potential of his own rascality for profit. No ordinary inflation could account for raising the price of beer in the Jersey Lilly from five to thirty-five cents in only a few years; the astronomical sum included admission to see and speak with the man who fined a corpse forty dollars for carrying a concealed weapon. He appeared on the stage of his front porch every day at 3:00 P.M., just as Lillie Langtry turned out when the curtain rose at the Lyceum at eight, in full wardrobe with prop in hand (a jug of whiskey) and all his lines committed to memory. You were disappointed if he didn't short-change you.

Good ol' Roy, what're you gonna do? Not a damn thing. He can't last much longer, and he's good for tourism.

The story of Lillie Langtry eerily parallels Roy Bean's, even if it runs in the opposite direction. She became famous almost immediately, and just as she was learning to exploit her fame, it left her. Along the way she made money and lost it, behaved outrageously, and blazed her name across three continents, only to see it smolder away in her own lifetime. Roy painted his on a sign, did most of the things she did, and got his page in history without ever leaving his little patch of Texas. Today, the name Lillie Langtry brings vague recognition in most circles (she's often confused with Lotta Crabtree and Jenny Lind), but leaps to most tongues almost without thought whenever Roy's comes up. It's a mismatch made in heaven, *Beauty and the Beast* and *The African Queen*, only with a tin-tack piano tinkling in the background.

They never met, a revelation that often comes as a surprise. But that seems to be the source of the story's allure. Their meeting would have been a disaster—or worse, a non-event. Her breezy disdain for proprieties might have shocked the old reprobate out of his crush, and his habit of chewing tobacco with his mouth open might have cured her of her amusement. Or they might have murmured a few banalities and parted, and for some reason felt emptied by the encounter. I prefer it this way. Unfinished business leaves room to daydream. Theirs is the ideal love story, because it never had the chance to be anything else.

In *Roy & Lillie*, I've tried to steer close to history, but I had to veer off course to fill blanks in the chart. That's the difference between history and historical fiction. I confess to having ghost-written the letters I've quoted between Roy and Lillie. Thanks to James Crutchfield, a close friend and eminent historian who did the spadework, I was able to establish that none of their corre-spondence is known to exist. Had any of it survived, I would certainly have used it, but that gap in the record gave me liberty to suggest an intimacy they may never have had, but one that adds another dimension to their long-distance relationship; that of two relative strangers exchanging confidences they would never have shared with close associates. If this is overstepping the bounds, I plead guilty and throw myself on the mercy of the court. (Not Roy's, I hope.)

The reader may enjoy separating Roy's real adventures from apocrypha, and Oscar Wilde's authentic quips from the ones I made up. Fortunately, they supplied reams of appropriate mate-rial on their own, and the triangle of Edward, Lillie, and Albert Edward, the Prince of Wales, is a melodramatist's dream.

I admit to a dislike for James McNeill Whistler unfelt by Lil-lie. He was a dull painter at an exciting time in art history, and repaid Oscar's friendship with crude jokes in his hour of trou-ble. I take comfort from the fact that his mother is more famous than he ever was.

I don't know who fathered Jeanne Marie Langtry; do you? Some say Bertie, some another member of the royal family, oth-ers a former sweetheart from Lillie's childhood in Jersey. I say why not Edward Langtry? She was uncertain enough herself not to connect Oscar's suggestion that she play Mrs. Erlynne, the mother of a grown illegitimate daughter, in *Lady Windermere's Fan*, with her own situation. Most accounts accept Oscar's version, that she was offended to be asked to play a middle-aged woman. She was thirty-nine at the time, a difficult age for actresses then and now.

I don't know if John Bean was Roy's flesh-and-blood son; do you? Maybe the Judge didn't either, which is how I chose to present the situation. His loins were sufficiently potent to produce four legitimate children, and there's no evidence he practiced safe sex when he was tomcatting among the señoritas, or that he interpreted his marriage vows any more strictly than he read the law. I'm just saying.

Most of what we know of Judge Roy Bean was mined from original soil by my late friend C. L. "Doc" Sonnichsen, author of *Roy Bean: Law West of the Pecos* (New York: The Macmillan Co., 1943; reissued by Fawcett Gold Medal in 1972 as *The Story of Roy Bean*). Archival material was more readily available when he researched it than it is now, although digging it up has never been easy, and after just forty years there were still people around who knew Roy and agreed to be interviewed. The book is surprisingly light on documentation, given Doc's other scholarly work, but enormously entertaining, filled with anecdotes set out in an order that may at first seem random but quickly forms a fully fleshed-out portrait of its unique subject. It's 100 percent free of the moldy stench of academia, and recommended. The historian credits Everett Lloyd's *Law West of the Pecos* and Ruel McDaniel's *Vinegarroon* among his sources, and acknowledges Horace Bell's *Reminiscences of a Ranger* and *On the Old West Coast* for clearing up the mystery of Roy's time in California.

Stan Hoig's *The Humor of the American Cowboy* (Caldwell,

Idaho: The Caxton Printers, Ltd., 1958; reissued by Signet in 1960) is worth ferreting out from the stuffy top floor of a used-book emporium in Fort Worth or Denver (or the Net, if you have no adventure in your soul), as a kind of Cliff's Notes recap of Sonnichsen, with a lot of unrelated frontier knee-slappers and blanket-stretchers thrown in. It gave this author his first taste of Bean.

The Jersey Lillie: The Story of the Fabulous Mrs. Langtry (Englewood Cliffs, N.J.: Prentice-Hall, Inc., 1958), by Pierre Sichel, is highly readable and sympathetic to its subject, without sacrificing journalistic objectivity. It's a straightforward cradle-to-grave look at one of the brightest gems in the setting of the Gilded Age, with pictures and a no-nonsense index. (Sonnichsen's book on Roy has pictures but, maddeningly, no index.) Other, more scandal-conscious biographies have appeared, but read more like tabloids than serious history. Langtry's autobiography, *The Days I Knew*, published in New York four years before her death, is warmly written and surprisingly well detailed for a personal memoir covering so many decades; her account of her visit to Langtry is enthusiastic and affectionate, and required little tweaking in these pages. (Roy's phantom cameo is an authorly indulgence; but surely he would have made the effort!)

From a historical standpoint, the character of Roy Bean (if not the particulars of his life) has been better served by Hollywood than most gunmen of the Old West. Screenwriters seem to have realized that leaving the bark on him played better than any attempt at refinement.

Using an original story by Stuart N. Lake, the fabulist whose *Wyatt Earp: Frontier Marshal* drenched its subject in a sainthood that more responsible research has all but eradicated, *The*

Westerner (United Artists, 1940) gloried in the Judge's rascality, uniting him in an unlikely but somehow plausible friendship with Gary Cooper's decent (fictional) drifter. The plot is a re-hash of all those cattlemen-versus-farmers yarns that had been around since the first horse galloped across the silent screen, but Walter Brennan's irascible Judge earned him a well-deserved third supporting-player Oscar (a record that still stands after seventy years), and made full use of his peculiar application of the law and near-psychotic worship of Lillie Langtry. (A "linch-pin" scene has Cooper bluffing his way out of his own hanging by promising to deliver a lock of Langtry's hair.) Lillian Bond has no lines in her brief scene, but her bejeweled beauty is quite appropriate to the Jersey Lily's reputation. Film lore says that Cooper refused to participate until more scenes were added to place his character in a charming light, to prevent Brennan from stealing the picture—which he did, but this compulsively entertaining outdoor drama presents two greatly underrated actors showing off their comedic talents.

No one but the idiosyncratic John Huston would ever think of casting Paul Newman as Roy, but *The Life and Times of Judge Roy Bean* (Warner Brothers, 1972) gives him carte blanche, and a gruff, prairie-wise, roguish Law West of the Pecos is the result. There's very little more history here than in *The Westerner*, and even more claptrap (Stacey Keach's gratuitous Original Bad Bob is painfully camp), but Newman's Judge manages to be more murderous and less venal than Brennan's, and Ava Gardner's turn as Lillie in the final scene is worth the price of the rental. (The paperback reissue of Sonnichsen's book claims to be the basis of John Milius's screenplay, but it would take a DNA test to find the connection.)

Judge Roy Bean (1956–57), a syndicated TV series, starred

veteran character actor Edgar Buchanan through all thirty-nine episodes. It's fun to watch, and although it reinvents Roy as a humble "storekeeper" out to bring justice to West Texas, Buchanan's cuddly old curmudgeon parlays Roy's more harmless quirks into great comedy-drama. (His call-to-arms to his deputies is his red flannel long-handled underwear flying from the flagpole of the Jersey Lilly.) Jack Beutel, the worst Billy the Kid ever in Howard Hughes's infamous *The Outlaw* (RKO, 1943), fares better here in a recurring role as one of Roy's deputies.

Not surprisingly, both films and the series ignore Roy's real-life family. Brennan's Judge is a childless bachelor, Newman fathers a daughter (Jacqueline Bisset) out of wedlock, and Buchanan's pretty, virginal niece takes care of his domestic arrangements. Roy's thorny marriage and unruly offspring were anathema to the sprightly pace of genre entertainment in those days. (Lillie's name is misspelled "Lily" in the movie credits, despite being spelled properly on the posters in Paul Newman's saloon.) All three versions propogate the myth that Roy was a self-appointed official with no credentials.

In 1978, Francesca Annis starred in *Lillie*, a thirteen-part production airing on London Weekend Television. The budget was modest (the fire that destroyed the Park Theatre is portrayed by a red electric bulb glowing through the window of Lillie's New York hotel suite), but it has a lavish look, and Annis is excellent. Peter Egan sparkles as Oscar Wilde, and one could not hope to find a better Prince of Wales than Denis Lill. (He played him in two other British miniseries, including opposite Annis's Langtry in *Edward the King* in 1975.) Tommy Duggan is an electric if somewhat natty Roy in his only scene; but the Judge gets short shrift, with one other brief mention and no visit to Langtry, which by all accounts including hers was a highlight of Lillie's life in the spotlight. Anton Rodgers is commanding in the thankless role of Edward Langtry, equal parts detestable, pathetic, and tragic. Whenever he's on screen, it's his film.

The Westerner and *The Life and Times of Judge Roy Bean* are both available on DVD, and episodes of *Judge Roy Bean* are staples in inexpensive omnibus packages of TV westerns on disc. *Lillie* was released in a four-disc set by Acorn Media in 2007.

Death has prevented me from expressing my gratitude in person to Fred Bean, Roy's direct descendant and a gifted writer, whose innate decency convinced all his friends that Roy could not have been all bad. It was only in the last quarter of Fred's life that he felt free enough of family restraint to talk about his notorious ancestor, ruefully and with wit. He left us too soon.

One final note on Roy and Lillie in Hollywood: Industry hubbub has it that romantic sparks flew between Newman and Gardner while on location for *The Life and Times of Judge Roy Bean*. One hopes nothing came of it, for the sake of Newman and Joanne Woodward's own legendary love story, and there's no reason to believe anything did; but on some cosmic level it's comforting to believe that Roy and Lillie hit it off, if only by proxy.

ABOUT THE AUTHOR

LOREN D. ESTLEMAN is the author of more than sixty novels. He has netted four Shamus Awards for detective fiction, five Spur Awards for Western fiction, and three Western Heritage Awards, among his many professional honors. He lives with his wife, author Deborah Morgan, in central Michigan.